...Last Minute of Play

Tales of Hockey
GRIT AND GLORY

Author Ross Brewitt behind the bench coaching the NHL OldStars.

...Last Minute of Play

Tales of Hockey
GRIT AND GLORY

Ross Brewitt

Photographs by Robert B. Shaver

Stoddart

Published in 1993 by
Stoddart Publishing Co. Limited
34 Lesmill Road
Toronto, Canada
M3B 2T6
(416) 445-3333

Canadian Cataloguing in Publication Data

Brewitt, Ross, 1936–
Last minute of play: tales of hockey grit and glory
ISBN 0-7737-5594-2
1. Hockey — Canada. 2. National Hockey League.
I. Title.
GV848.4.C2B74 1993 796.962'0971 C93-094207-8

Cover Design: Brant Cowie/ArtPlus Limited
Cover Photograph: Robert B. Shaver
Typesetting: Tony Gordon Limited
Printed and bound in Canada

*Stoddart Publishing gratefully acknowledges the support of the Canada Council, Ontario Ministry
of Culture, Tourism, and Recreation, Ontario Arts Council, and Ontario Publishing Centre in the
development of writing and publishing in Canada.*

For my family, the people who never gave up on me

Contents

Preface

HE SITS ON THE BENCH throughout the final game of a losing season for his once-proud team and suddenly comes to the realization that the fat lady is about to sing. Hunched over at the end of the padded bench, out of sight and out of mind, one gloved hand hanging over the boards, he understands. The end of a long career has come, the beginning of a new life has arrived.

"Last minute of play in the game . . ."

For an instant he remains frozen. Then he rises, looks at his long-time coach, and points a finger at the clock and at his own chest. The coach slowly nods in recognition. At the next whistle the older player climbs over the boards while the coach puts a restraining hand on the shoulder of a young, confused winger. The retiring veteran finishes his final 60 seconds of play on the ice — one of the fortunates.

Every player vividly remembers his first game in the NHL. The national anthem. The brilliant lights and sparkling glass, the thrilling colours of his uniform. He recalls the rush of expectancy, the surge of determination, the anticipation of a career, the heavy responsibility of a one and only first time.

As a rookie, he suffers the pangs of inadequacy when he sees the famous faces on his bench and the ones across the way. He is secretly envious of their offhand gestures, the seemingly easy, indifferent acceptance of the task to come. But in his heart he knows there are thousands of minutes of play ahead. What he doesn't realize is that when it's over he'll hear it loud and clear.

With only a few exceptions all of the people in this book have endured that last minute of play.

90-Second
All-Stars

WHERE POSSIBLE, all the people in this book were asked to select a 90-second team (approximately the length of an on-ice shift). The situation given to them was this: "Score 0–0, 90 seconds remaining, the obvious idea is to score, but not be scored upon. The entire season rests on the next minute and a half. The players selected must be from your playing days, on your team, or any other team, but you can't pick yourself." That was it.

The results were predictable in a lot of cases, most often they were tinged with personal favouritism, a few were thoughtful in their selections, others went with the flow.

One player mulled it over for a moment, then asked, "Is this a regular season game or playoffs?"

"Does it matter?" I shot back.

"Damn right! I know guys who played one way during the season, then played like they'd grown a foot in the playoffs."

You will note there are selections based on firepower, some on defence. One thing they had in common was the strength of the line-up. As one gentleman said, "If I've got these six to throw over the boards . . . hmm, all I got to say is you're gonna have a hell of a time beatin' me. These guys sure as hell won't beat themselves."

Given the boundaries, and the personal experiences these men had with the selected players, don't be surprised if names come up that seem to fly in the face of rationale.

Prologue

HE INSPIRATION FOR THIS BOOK wasn't a bolt from the blue, a dawning of such impact that I had to sit down and begin before I lost my train of thought. It is simply a collection of personal observations of a group of people who, although totally different from one another, have a common denominator — professional hockey.

That they survived and are able to laugh at it in most cases is an accomplishment. Make no mistake, playing pro hockey isn't the glamorous, never-ending ego trip it seems to conjure up for some people. The naive zeal a player begins with is usually replaced between his last junior game and the first two weeks of his rookie NHL season by the realization that he's in a very tough, unforgiving business. Even those who come out of college hockey, although probably better prepared for the afterlife, realize it isn't much more than a skilled trade. What we are dealing with here are dreams, which eventually become real life, making the dreams the first casualties.

For those fortunate enough to have star quality, additional benefits may come with celebrity, but in the main, nothing is forgotten more quickly than an ex-player. The majority arriving late from the bubble of professional sport will find their clippings worthless except as

1

reminders for later on in life. In a way it's sad, but as a legion of ex-athletes can attest, it's true, and *legion* is an excellent descriptive word, because if there's a saving grace, a value aside from the fame, it is in the fact that they were "there."

Much like Legionnaires, they are veterans who have suffered and survived together. They can lay claim to a status not afforded ordinary fans, backyard phenoms, road hockey marvels, the guys who won the Atom A house league trophy, others who were sent home from a Junior B tryout, and those "used-to-be" players who revive the vision every Thursday morning at 1:00 a.m. with a group of mixed sweaters and mismatched socks.

So who are these people who have become household names in some cases, curiosities in others? Whatever became of them since they left Dauphin, Elliot Lake, Campbell River, and Valleyfield? What are they like now that the game is over, and what in hell do they do, anyway?

It's rare now to see an active or retired player "go home." Most often they opt for the cities where they have made their marks, gravitate to better job and business prospects, or move to warmer climates. The places of birth, so proudly pointed out by the folks in Tisdale, Sydney, Cornwall, and Brooks, don't get to see their "boys" very often.

For a while my position kept me in touch with the active players. I was fortunate to have a job with Maple Leaf Sports Productions that put me in close liaison with the Toronto Maple Leafs of the late sixties, and later I was to go through the birth of the Buffalo Sabres, which broadened the base and opened the door to a whole new group of everyday players. And as these men were traded or retired, my file of contacts grew to every team in the league and every part of Canada and the United States. Settling into my own promotion business in the mid-seventies, I was available to hatch both the Molson ProStars, a fastball team of current Maple Leafs (plus added NHL friends), and later got the NHL OldStars off the ground at the urging of Ed Shack. The OldStars evolved into the Labatt's Original Six team and, coupled with my ongoing speaking engagements, plus the representation of speakers like Dennis Hull and the constant scribbling I hunched over in every spare moment, I came to the conclusion that I had accumulated treasured associations over many seasons come and gone, with thousands of anecdotes and stories, sidelights and observations, spelling out loud and clear the characters and situations shaping these lives. I was determined someone should tell it, so I picked me!

The idea settled and simmered in the back of my mind for a long time as I continued to look for the thread joining all the pieces. Like most revealing, illuminating ideas — the ones cartooned as light bulbs clicking on brightly overhead — this one came naturally enough in Maple Leaf Gardens, where earlier I had said good morning to some of the usual practice visitors in the outer hallway — media people, agents, equipment and stick suppliers, and a father escorting a daughter I guessed to be 12, autograph book clutched tightly to a newly purchased number 17 Leaf sweater.

Dad was proudly pointing to a wall photo, saying, "He used to live up the street from us when I was a kid. . . ." The little girl only frowned, as if to say, "Who cares?" She was interested in the "cuties" sweating it out on the ice only yards away, but I could see the smiling, distant, unaware father reliving the past, back in a small Ontario hard-rock mining town. As I glanced at the picture on my way past, I knew he was referring to a street in Kirkland Lake and a Leaf player who had never returned.

I put the thought aside and made my way into the arena, looking back up into the seats for the man I was supposed to be meeting. As I spotted him and climbed through row after row of empty seats, the thread I'd been searching for peeked over the horizon.

Where did "they" come from?

My companion didn't know it at the time, but he was going to trigger a flood of recollections and a lot of late-night writing for me.

Seated with Dennis Hull near the top of the reds, I watched as the San Jose Sharks skipped briskly through their morning workout. The few veteran NHLers on their roster were easily identifiable in the group — a bad sign. Dennis was with the broadcast crew in the Sharks' first year, and he sporadically aired out new lines on me in preparation for the coming banquet circuit.

3

"St. Louis has Hull and Oates," he said, eyes following the players, "but we've got Presley."

"Too reliant on a perfect sound system," I cautioned him, "and besides, it'll only work with a clued-in hockey crowd." I doubted if he'd run across many well-informed Shark fans this year, or anybody closely scrutinizing the career of Wayne Presley.

"Okay . . . we're last in power play goals but first in T-shirt sales," he said, plowing on, undeterred.

"Might work," I told him as I watched the San Jose netminder in what appeared to be stiff, brand-new pads. Pat Falloon cruised over the blue line and cuffed a casual snap shot toward the net. The pads sounded hollow up where we were sitting.

The Sharks split up into teams for a closing scrimmage, and the coach went to centre for the face-off. "He always has them scrimmage at the end of a practice," Dennis cracked with a straight face. "This way at least half the team will get the winning spirit."

"Better," I said, nodding, "much better." I figured it could be used on the Leafs, too, the way things were going at the time. Then, as the Sharks went into a feeding frenzy below, Dennis pointed out a winger, number 15, coasting along the boards, alone and unguarded.

"They should give him the puck now before he grows moss down his north side," I said, thinking he was only indicating a man in the open. The puck whistled over to 15 as if on cue.

"Yeah, sure. Only I meant he's from your hometown," Dennis explained. "Thunder Bay. Dave Bruce. Nice kid, good kid. You know him?"

I shrugged. No. It had been a long time, and as we sat there amid the muffled sounds peculiar to big league buildings, the noise swallowed up in the space for 16,000 people, I realized how blasé we'd become, how far we were from the small-town arenas, ringing and booming with activity, the tinny crackle of sticks and skates, the clank and bonk of pucks shot by kids who could only make the back bottom bar of the net because they still weren't strong enough yet to lift the disc off the ice and into the netting.

We all started there, I thought, drifting off in time, daydreaming, my mind's eye returning to buildings with seats on only one side, hardier fans standing in the corners where the frost from the ice plant covers the concrete floor. The dressing rooms are one size, small, benches bolted to the floor, one tap in the sink, and no mirror. And, always, there's a shortage of black rubber mats. Players tiptoe in skates to find the next pathway, or an island of user-friendly wooden floor. Is there any noise more dismaying to a hockey player than the sound of a bare skate blade on uncovered concrete?

Arenas are like ant farms, and weekends are prime time. Early mornings, all day, and throughout the night the Zamboni emerges through end boards every hour on the hour like some mechanized cuckoo. There is always one warm, crowded foyer complete with trophy case and canteen aromas, the latter wafting back and forth like good backcheckers. Hot chocolate, hot dogs, popcorn. And they never oil the front door hinges.

That's where we all came from.

In the small towns an arena is *the* place, the hub of everyday life for kids. It's where the dream starts, it's where legends begin, it's where hearts are broken and heroes are made.

In a big city like Toronto it's still an area arena, maybe several if you were in the elite leagues. Pine Point, Doublerink, Chesswood, Westwood, Ted Reeve, Cawthra Park, Forest Hill, many different uniforms and full parking lots. Glum fathers, screaming mothers, one set of teams going home, one set arriving, the exchange of parking spots never-ending.

I remarked to Dennis about my thoughts as the Sharks streamed off the ice, and he laughed, remembering the freezing mornings when he and his brother would have to walk a couple of farms down the road and wake up the bus driver to take them to their games in Belleville. "It's them goddamn Hull kids," the driver's wife would groan to their persistent 6:00 a.m. knocking on the front door.

"We used to start the bus for him," Dennis recalled, "and the damn thing never got warm till we reached the arena. What the hell was the sense in starting it early?" he asked, giving out a laugh for an answer.

"Yeah, I know," I agreed. "Tony Kaplanis and I used to get dressed in full equipment at his place every night we could. Then we'd walk in our skates through backyards to Miles Street and plow St. Stan's school rink ourselves. The streetlight made a shadow down the boards and you couldn't see the puck. It was like a black hole on that side. Talk about dumb, really dumb, now that I think of it."

What I left out was even dumber. Kaplanis and I would walk, skates around our necks, passing a puck, a tennis ball, a chunk of ice, all the way up McKenzie Street to Minnesota Park, or even farther, over the bridge and down into the end of town known as the "coal docks" where the East End Rink was our home ice. We'd walk in any kind of weather, holding on to the belief that just because it was snowing on our street it might not be when we arrived a mile or two up the road. See, back then all the games were outdoors, where whistles froze as often as fingers and toes, and a light dusting of snow made the puck seem like a mole from hell, burrowing under the snow on its blind way to another stick.

Later, when you got real good, you played in the Fort William Gardens, a state-of-the-art edifice, as far as I was concerned, certainly a hell of a lot better than the Winnipeg Amphitheatre or the Regina barn that passed for an arena. It was light-years ahead of the dumb-ass Duluth rink, which was on the second floor, boards about thigh-high, perched on top of a curling club. No, we had it all at the FWG, and over four or five years we would get to know it intimately, like a friend, a haven, an alternative to the Top Hat, Schmerg's, or Carter's, billiard halls of learning where hockey players of all ages sported team jackets and learned how to smoke and swear over a challenging game of blue ball at a dime a blue.

Everybody followed the kids' playoffs and knew the scores all the way down to Bantam. It wasn't tough to follow — the results were right there in your *Daily Times Journal.* Upsets were greeted with glee, beating Port Arthur at any level was considered a religious experience, dynasties were born, careers hatched, and winners were treated like visiting royalty all summer long.

Saturday night was hockey night; dances didn't get going until the macho crowd surfaced after the final whistle on TV. Social plans were built around the NHL TV schedule. Winter wedding receptions were unwelcome infringements on most of the male population.

That's the way it was. It didn't matter where you were from; only the towns, teams, jackets, and pool rooms changed. Estevan, Dauphin, Walkerton, Jonquière, Kentville, and Noranda, I've heard the same story over and over, and it's a revelation to listen to hundreds of NHLers tell similar stories.

But the Labatt's Original Six old-timer team, which played as many as 40 to 50 games a year, says more about the roots of hockey than anything I could say. In crisscrossing the country we would sometimes play in the hometowns of our players, where the stories would start, the landmarks would be pointed out and, invariably, there would be some heartfelt moments when a familiar face from the past turned up or a long-forgotten arena turned out to be as good as the refurbished memory.

I remember one old dressing room in particular: the one in the arena in Schumacher just on the edge of Timmins, Ontario, where the Mahovlichs began. It brought all of us back to our own special arena, our one rink where it was still magic, still a dream, and still the place where they never oiled the hinges on the front door.

During those OldStar years, I was fortunate to meet a wide assortment of people who made a living in the sport, the good ones, some bad, some totally the opposite of what you'd expect. They all had a story, and as we went back and forth across the country, I not only got to know them better than ever, but no matter where we went we always drew other ex-players who came by to say hello, relive the good times, and lay new material on us in one form or another. It was an ever-changing composition that grew larger with each trip. Naturally there were some favourites, stories that always drew surprised laughter or caused frowns of concern whenever I got into the mood and related the experiences. Of course, there are a few tales that can't be told and others that fall by the wayside because, well, you had to be there. The team, regardless of the makeup on any particular trip, was a beehive of yarns and anecdotes. Each time a new member was drafted we got another batch of fresh material.

The OldStars played everywhere, literally — Vancouver, Edmonton, Saskatoon, Halifax, St. John's, London, Toronto, the cities of note all over the nation. And the little towns, the ones all of us remember the most — Dawson Creek, Edmundston, Shelburne, East Musquodoboit, and the place where we suffered our first loss ever.

That was Nipigon, located 60 miles east of Thunder Bay along the rugged north shore of Lake Superior. Their old-timers lined up against our high-priced talent, which included Norm Ullman, Pat Stapleton, Bill White, Ed Shack, Fred Stanfield, and the never dull Jim McKenny. On arrival McKenny, finding the cold more potent than his insulation, went on a shopping trip and returned with a new set of purple-striped long johns, a purchase that might have spelled disaster. Stripping down after the game, Jimmy bemoaned the buildup of lilac-coloured lint in the general area of his butt cleavage, claiming it might have hampered his "aerodynamics and mobility. I should have waited until they were broken in," he remarked remorsefully.

Nipigon, with some help from "our" referee, our suddenly generous goaltender Marv Edwards, and some shoddy, befuddled play by our defence, had us down 13–9 with three minutes remaining. Perfect planning. Glancing at the clock, Ullman said, "Let's turn it on, boys, and give them a show." It was supposed to be a goal-scoring fireworks display just in time to nip the locals. No problem.

Tommy Naychuk, an old acquaintance from the Fort William Canadien Juniors, led the standoff up front, while A. Jorgenson played flawless goal. I alone must have known at least 10 A. Jorgensons in northwestern Ontario, and nine of them couldn't stop anything but a pulpwood truck with their foot on the brake. Unfortunately this one was an ex-goaltender of note, and Arnold played so well that Pierre Pilote said, "We could've thrown a handful of sunflower seeds at him and he would've stopped them all at once." The result: 13–12 for Nipigon. Was there dancing in the streets? Nope. Too damn cold.

After the game, Naychuk graciously directed us to the nearby hall where the usual postgame libations were being served. When we arrived, shouldering our first loss, we found the place packed wall-to-wall, everyone glued to the TV sets strategically located around the room. *Hockey Night in Canada?* Wrong. The centre of attention was the *Dallas* episode in which J.R.'s killer was revealed. When our bus left for Thunder Bay, I don't think anyone even noticed.

8

But I do believe they still talk about that game — the night Arnie Jorgenson stoned the big shooters. Just a small-town legend that took place in a dingy old arena where they never oil the hinges of the front door.

Hopefully my perspective will shed a little light on the people we revere in this country of ours where hockey still rules the roost. The subjects are only everyday folks, the same kind of people who attend Rotary meetings, the same sort you saw in your section at a Blue Jay game. They might have been bigger and more athletic for a while, but they still have similar feelings, fears, aspirations, challenges, and concerns. They have kids in school, wives at home, the roof needs shingling, the car breaks down, the shower drips.

These profiles are only a few from the large cross-section I was fortunate to meet in the game of hockey. For a variety of reasons they left an impression, but by no means is this book meant to be a who's who, a whitewash, or a fairy tale about hockey.

It's a collection of stories. About real people.

Jim McKenny

Prince of the
Put-down

JAMES CLAUDE "HOWIE" MCKENNY is in the leadoff position only because he personifies the totally different public and private sides of the group that makes up this book. He flies in the face of "what you see, is what you get." He was talented but erratic, vociferous but brooding, bright yet mindless, sensitive and callous all at once. He was a genial host, or drinking buddy, and still managed to get in a slice of boorish behaviour. He was well read, well informed, yet at times seemed to be totally out of touch with the world around him. Flaky and unreliable off the ice, he was a trusted and staunchly loyal teammate in the rink. He openly admired and revered misfits, team clowns, and other recalcitrant players. The against-the-grain people of the day were his idols, often his closest friends.

I never heard him field a direct compliment that he didn't invert into a put-down of his own talent and skills. I never heard him accept a sincere evaluation of his abilities without immediately turning it into the joke of the day, and in many ways the facade he erected around his private image was one of part buffoon, part court jester, a guy who ran on laughs, who basked in limbo, a player who could make his peers chuckle at their predicaments because his was a lot worse. He also made them shake their heads time and again, wondering why a talent

Maple Leaf turned CITY-TV sportscaster Jim McKenny (right): *"he was irreverent, pulled no punches, and loved to deflate the inflated."*

like his was being wasted, amazed that he could weather any drinking bout, then survive any torture a coach could dream up in practice the morning after. It was almost as if he wanted to criticize himself before anyone else got the chance.

As a result, he appeared to be bigger than any of the giant misfits he apparently held in esteem, was the stuff backhand legends are made of, and was his own worst enemy. It had been that way since he arrived from Ottawa as a 14-year-old phenom at the Toronto Marlboros camp. Those Marlie salad days with Jim Gregory were the forerunner of a career spanning 14 professional seasons, an accomplishment that takes on new relevance when you consider the conditions he put himself through over those years.

During those Marlie games, his considerable abilities were repeatedly compared with another young defenceman named Orr out of Oshawa. It was a burden he would carry to the NHL. Fans demanded to see evidence of why such a comparison was ever made. While they may have been on a par as youngsters, Orr and his once-in-a-lifetime talent went one way, McKenny and his "you've seen one, you've seen 'em all" attitude went the other.

We first met at the 1969 Maple Leaf camp, the last held in Peterborough, and the first for John McLellan and Jim Gregory, elevated to coach and general manager respectively the year after Punch Imlach was deposed. I only knew one man in the Leaf dressing room at the time — a power-hitting first baseman named Bruce Gamble from my Thunder Bay baseball days. At that time "Bates," as he was known, (a tribute to his favourite country singer, the obscure Smiley Bates), was the number one goalie for Toronto, having taken over the lion's share of work from John Bower the previous year. He was my introduction to the players of the day — Rick Ley, Pat Quinn, Dave Keon, Murray Oliver, Marv Edwards, Jim Dorey, Brian Glennie, and Jim. Aside from the dressing room and practice meetings, the only time we saw each other was at a house party, a Molson function, or in a bar, basically all one and the same, and it wasn't new for McKenny to be in a bar. As a teenager, he was known to have performed beer-drinking feats that would have buried a seasoned downtown wino.

That he even got a sniff of the NHL, particularly the Leafs, in an age when the Imperial Grand Wizard was Punch Imlach, was remarkable in itself. At the age of 19 the Toronto brain trust gave him a one-game tryout with their Rochester farm club. They even brought him up for two games with the Leafs before sending him down for a few playoff games with the McLellan-coached Tulsa affiliate in the Central Hockey League. In those four games he had two goals and two assists. During his first year as a pro, he did the trip in reverse, playing 45 games in Tulsa, six with Toronto, 19 with Rochester, plus dressing for seven of their playoff games. But already his erratic side was beginning to show, and while others would ascend to the NHL, he would continue to bounce between Rochester, the Leafs, Vancouver, and Rochester all over again.

His reputation was beginning to precede him, gaining howls of laughter from the players and blank stares from the likes of Punch and Joe Crozier, Imlach's overseer in the minors. But when McLellan and Gregory became the Frick and Frack of Toronto in 1969, McKenny was swept in with them and directly onto the starting lineup. He played brilliantly for stretches, occasionally perpetrating a gaffe loud enough to be heard around the league. He one-lined and quipped his way through eight solid, productive seasons that would have been high watermarks for many other defencemen. But he was the guy compared to Bobby Orr, remember. Everybody wanted more.

If anything ever held McKenny back, it was a blind eye toward danger. While his play and offensive skills were the envy of his peers, the rash cut in front of his own net, or an attempt to make a picture-perfect deke when he was the last man out of the defensive zone, made everyone's shit list. When he allowed a giveaway, nobody worked harder to get it back, but it was still a giveaway. He was more often in the doghouse than not with McLellan, a soft-spoken, velvet-gloved coach who couldn't fathom the paradox that was Jim McKenny, nor understand why he chose to joke about everything from benching to threats of demotion.

Joking was McKenny's forte. He was quick and his wit and repartee were unmatched anywhere in hockey — delivered with incisive inflections, deadpanned, and perfectly timed for the best result. To add to the effectiveness, he was irreverent, pulled no punches, and loved to deflate the inflated.

One such deflation I have always remembered concerned a start-of-the-season team press reception put on by Molson's. For some strange reason football rarely lets you see the players, much like baseball, where one or two individuals, usually losers in the dressing room elimination name draw, are forced to represent the entire team. Hockey has a different set of rules. It's called "be there or else," and on this particular day all of the Leafs weathering training camp were there, including our Jimmy.

A few short months earlier, in my role as general manager and editor of the Maple Leaf Gardens magazine, I had elevated a receptionist at our office to the position of editorial assistant. She had primarily worked on the CFL magazines we produced that year, and this was her first chance to venture forth into the wonderful world of hockey. It had always been my belief that staff members should be familiar with the faces they come into daily contact with on the phone. Pictures didn't do the trick, so Georgina was simply another of the production crew who had to meet some of the "names" at the press reception.

After two or three glasses of wine, Georgie became slightly theatrical. She overemoted on each and every introduction, batted eyelashes here, gasped in phony surprise there, and generally played her way into the minors. When it came time to meet Howie, she gushed, "Oh, oh, I've heard about you . . . so much about you. Why, I feel I almost know you." At that point she put one hand on his arm, as if to allay any trepidation he might feel that his past had been laid bare. Then, placing the other hand to her throat in mock concern, she glanced at the beer in Jimmy's hand, widened her eyes, and said chidingly, "This *is* a surprise. I didn't know hockey players drank."

Jimmy shrugged and replied, "I know just how you feel. I was 23 before I found out girls farted." The remark cooled Georgina out for the entire luncheon.

McKenny could also break up a dressing room with one feigned stab at sincerity, counterfeit bravado, or thinly masked righteousness.

His style didn't begin and end at the arena; it carried over into the family, as well.

I was at his house to do an interview for an article one afternoon during which his son Jason, only four at the time, absently watched us with interest while attempting to climb onto a glass coffee table. In doing so he repeatedly put one little red rubber boot on the tabletop. A hint of caution in his voice, Jim politely told his son, "Take your foot off the table, please."

Jason removed his boot for a moment, then proceeded to run through the routine again.

"I *said*, get your feet off the table!" McKenny warned, a bit louder this time, but only a moment or two passed before the boy did the same thing once more.

"Put your fucking feet down!" McKenny commanded menacingly and loudly.

Jason stood stock-still, this time suitably chastened and attentive.

Jimmy leaned back and observed, "He's a good kid. You just have to get his attention."

A few years later Jason would be involved in another, much repeated story, certainly one of the McKenny family benchmarks. Jason and Darryl Sittler's son Ryan were batting a roll of black tape around the hallway outside the Leaf dressing room door as kids with hockey sticks are bound to do. When Coach Red Kelly came out of the dressing room on his way to the practice ice, he told them to stop. They halted their mini-game long enough for Jason to fix Red with a child-like glare and say, "My mother says you're nuts." Kelly, surprised but ever the gentleman and a father himself, shooed the two away to the outer hall.

The story was subsequently relayed to McKenny on the ice by the Leaf trainer, a laughing, teary-eyed Joe Sgro. From there the incident went around the ice like wildfire. Later, as the players trooped in and took their seats for a postpractice talk from Kelly, McKenny stood and loudly announced, "Red, there are a lot of things my wife and I are not in complete agreement on." For a lot of guys it became a part of hockey lore.

Sometime later we flew to Philadelphia on the Maple Leaf charter. The next day, with time to kill before the evening game at the Spectrum, McKenny and I took in a Swedish triple X movie at a theatre within walking distance of our hotel. One particular scene stayed with Jimmy as we left, and he cut up the "acting" all the way back to the hotel, twice leaving me laughing helplessly and hanging on to parking meters for support.

That evening Toronto led the Broad Street Bullies 3–1 going into the third. On two successive shifts for Brian Glennie and McKenny the Flyers scored to finish with a tie. During the homeward-bound plane, McKenny admitted it was a godsend the game hadn't started at 7:00, otherwise he would have had that "scene" from the movie replay in his mind two more times, "and who knows how many the Flyers would have banged in then?"

On another midwinter night in blustery Buffalo, Toronto was being victimized by the great Gil Perreault, who had already scored twice, burning McKenny at least once. "Jeezus, Howie," the frazzled McLellan exclaimed, "do something out there. We're paying you a lot of goddamn money to stop guys like Perreault."

On his way back to his stall after the usual between-period smoke in the can, McKenny replied in an offended tone, "Don't get on me, John. You're after the wrong guy. Get on Imlach. He's paying Perreault a hell of a lot more to get around me."

Then there was the morning the Russians, in town to meet Team Canada '76, lounged along the rail seats and caught some of the Toronto practice. As the Leafs went through their workout, one of the players commented on how happy the Soviets appeared. McKenny looked over and announced, "Yeah, they think they're playing us, but wait!"

In a game with Montreal Billy MacMillan caught legendary tough guy John Ferguson with a tremendous shoulder check as Ferguson emerged from behind the Canadiens' net, intent on carrying the puck out of danger but not seeing MacMillan heading toward him. Fergy was caught squarely and bounced first off MacMillan, then the boards, crumpling to the ice as play went on toward the Toronto zone without a whistle. Seconds later play reversed, and as Ferguson, a wheezing, shaken man, headed to the bench for relief, McKenny was by this time the closest Leaf and almost in the direct path of Ferguson's beeline. Seizing the opportunity, Howie hollered out, "It wasn't me, Fergie. It was number 12," thereby eliminating any excuse for mistaken retaliation on the part of Big John. Both benches got a suppressed laugh out of that one.

The media was another group that benefited from Howie's droll wisecracks. When McLellan felt he'd seen enough of McKenny's antics, he installed Jimmy at the end of the bench for a few games. Then, in an apparent change of heart, he announced before a morning practice that he was going to turn McKenny loose on the visiting Canadiens the following Wednesday night. He advised the media but neglected to inform the now diligently hardworking, born-again defenceman. During the scrimmage, McKenny returned to the bench after a shift, perspiring and panting with exertion. He was approached by a clued-in writer who asked for an interview. "Sure. But why don't you come down and see me during a game when I have more time?" he deadpanned.

On another occasion a misguided young journalist made the incorrect assumption that McKenny's long-standing nickname of "Howie" must be connected to another ex-Leaf, Howie Meeker. McKenny straightened the kid out with a terse retort. "It was Howie Young, my idol. We got the same red face when we made a rare faux pas. Two different Howies, pal. Besides, Meeker played for a guy who knew something about hockey — Conn Smythe. Fuck, all I have to work with is Ballard."

When asked about the chances for the upcoming Toronto season, particularly in goal, McKenny pontificated in typical fashion. "I'm glad you asked me that one. I know my stuff. I've kept a lot of goaltenders in the NHL. Unfortunately none of ours."

A lot of players voiced their sentiments on Harold Ballard, usually obscene, sometimes vile, always behind closed doors, off the record, and in hushed tones. Jimmy was open, undaunted by the power of the owner, and took his shots, like a mouse at an elephant. Ballard, never beyond cutting up his team in the press, one day referred to the Leafs "as a bunch of fat cats," an allusion to the money he was paying them for little in the way of results. It was on a Wednesday home game against the Bruins that the equally irreverent *Hockey Night in Canada* host Dave Hodge had McKenny as a between-period guest. To close out the interview Hodge had devised a "name association" test, and the last two questions were the hit of the evening.

"Bobby Orr," Hodge prompted.

"Oh, Jeez, my archrival," McKenny retorted.

"Harold Ballard," Hodge offered, expecting the worst.

"Last of the fat cats," McKenny shot back with no hesitation just before the fadeout to black and the unheard laughter of hockey fans across the network.

Everyone has Jim McKenny stories. But as the end drew near it became apparent the best was long gone. The humour was still there, but the game wasn't. Nevertheless, as with most players, the realization came as a jolt to Jim's psyche. At one point he asked to be traded and was told the Leafs had already tried many times. Then he asked to be put on waivers to see if another team was interested but was informed that, too, was a no-go. The Leafs had put him on waivers without recall and no team had bitten. To any player, that's a stunning blow, not only to pride but to perspective. It fell to Roger Neilson, McKenny's fourth Toronto coach, to call him in and announce the bad news, albeit with some tact and a bit of diplomacy.

"We're sending you to Dallas," Neilson said, purposely not using the dreaded words, "sending you down."

"What for — seasoning?" At the age of 33, after eight strong seasons, even the excuse of a minor injury that had hampered him from the start of the season wasn't enough to save his year, or eliminate a note of sarcasm. "It's just this injury," he told Neilson. Then he added, "I'll be back."

Neilson simply said, "No you won't," and rang the final bell on Jim McKenny's days as a Leaf.

There would be a brief 10-game stint with Minnesota, but the balance of the season was spent in Oklahoma City. Toronto picked up most of McKenny's contract for the North Stars and in return received the rights to Owen Lloyd. You remember Owen, don't you?

When the last season comes, as it does to all hockey players, it comes in stages. Rarely does a player get to choose the announcement of his retirement; instead, it is thrust upon him. For McKenny there was a brief respite playing hockey in Europe, but the years after Oklahoma City were a mixture of searching and attempting different ways to survive in a hockey afterlife. He took a fling at becoming an actor and a model, went into selling Canadian-content TV programming, and then was offered an opportunity in computers or radio broadcasting. He couldn't choose, so he called on old roommate George Armstrong, someone whose opinion counted.

"I don't know anything about computers," the Chief offered, "but radio's gonna be around forever. Go on radio."

He did, and that led to television, where he became a sports fixture at Toronto's CITY-TV.

With that job came as much security as it is possible to have, especially for an ex-player, particularly one trying to drop the bad habits of the past. Gradually the focus adjusted and McKenny joined Alcoholics Anonymous. A few years later he even sought help for the smoking habit that was beginning to bother him, gravitating to a hypnotherapist who, in doing some research into McKenny's background before attempting any treatment, recognized other, more intense problems and recommended a different kind of therapy — analysis.

The last meeting Jim and I had was in a small café on Queen Street West in Toronto, not far from CITY-TV. He's as publicly recognizable now as he ever was as a player, the wit is still razor-sharp, and the one-liners are tossed off with the usual abandon, which is great for a guy like me because I've been using them in my after-dinner speeches for years. Jimmy has sort of been my in-house writer.

"Happened a few years back," he said, referring to the psychoanalysis over a cappuccino. Our window table afforded passersby the opportunity to see, recognize, and occasionally offer a wave. "See," he said, tilting his head toward the window and the unknown friendlies outside, "that's okay now. But before, well, my reaction was to run away, mentally hide. I'd run from the pain of failure, of not being accepted. I thought everything was my fault. When we lost, it was my fault. When the team was going bad, it was because of me. I couldn't control my fear, so I buried it under being probably the most irresponsible person in the world. That's right, I was the most irresponsible person *you'll* ever know.

"I had this fear that everything was gonna turn on me, a sense of abandonment. I was really fucked up, believe me. Down deep I admired the strong guys, the ones who could handle the game, like Sittler. Now there's a player who shouldered a lot of the load for all of us. Then there was a guy like Booter [Pat Boutette]. He was tough. He could handle the game. Those are two examples of people who could control their emotions, because everybody has fear in one form or another. So I was always blaming other guys for mine. On every team I ever played for I always hated one guy — for my own protection. If I could be down on him, then I was still okay, see?"

"Who was it on the Leafs?" I asked, curious.

"Rod Seiling, while he was there. Why? I don't know. Just handy, I suppose. Now I see him for what he really is, and was — an okay guy. Someone just trying to make his way like the rest of us. I had no valid reason to feel the way I did."

After an hour of conversation, I realized this was indeed a new Jim McKenny. Certainly someone I was unfamiliar with and definitely not the guy who got us thrown out of Mother's Bakery in Buffalo years before. We had spoken at a convention luncheon in Niagara Falls that day, and I decided to cross the Peace Bridge and see some of my old buddies, make a victory lap around the bars, so to speak. Ed Kilgour, a local sportscaster was in Mother's, and when I drew Howie's attention to this fortuitous happening, he launched into a perfect impersonation of *Bowling for Dollars,* a time-wasting show that Kilgour also hosted. A bartender the size of the Bills' defensive end, Bruce Smith, suggested it would be a good idea if we left. We heeded the helpful hint, and as we hurried through the door, Jimmy yelled over his shoulder in traditional, true-blue *Bowling for Dollars* style, "These are some of my friends in the audience, Ed, and I'd especially like to say hello to my aunt in Vancouver, my cousins in Perth . . ."

But that was a long time ago.

When we went our separate ways on the street, me to my car, Jimmy walking back to CITY-TV, I told him I had been surprised to find his career had spanned 14 pro seasons but only 600 NHL games.

"Yeah, me, too, and I only remember half of them." It was typical, vintage McKenny.

A truly new Jim McKenny, to be sure. Next time you see him on TV, think of how lucky you are. Here's a guy who had a pretty good NHL career and doesn't quite remember it all.

90-SECOND ALL-STARS

G — **Johnny Bower** *". . . a battler all the time."*

D — **Borje Salming** *". . . incredible two-way player, game in, game out."*

D — **Bobby Orr** *". . . if it can't be me, it's gotta be him."*

C — **Darryl Sittler** *". . . you need a goal, you'll get one."*

RW — **Lanny McDonald** *". . . no worries with Lanny."*

LW — **John Ferguson** *". . . his check will never score. He'll be too scared to make a move."*

Harold Ballard

Carlton Street
Conundrum

PAL HAL. A real poser. A bona fide conundrum. Even when I first met Harold Ballard I realized all the tags were inadequate.

"You work for that goddamn Whalen" was his only response to my self-introduction. John Whalen was the head of Maple Leaf Sports Productions, and my boss. MLSP was a part of Maclaren Advertising, much like the bigger and better, new and improved dinosaur called Hockey Night in Canada Productions. MLSP was merely one of the pieces of endless paper leading from the offices on Richmond Street and back to the Gardens. Our job was to sell advertising, produce the program and guide book, and do anything else that might show a profit and cover a stiff rights fee.

As the latest salesman on the block, my first assignment was to secure a new set of 20 odd TVs for the Gardens and the Hot Stove Club. I never was told where the old sets had gone. The only thing I knew was that when you walked through the Gardens' hallways you saw mounted, boxlike platforms with gaping holes where television sets once glowed.

Additionally our group handled advertising on the old Alphalite "moving message" signs at either end of the arena, but as time passed,

Harold Ballard (left) in his Maple Leaf Gardens bunker: "salty, gruff . . . intolerable, rude, crude . . ." Ensconced on Pal Hal's left are Jim Gregory and John McLellan.

and I advanced my area of responsibility, I learned that no written agreement could sufficiently cover negotiations at the Gardens without the Man's okay. Over the next few years I was never sure who bossed whom, and I know I wasn't alone. Ballard, and the Leafs as a property (despite their so-so station in the standings), called the tune.

Salty, gruff, irreverent, insensitive, intolerable, rude, crude, and even dumb were terms I heard used to describe Harold. I also frequently heard generous, funny, and caring. But they were only a means to get what was his main meat — the limelight.

He obviously thrived on being some sort of front-page pariah, always greeting a new day by finding himself in the middle of controversy. God knows he heaped a lot of controversy on the team and management.

But under all the bluster and blather he was, most of all, two things: a great friend and a terrible enemy. And I saw a lot of both sides.

He could be arrogant and vain beyond acceptance. There was the day a photographer arrived intent on getting a shot of the Gardens' centre ice, which was newly painted with a Maple Leaf insignia on one side and a Tiger-Cat emblem on the other. Since Harold was nowhere to be found, the intrepid photographer convinced one of the door watchers, complete with ratty blue cardigan and outmoded white usher's hat, to stand on the ice and point at the two logos. The recalcitrant doorman was dressed down later and told by H.B. directly, "If any more goddamn pictures are taken around here, I'll be in 'em."

Another full-time employee had a name for Harold that was not supposed to be known to the Man. B.S.

"Here comes B.S." would be the whispered warning when the boys were cleaning the arena glass or polishing the endless rows of old photos lining the halls.

But it was rare for anything to escape Ballard's notice around the Gardens, or as loyal Stan Obodiac, the Leafs' PR man once coined it, the Taj Mahal of Canada. In one of his meanderings through the building Harold confronted the workman and demanded a translation of B.S.

"Big Shoes," the man replied, never missing a beat. "Big Shoes. Like big shoes to fill . . ."

Harold only paused for a moment, his face breaking into the famous hearty smile. Then, turning away, he said, "Not bad, goddamn it, not bad by a long shot."

But if you lined up on the bad side, he could be incredibly petty. One day, at about 11:00 a.m., I walked from the parking lot on Church Street into the Hot Stove Club lounge on my way through the back kitchen area to a Leaf practice. I found Big John, one of the long-serving bartenders, up to his elbows in beer bottles. He had an ordinary dinner knife in his hand and was busily scraping the labels off pints of Molson Export and Canadian — on orders from Harold, naturally, for some slight or hitch in negotiations with the brewery. For almost a week the product was available, but sans ID.

Yet, for me, the one incident that revealed the most about H. Ballard concerned the cover of the hockey program. Back in the early seventies I had to select eight colour photographs to be used as the entire season's covers. The cost of colour separations, plus the savings in doing them eight-up, as they say, was a key in showing a profit or loss. The selection had to be weighed carefully to ensure "safe" players, those not expected to be traded, or more important, those expected to finish the season. At best it was a crap shoot. The second problem was the photography itself. Technology was still pretty primitive when it came to action shots. Naturally the photo had to represent the Leafs. Eight times. But on a team with few stars, and even fewer name players, that was a tough job.

Therefore, picking a shot of Dave Keon was easy. He was a lock. Keon's cover came out in mid-February of 1971, beginning with a visit from the North Stars. I still have clear memories of that particular magazine. Davey was front and centre, while an obscure Minnesota player, slightly out of focus, and without identifying numbers of any kind, was barely visible behind him. He was simply a North Star body, vintage unknown.

Back in those days of Johnny McLellan and Jim Gregory, the media room was what is now the coaches' office. Scouts, visiting team civilians, press boys, TV personalities, and broadcast voices would gather for pregame sandwiches and coffee. On this particular occasion Harold was in a huddle with a couple of senior scouts (Harold "Baldy" Cotton was one), while King Clancy stood nearby, rehashing one of his refereeing anecdotes. I had just gathered up a game lineup and the latest of Stan Obodiac's "Maple Leaf" releases and was talking to Bob Pennington of the *Telegram* and CBC broadcaster Fred Sgambati.

In marched Wren Blair, North Star boss of bosses, brandishing a battered and abused program. He headed directly for Harold, slapped the magazine on the table, pointed at the cover, and asked loudly, "Who put this crap out?"

The only crap visible was the blue Maple Leap proudly worn by an earnest-looking Dave Keon. Before Harold or anyone could answer, Blair took it a step further.

"See that guy in the background? That's Mike McMahon, for Christ's sake. He hasn't played for us since goddamn '68. Never played very well when he was with us, either. Whoever put this on the cover oughta be canned. Jesus, what a goddamn insult."

Ballard looked perplexed. Clancy looked mortified, as only Clance could. Baldy merely blinked. Most of the others simply appeared bemused. Then Harold, catching my eye as I made my way toward their table, proceeded to blast me.

"What the hell are you doin', anyway, buying old pictures an' shit? Don't you bastards make enough money to get the good stuff?" And more words to that effect. He alluded to firing me if it were up to him and vowed to everyone within earshot that "those clowns at Maclaren were gonna hear about this." He turned to placate Blair for the offence, while I was left sputtering the fact that it was impossible to check on every player in every photo background, only to be waved off by Ballard. I also got a parting shot in the form of a muttered "bullshit" from Blair.

Steaming, realizing I would soon say something to make the situation worse, I barged out of the pressroom, red-faced and frustrated. As I stormed into the hallway between the *Hockey Night in Canada* studio and the Leaf dressing room, I was intercepted by the *Globe and Mail*'s Dick Beddoes, wearing a cape or some other outlandish get-up that he affected in those days. The jaunty homburg and 32-tooth smile weren't what I needed at the time. Still, I gave him the whole garbled account, anyway, and being a close buddy of the Man, he cautioned me to take the whole affair with a grain of salt, suggesting that it would blow over in no time. Thankfully Dick managed to cool me out enough so that I was able to wedge into a pay phone booth, call home, and recite to my wife the famous line, "They can take this job and shove it."

Fifteen minutes later I was wandering the east side hall, considering whether a bit more discussion was needed or a vacation of the premises was more prudent, when Harold and Clancy flagged me down on the way to their bunker at the north end.

"Don't let that little yapper get to yuh," Pal Hal told me, "and see if you can dig up any more of those pictures with McManus in them."

"McMahon," Clancy corrected.

"Yeah," the man shot back. "I love to see Blair riled up." Then, laughing, they walked away. Seems I was just part of another prank that might make the rounds at the owners' meetings. Even I found it funny later. Much later.

That incident said a lot, at least to me, about Harold Ballard. He loved to have fun, to enjoy the moment, even if it was at someone else's expense. He went with the flow, although most of his time was spent rowing upstream.

Make no mistake, though. He may have loved a laugh, but he was bad for the team, bad for hockey in a city ready to accept anything in blue and white. While his intentions were good, his actions weren't. And there was never a chance it would change regardless of who was in the GM seat, for Harold treated the Leafs like a kid with a new computer game. He couldn't leave them alone.

Many years later Dick Beddoes gave me a copy of his Ballard biography and wrote on the inside cover: "To Ross — who knew Pal Hal as a rogue, and loved him for it."

Dick liked to stretch a point, a trait that kept him in the forefront of sportswriters, but he was only partially correct. I had respect for Harold Ballard, liked him for a lot of things he did, and some things he didn't do.

When it all comes down to a decision, though, I always go by how the other person treated me. Harold was always good, helpful, offering advice in an abrasive tone, taking time to chat, opening up on a good quote for my speechmaking file. He showed his regard many times by simply remembering my name, acknowledging that I was in the room. He didn't always do that for everyone.

I disliked what he did to the Leafs, since it was all so unnecessary. The franchise, the team, people a lot closer than I ever was, were the ones most often hurt, the victims of his ego.

Because despite a work ethic that would have felled other men of his age and health, despite the good things he did for a lot of causes and cronies, despite some glitches in his personality, I have to believe we all knew the drive was toward one thing.

Publicity.

He loved it. Good, and bad.

Even at the expense of his hockey team.

Jacques Plante

Snake between
the Pipes

S CLOSE AS YOU THOUGHT you were to Bobby Hull, simply because of his outgoing and friendly demeanour, you were, conversely, just that much more separated from Jacques Plante. That doesn't mean he was an unfriendly guy, but he was reluctant to acknowledge anyone unless sufficient time and facial exposure had been registered. If you said hello, he would respond in kind. If you were part of an along-the-boards discussion or a hotel lobby confab, he would listen, offering opinions and general discussion as if you were an accepted member of the group. But the next day it was back to square one. For you. Not him.

Goaltenders have been categorized as everything from crazy to morose. Both labels are accurate, as is almost any designation in between. Their excuse for whatever character traits surface is the knowledge that they alone labour in the most stressful position known to team sports. The only other professional career to come even close is that of a major league pitcher, and in baseball the main risk is ego. When a 90-mile-an-hour fastball is taken downtown for a home run, the only personal injury is to pride. On the other side, facing a 100-mile-an-hour frozen puck, fired from any conceivable angle, makes permanent, career-ending injuries a real, not imagined consideration.

The legendary Jacques Plante as a Maple Leaf: "a bone rack in an oversize sweater."

Yet in goalies, as in baseball pitchers, self-recrimination is a constant companion. The ones who last the longest learn to handle the load, spreading it among teammates, accepting the fact that both sports are games of mistakes. The survivors never forget that it's best to consider the game over the long haul rather than fret about any given moment.

I recall one particular Saturday night in October 1970. The Leafs had just dropped their second game in three outings after a listless 6–2 loss to the New York Rangers. A charter was waiting at Toronto International Airport to take the team to Philadelphia. Even before the plane was ready to taxi, Bruce Gamble, the Toronto netminder that particular evening, was unconcernedly asleep in his window seat while his compadre, Marv Edwards, was peeling an orange and was deep into the sports section of the *Toronto Star.* They would lose again on Sunday night to the Flyers, and the routine would be the same on the flight home.

Their dispositions weren't lackadaisical; they were merely two veterans handling the 76-game schedule. Edwards was an on-ice chirper, constantly chattering and cajoling, a bundle of nerves. In a game Gamble was intense, combative, a red-faced workaholic who battled every shot. But for both of them, like most other goaltenders, when it was over, it was over.

After Jacques Plante and Bernie Parent arrived in Toronto, I had the opportunity to watch them play, practise, and work together before Bernie returned to Philadelphia from whence he had come. It was akin to watching a father and son, or an accomplished musician with a young protégé. Later, after Bernie jumped to a bad team in the World Hockey Association, then returned to the Flyers, picked up two Stanley Cups, the Vezina twice, and the Conn Smythe Trophy, I often wondered how much was due to the Flyers and Fred Shero and how much was due to Jacques and Bernie himself. The two goalies were like facing mirrors. But Jake the Snake was the grandmaster, and by action and play you knew he was above the standard.

Although six feet tall, Plante was gaunt by his teammates' standards — a bone rack in an oversize sweater. Filled out by his pads and mask, he often reminded me of the golf adage that says most of a tree is air. Shoot through it if there's no other way around. Plante gave you the same impression, although obviously to opponents he had much more substance when facing pucks.

He had a way of skating without moving his feet, perceptibly, anyway, and a habit of bouncing along as if he were on shock absorbers. The Snake always seemed to be flat to an oncoming puck, and he subscribed to a few rules for being a successful stopper, rules that he made known in a variety of ways to the likes of Ley, Pelyk, McKenny, Glennie, and even the veteran Boomer Baun. He once said he could stop anything he could see, an admonishment to his own people who tended to arm-wrestle opposing players instead of putting them down. Another old reliable was to keep any shooters out of the centre, making them come from an angle. Angles were his forte, he explained. And if this superstar and innovator of the game was anything, he was a calming influence. On a team staffed by blue-liners who, with the exception of Baun, were in their early twenties, this was a stabilizing quality.

Plante rarely appeared herky-jerky or panicky in goal mouth scrambles. Nor was he ever flustered by the never-ending pressure in the Leaf end, a trademark of the team in the early seventies. The eighties and nineties, too, come to think of it. His movement around the net, his instructions delivered from behind the signature mask were terse and to the point, something the fans couldn't hear but errant defencemen had no problem in picking up.

Two moments stand out when trying to summon up who Jacques Plante was and what he meant to the people who shared his daily routine. The first was on New Year's Eve, 1970. The Leafs had knocked off the visiting Oakland Seals the night before and weren't scheduled to play until the second day of the new year. Plante decided to stay in Toronto rather than return to Montreal for the holiday. He was sitting in the dressing room after a light workout with the remnants of the team still in the city — mostly walking wounded and stragglers who only had plans for the evening.

Plante, in a suit, sat in front of his cubicle reading the *NHL Official Guide and Record Book*. Looking up, he asked no one in particular, "Does anybody know 'ow many wingers 'ave moved to centre and scored more goals dan before?" His accent was there, but less noticeable than one would expect, his voice low yet nasal, sounding as if he had a slight case of laryngitis. If he expected anyone to know the answer to his question, he was mistaken.

"All of them," said a laughing defenceman finally.

"Wingers are too stupid to be centres," growled a centre, acting as if the whole suggestion was too impossible even to entertain.

"Who gives a shit?" piped up another defenceman.

At that Plante cocked his head to one side and said softly, "Well, I do."

"Does it say anything about centres who moved to wing and then out the door?" asked the team captain to derogatory heckling from the two remaining centres.

As Plante stood to put on his coat, I noticed that the book was dog-eared and crinkled, much like a sportswriter's. I also noted that he slipped it into his coat pocket. The man was obviously a student of stats.

The memory of that moment came back on April 15 later in the same year. The Leafs were at home and down to the Rangers three games to two in the first round of the Stanley Cup playoffs. The game went into overtime at 1–1. New York captain Bob Nevin stepped across the Leaf blue line with a Leaf defenceman bearing down from the left side. Plante, gliding far out of the net almost to the hash mark of the face-off circle, seemed to have the situation in hand, only to have the heads-up Nevin stride a step deeper and bury the shot into the back of the net. The puck never left the ice. Game, set, match. And Plante didn't look back. He simply kept on going to the centre ice door and into the dressing room.

During the postgame bloodletting, crusty Red Burnett of the *Toronto Star* was the first to ask, "What happened?"

With a shrug Plante said, "I guessed wrong." Burnett's head shot up as if he'd been goosed. Most of the other media types did the same thing. Candour is a rare commodity in a dressing room.

"I 'ad 'im down to shoot in dat situation. You know, we go back a long way, eh? But I guess wrong." Again he shrugged.

He stood alone, a bone rack in soggy underwear, barefoot, but still wearing his hockey pants, unrepentant and refusing to hide in front of the stricken stares of the Toronto press.

It was a time when his mental file cabinet of stats failed. He never revealed how many times it had served him well.

Chico Maki

Sultan of
the Shadow

IFIRST MET CHICO MAKI at the Markham Arena in Metro Toronto when Gerry Patterson of Special Event Television was shooting the Original Six Hockey Heroes series. He was perched on a table outside the Chicago Blackhawks' dressing room in full uniform, smoking one of those brown cigarillos. Colts, I think.

Maki looked compact and fit as he flashed a lopsided grin every now and then to a rink security guard. He seemed genuinely interested in whatever the man was saying, and I remember thinking to myself, Seems like a nice guy.

"Dale inside?" I inquired, breaking the ice but really looking for Dale Tallon, an old pal from my ProStar fastball days.

Maki looked directly at me without answering for a second. "Prob'ly not, since it's only a half hour till game time. He always likes to start half dressed," he finally said after taking a long drag on the Colt.

Isn't this nice? I thought. Smiles at everybody but me and then gets sarcastic. It wasn't as if I needed his permission to go into the dressing room, since I was the "player coordinator" and all. I looked at the roster of my clipboard. "Sixteen, huh? You must be Maki," I said innocently, watching to see how he liked that one.

The Shadow at work. Chico Maki "literally grafted himself" to the hip of an opponent.

"I used to be Hull, but then we changed numbers," he shot back, Colt wedged firmly between his teeth. The remark was followed by dead silence. Even the security guard turned away.

We both started to laugh about the same time, and I turned and walked into the miniscule dressing room.

That little incident was pure Chico.

He never got a lot of credit for playing 13 or 15 years, according to whichever NHL guide you subscribe to. And even then the same book would list him at five-nine or five-ten, depending on whether it was the team roster or the player bios. Some people get no respect. Or recognition. But as a matter of record he spent most of his career as the checker on Bobby Hull's line, and was Bobby's roomie for much of that time.

Chico was the silent type, and in the years he played with the Labatt's Original Six team across Canada and the States, he could be relied on to become animated and enthusiastic only when on the ice. His speed and mastery of checking developed one of the stunts that became a standard for our team.

In our travels from one end of the country to the other we were always confronted by at least one individual who was bound and determined to show the boys why it had been a terrible miscarriage of talent evaluation for him not to be drafted and play in the NHL. It became my habit to ask someone local, with a knowledge of our opposition, which guy was taking the game a tad too seriously.

We were in Bridgewater or Yarmouth or Kentville, I can't quite remember where, but it was definitely Nova Scotia. When I popped the question to the arena manager, he was only too happy to oblige.

"Shit, that's a goddamn cinch. It's that silly son of a bitch Jamie," he volunteered. "Fool's been out joggin' fer weeks, rentin' the goddamn ice by himself, jus' skatin' into a lather. Ever since you guys said you was comin', he's bin poundin' them poor legs into a coma," the man said, laughing so hard that he wheezed. "I even thought he was gonna give up drinkin' fer a while," he added, gasping into another fit of laughing.

In the warm-up it was obvious, even without a program, who Jamie was. He zipped and darted through the pregame stuff, steely-eyed and relentless. Every practice shot was a Stanley Cup winner, every stride an explosion of sheer power.

The first period went as planned. The boys put on a show, the fans had a great time, and we were up 7–1. But Jamie was in a blue funk. His sole golden opportunity was a wide-open attempt to one-time a soft pass in the slot. However, his slap shot attempt hit so far behind the puck that his stick splintered, while the puck merely continued, unhampered, on its way to the corner. Red-faced, he made a flailing pass at his bench, reaching for a replacement stick that was never offered. After two fruitless circles, he left the ice in a snit.

By the middle of the second period he was almost in a rage, trying to carry his team by getting no help from his mates, who seemed to be content to roll along, having a good time and watching what they seemed to think was a pretty entertaining show.

Their bench was adjacent to ours, and Jamie's intensity could be seen by all of us. Rocket Richard never looked more determined, nor more beady-eyed. Their coach sent both benches into gales of laughter, when he announced in a foghorn voice, "Jamie, yuh better take 'er easy or yer gonna pop one of those hemorrhoids."

We worked something out on our bench, and on the next shift change I made a show of calling Chico over to our gate. In what was almost a pantomime for the crowd I pointed to Jamie, then tapped Chico on the chest. Next, palms together, I made weaving motions with my hands, indicating that he was to stick with Jamie wherever the guy went.

Chico put on a shadow better than he had done with any of his assignments in the NHL. Every puck that came near Jamie was deftly deflected at the last possible instant and every avenue of open ice was repeatedly blocked. Jamie's stick was lifted, his elbow was nudged into mishandling the puck, he was herded and delayed, fenced in and forced out. It was a blanket job. Chico literally grafted himself to Jamie's hip, paying absolutely no attention to the play or his own chances on offence. Finally, tired of the attention, frustrated at his lack of puck control, and obviously bone-tired, Jamie made a disparaging gesture and skated to the bench for some relief. As he neared the gate to change on the fly, the door was opened, and unknown to him, Chico, true to his role, followed and sat down, too. The crowd roared.

"Did you see that little asshole all over me?" Jamie moaned to the rest of his team, oblivious to the crowd's laughter. He almost jumped out of his sweater when he turned and found Chico, lopsided grin and all.

We kept the trick in the act everywhere. The gimmick wasn't just funny; it was a tribute to Chico's skill, something most players or fans have no appreciation of unless it's done by a master.

But the event I remember most concerned the matter of recognition and respect. When Chico was living on his farm outside Simcoe, Ontario, his son played minor hockey with other kids along the rural route. Apparently the team needed a coach, so Chico applied, explaining that since he was taking them to practices and games, he might as well get totally involved.

They called and asked what his coaching level was.

"Level?" Chico countered, puzzled.

"Your CAHA Coaching Certificate, Mr. Maki."

Chico admitted to not having anything like that, and they regretfully had to decline his application.

Seems he had applied, as the form asked, with his given name Ronald. Ronald Maki. The Ronald Maki with 13 or 15 or whatever years in the NHL.

Even when they called back he declined.

Pure Chico Maki.

90-SECOND ALL-STARS

G — **Glenn Hall**

D — **Bobby Orr**

D — **Larry Robinson**

C — **Stan Mikita**

RW — **Gordie Howe**

LW — **Bobby Hull**

"I think we just won."

Ed Shack

Windmill on Skates

THAT'S HOW HE SIGNS his name. Not Eddie Shack, not "Fast Eddie," nothing cute, just plain and simple Ed Shack. For someone who can only write his name, he's got very compact, stylish handwriting. And he can't read or spell, either.

There are a lot of people Ed's never met who tell stories to bear out the fact that he's illiterate. Invariably it's the yarn about spelling the world *score,* or was it *goal?* No one seems to agree. They "know" he said it to Punch Imlach in response to the Leaf coach's charge concerning Ed's lack of scoring, reasoning if he couldn't spell it, how could he do it? Some say he was wearing a Beatles wig, and they feature him either playing for the Leafs or visiting while with the Bruins. It doesn't matter; they always sound genuine, as if they were there. I've personally heard the story hundreds of times, from St. John's to Victoria. Eddie must have heard it more often than I have, and in more places, too.

What makes a grade-three dropout so unique? How can someone who can't read an airline ticket or street signs travel across the country? Who else has total strangers think it's perfectly all right to bellow "Clear the Track, Here Comes Shack" into his ear at restaurants, airports, and hotel lobbies? What can you say about a guy who considers newspapers

Eddie Shack mixing it up nose-first: "the one player people will pay to see for no other reason than to enjoy the game with him."

nothing more than fish wrapping, but is the first one singled out for an interview he won't be able to read?

The answer is simple, Ed Shack is a legend with an inbred sense of humour. I always maintained if Eddie had been born in Florida instead of Sudbury, he might very well have run away to the circus and become a clown. Perhaps the world's best clown.

I mean no disrespect. Shackie has a gift of making people laugh, making people enjoy their surroundings, making them see the humour in their everyday lives. Despite the fact that he has accumulated financial success, he considers himself one of the working stiffs, the guy who has to battle taxes, the recession, the cost of gasoline. Despite his notoriety, which rivals all of the greats in the game, he still gravitates to the regular people, and they sense it, too.

There's a reason. He's successful despite his shortcomings because he doesn't mind working. Unlike a lot of people who have more education and knowledge and the opportunity to apply those advantages, he's taken his limited gifts and made them pay off in a way that's the envy of more than a few of his peers in the hockey trade. This gift for people smarts won't result in a cure for the common cold or turn out a screenplay, but it gets him past the concerns of not being able to read and write.

Once, when we were in Hy's in downtown Vancouver, a snooty waiter, complete with tuxedo, handed out expensive 10-pound leather menus to myself, Shack, Bob Nevin, and Keith McCreary. The guy in the tux unfolded the cover with a flourish, causing Shackie to look at him caustically and ask, "What am I supposed to do with this? Catch up on my goddamn reading? I want a steak!"

The waiter was taken aback until Nevvie said, "Now, Ed, they have the beef medallions . . . or how about Stroganoff? You like that." During all this, the waiter, happy to have an ally, watched hopefully.

"Is that the stew?" Shack inquired, interested now.

"Exactly," Nevin said.

The tuxedo took the order, visibly chagrined at having his Stroganoff referred to as Mr. Chunky or less, but he swallowed his annoyance and we discreetly enjoyed his deflation.

Which brings us to a revealing point about Eddie. Any time I've ever been with him, be it airports, bars, restaurants, or speaking functions, I have never heard him ask for help, except from those who know him. If he has a fault, it lies in the fact that Eddie assumes, incorrectly, that his handicap is well-known enough to excuse his combative stance. From his side it's also true that most people assume everybody these days can read.

However, Ed does recognize the word *Shack* quickly enough, in all forms and type styles. Case in point. We were on a bus with the NHL OldStars on our way to downtown Edmonton from the airport when Shackie suddenly bellowed, "Look at that! The bastards use my name and I never get a goddamn nickle." To a man we turned left and saw that we were idling outside a Radio Shack.

What's more, the printed word, and its strange working wonders, is a constant source of amusement and fascination to him. When he lived in a home along the 16th fairway of the Bayview Golf and Country Club, he had a stained glass basement window installed on one side of the rec room overlooking the pool table. The coloured pieces were arranged in a number 23. Eddie was amazed and thrilled to discover that from the outside the 23 became a styled "E S." To this day, according to buddy Bill May, Shack considers that the pinnacle of typesetting.

Ed can't make use of the normal schooling tools such as dictionaries or thesauruses. And naturally, for a person who can't read, Funk and Wagnall's could be a law firm for all he cares. So the fact that he has a good vocabulary lies in his talent for listening, his ability to pick up on other people's conversations. He simply has no other source of input, and occasionally has a problem grasping the right meaning for words, or the actual words themselves.

For example, on his own golf course northwest of Toronto he hit a ball that tailed along the white marker stakes. From our viewpoint on the tee, it appeared to be a borderline, out-of-bounds shot. After a quick survey, though, Eddie elected "to hit a provincial, just in case."

Bobby Nevin, ever the mediator, asked "You mean you're going to hit a provisional?"

Eddie's answer was an indifferent nod.

On an Air Canada flight bound for Winnipeg it was announced: "Not enough lunches were taken on board in Toronto for the entire passenger list, so would anyone who has already eaten, or those willing to voluntarily pass on lunch, please notify the cabin attendants and we will issue those passengers a meal voucher, good in any airport in Canada."

Dale Tallon, a fun lover of the first order, heard Eddie grumbling about our chances of getting such a freebie, and naturally prodded the big boy to an agitated pitch. By the time we landed, Shackie was primed for our exit from the plane. As we filed off, the crew chimed in with their interminable goodbyes and eventually came to Eddie, decked out in leather jacket, cowboy hat, and boots, suit bag over his shoulder, carryon in hand. He asked the crew chief, a robust woman of some seniority, "Where's our meal vultures?"

Caught in mid-goodbye, she did a double take. "Vulture?" she queried.

"Yeah, where's the meal vultures you promised," Eddie shot back suspiciously, expecting a scam. Meanwhile Dale and several others in our group had folded to the floor or nearby seats in a laughing fit. But we did receive our "vultures." Thanks to Eddie.

Then there was the time Shack demanded to see "the head poncho." I couldn't let it slide. "It's head honcho," I corrected to no avail.

"Yeah, I knew it was Mexican," he offered, undeterred and equally unenlightened.

Again, on one of our westward flights, someone said it was great to gain the hours going out but complained of the jet lag on the return trip. Later that week Eddie was heard saying to a reporter that he always worried about his playing time in L.A. and the damage "jet legs" had done to his career.

Or how about the night we were in Lloydminster, home of ex-NHLer Skip Krake and his Neversweats old-timers team. At the postgame get-together it was suggested that the guests remove their cowboy boots to save the carpeting in our host's beautiful home. One of the wives of the old-timers steadfastly resisted any suggestions from her husband that she should take hers off. Shackie, noting the mild disagreement, said out of the side of his mouth to a few of us nearby, "Maybe she's afraid to because she's got vertical veins."

One day Jim "the Bird" Pappin showed up for a road trip sporting an angry cold sore, and Eddie volunteered the opinion that "Bird's got the Kirbys." Nevin translated the remark to the rest of us as "herpes," an affliction that was much in the news at the time.

If Eddie has problems with the written word, he has absolutely none with numbers. An excellent bridge player, he was a studious, abnormally quiet participant in the eternal game on the plane or bus with Bob Nevin, Norm Ullman, Mike Pelyk, Keith McCreary, and a few others, depending on the team in transit at the time. The boys would routinely turn the front-to-back seats into a facing foursome, with the fold-down trays serving as the card table. As I said many times to curious civilians who came upon this new seating arrangement, "Don't try this at home. These men are trained professionals."

When it was his turn to sit out, Ed would usually park his large frame in the aisle and either watch or kibitz between hands. That's when I got to observe his people skills at their best.

On one western flight Ed was hovering over the card game when the call came to sit down and buckle up for landing. Without thinking he plopped into the vacant aisle seat beside two nuns. They were in blue habits and had been watching with interest and occasional smiles as Shackie heckled and criticized the players below him after every deal. I watched as he glanced at the sisters while doing up his seat belt.

"Nice uniforms," he said admiringly. The ladies nodded and smiled at the terminology. Then Eddie turned to me across the aisle. "Nice uniforms," he repeated, and began to laugh. Turning back to them, he sputtered through a mouthful of guffaws, "You oughta see ours. Real nice ones, too."

It was a line the rest of us couldn't have delivered without sounding like a smartass. Instead Eddie and the "girls," as he called them several times, had a good ol' visit right up until we reached the terminal.

Another time he was doing his over-the-shoulder card watch, when turbulence caused the cabin attendants to ask him to sit down. The plane was a DC-9 with three and two seats per aisle. Eddie obediently parked his butt next to a woman I had observed was not happy being trapped near what she obviously considered a group of overgrown children. Now the biggest kid on the block was going to be her seatmate.

Throughout the flight the woman read a pocketbook, glancing up from time to time just to show her displeasure. When Shack sat down, she literally leaned into the wall in an attempt to be as far away as possible from this big, rough type. Meanwhile Eddie groped for his belt, saying, "Tricky little devils, ain't they?"

I caught her glaring at him as if he'd stepped on her foot, and I remember thinking, What a prude. But as Shack settled in, nice and comfy, he looked over to her, smiled, and bobbed his head to signify he was fine, even if she didn't care. In answer, the woman gave him a withering look and put the book in front of her face, slowly and deliberately.

Undaunted, our hero said, "Don't mind the boys. They're only fooling around." Obviously he didn't include himself in any of her distress.

She put down the book and gave him a dirty look that I took to be her career best.

Eddie turned to me, devilishly quizzical, then looked at her again and asked, as if he had every right to, "You *have* fooled around before, haven't you?"

In that instant I recall thinking, Oh, God, she's gonna hit the button. We're gonna be up to our asses in attendants. Mounties will meet us at the gate!

Instead, in that same instant, she looked into Shackie's goofy grin and walrus moustache, blinked in thought, a hint of a smile crossing her face, and started laughing uncontrollably into her book. For my benefit and relief Eddie grinned and snickered, pointing alternately to her, then himself, indicating they were getting along aces.

An hour later she tripped through the airport corridor and loudly introduced her waiting husband to Eddie Shack from 50 yards away. I couldn't help but think, watching this little scene, that if any other member of our group had tried a similar stunt, he would have wound up in handcuffs.

When targets of opportunity don't arise, Shack is quite prepared to manufacture his own, such as the time he did the garbage bag commercial. The manufacturer was trying to show how tough their bags were, and Eddie's job was to punch the suspended competitor's sack, busting it and thereby proving how inferior the Brand X bag was by comparison.

"I musta drilled that bag for an hour. It went on and on, and by now I was sweatin', drippin' water, and gruntin'," he recalled, breaking into a fit of snuffles. "So I said to this twerpy little *di*-rector, 'Once more and I'm outta here. Enough is enough.' The guy clicks the board — take 51 — and I let go with a couple of dingers, but nothin' happens. The bag doesn't bust, so I kicked it. Perfect! They shoulda let me do it my way from the start." The commercial ended on a freeze-frame of the breaking bag, with Eddie caught in mid-guffaw. That photo should have won an award.

He did the Mark's Work Wearhouse commercials as a tap-dancing sheriff singing "I got Rhythm," and the Pop Shoppe series where he was billed as having "a nose for value." All of this by a man who couldn't read a scripted line, who only worked from improvisation, raw memory, a penchant for the funny side, trusting his instincts to do exactly the right gesture or voice inflection.

One of his best ideas never made it to air, but it showed how he could think ahead with an eye for the ridiculous, and a dollar.

"Remember my little dog?" he asked happily, holding two large hands 10 inches apart.

I nodded.

"I taught Foo Foo to sneeze every time I said, 'Scott.' You know, Scott tissues? I went to their ad agency, did a demonstration to those suit-and-tie floaters — Foo Foo and me." He confessed the executives were impressed but weren't buying. "Dummies," he added, dismissing their collective stupidity.

Then there was the time I saw him use a sales technique most marketing managers would kill for. It was his annual Christmas tree sale. This particular day he was operating out of the Shell station near his Toronto home. Not one to have other people do his job, he was out in the night, freezing, liberal flakes of frozen stuff hanging from his ample moustache, tucked under his ample nose. An elderly, blue-haired lady in rimless glasses and a mink coat hemmed and hawed over a tree, twisting this way and that, looking for the best angle to appreciate the foliage.

Impatient and cold, Shack finally made an offer. "Look, lady, it took eight years to grow the damn tree. Don't take eight months to think about it. I'll give you the tree at two bucks a foot and throw in a big kiss for nothin'."

She, too, broke into a grin. Her sales resistance shattered, she surveyed his encrusted countenance, passed on the kiss part, and drove happily away with the tree.

"It's the old Soos-berry charm. Gets 'em every time," he said, laughing raucously as her taillights pulled away.

That's the way he is — no more, no less. He's fun, a character trait that probably cost him a lot of bench time in the NHL. He was tough, and he had a role, a typecasting that belied his attitude. Some coaches and general managers didn't see hockey as fun. Remember, fans, the NHL is a *no-fun zone*.

For instance, in his days as Buffalo GM and coach, Punch Imlach would often use Tim Horton, Dick Duff, Floyd Smith, and Shack, older players he had gathered around to serve as examples for the youngsters. He would take one of these players aside and say, "Listen, I'm gonna give you shit in the room and you're gonna take it. The kids will say, 'Goddamn it, if he's not above criticism, then I guess I ain't, either.'" At least that's the way it was supposed to work, but Imlach should never have used Eddie in such a gag. He should have known better.

In a game at the Buffalo Auditorium Shackie did the one thing no player is supposed to do, namely, get a penalty in the first minute, or the last. He took one at 19:40 of the second period. Imlach was furious, but Shack thought it was merely another mock dressing-down.

Punch launched into a tirade the instant he came through the dressing room door, lacing it with more than the usual share of obscenities. His hat pushed back in the famous "pissed-off" mode, he had everybody's undivided, wide-eyed attention. Meanwhile Shackie continued to smile throughout the ordeal, albeit behind Punch's back, figuring this was another lesson for the kids, something not to be taken too seriously. Imlach ended the tantrum with explicit instructions to Ed.

"When the goddamn penalty is up, I want your ass off the ice. You come straight to the goddamn bench. Don't touch the fuckin' puck. Don't try to check anybody. Just get your sorry ass straight back to the bench. I don't want you on the ice. Got it?"

Shack, unsmiling, nodded his acquiescence, then his face lit up with the glow of an idea. "But, George, what if I get a breakaway?"

"I don't give a shit if you get three breakaways, Shack. I want you to go directly to the goddamn bench — and fast!"

Finished, an agitated Imlach left the dressing room, while a contented Shack merely bobbed his head at all the rookies, indicating his acceptance of shrewd coaching from an obviously shrewd guy.

As the last five seconds of his penalty were counted down, Eddie pawed the floor like a corralled mustang, adding race car revs to the consternation of the timekeepers on the penalty bench. Then, yanking the door open, he bolted out of the gate, roaring a long "Yeahhhhh!" A man possessed, he pointed his stick, spearlike, at the waiting winger, who was poised on the boards. Hair flying, moustache streaming, he grinned wildly, still roaring "Yeahhhhh!" as he dived headfirst over the boards and destroyed the stick rack, scattering the Northlands, CCMs, and Victoriavilles as if they were matchsticks. His plunge took out Gatorade dispensers, spare tape, towels, and the medical kit, plus bespectacled trainer Frank Christie. As the jumble of debris settled, a giggling Shack asked Imlach, "Fast enough, Punch?" over the laughter of the players on the bench and the cursing of Christie, who was trying to struggle to his feet and locate his glasses. Imlach walked a few tentative steps down the bench, looked at the rubble for a moment, tipped his signature hat forward over his eyes in disgust, and marched back to his spot, a beaten man.

Keep in mind, this was Eddie's 14th year. He was still a player who hadn't lost his zest for the game, who hadn't stopped deflating the sacred cows, who hadn't lost that intangible childlike quality we all had once when we played hockey in the streets.

For the record, there were five winters away from home in Junior hockey, a trip to Providence to begin a pro career, then 17 big league seasons. Eddie pulled an NHL jersey over his head more than 1,100 times, and there were 239 goals and 1,500 minutes in penalties. He has his name on the Stanley Cup four times and has scored over 20 goals for five different teams. The year he played with a youngster named Derek "Turk" Sanderson, he bagged 23 goals; Sanderson netted 24 himself and won the Calder Trophy as rookie of the year.

Later, on the Original Six old-timer team, we saw a showman, the one who commanded attention with his antics, the one who in short bursts showed why he was a feared winger, a runaway windmill on skates capable of whoop-dee-doing around players, friend or foe, and enjoying every moment of it. He was a player able to rip one of those laserlike wrist shots past skittish amateur goaltenders from one end of the country to the other.

His shifts became shorter as the seasons went by, and most people attributed the slowdown to age. For my part, I always said it was his hootin' and hollerin' on every rush, goal or no goal, that sapped his stamina. He was simply out of breath.

Or perhaps it was "jet legs" coming back to haunt him.

And, like everyone else in the world, including comedians, there are times when Eddie slips into a morose, sulky vein. The famous bigger-than-life grin fades and the gravelly, foghorn voice is quiet. He wears his feelings on his sleeve, so there is no mistaking his mood. There were times on the road when he wouldn't join in the never-ending heckling and banter within the group, times when total strangers were probably put off by his offhand way of signing autographs without so much as a vocal response to their platitudes. There were other times when, miffed at some real or imagined slight, his funny remarks went over the edge and became cutting, sometimes rude, and there were times when he was unreasonably stubborn and obstinate.

I would say to him, "Edward, you are being obtuse," just as a teacher would to a recalcitrant student. Sometimes it would raise a slight smile, because I was trying to slide a new word by him, and he knew it. But the best thing to do when these sporadic blue funks would hit was to leave him alone. Somewhere, sometime, something would trigger the fun button and he'd come back with a bang. Like the rest of us, he only needed time to sort out his feelings.

How do you rate an Eddie Shack? On a scale of one to ten? A to Z? Whatever yardstick you use, he was, and still is, "the Entertainer," the one player people will pay to see for no other reason than to enjoy the game with him. That fact in itself is a wonderful tribute.

He won't make the Hockey Hall of Fame with his numbers but, as I once suggested in one of my writing fits, Ed Shack should be designated a national treasure and as such should be protected by the Heritage Society. But I doubt Shackie will ever need any protection. And I'm damn sure he won't need any tag days, either.

90-SECOND ALL-STARS

G — **Johnny Bower**

D — **Bobby Orr**

D — **Tim Horton**

C — **Phil Esposito**

RW — **Gordie Howe**

LW — **Bobby Hull**

"I could look better than Imlach with these old bastards. Haw-haw-haw."

Henri Richard

Plastique with a
Short Fuse

IRST IT WAS "The Rocket," then came the "Pocket Rocket."

Red Burnett, the fedora-wearing veteran hockey writer for the *Toronto Star* back in the glory days of the Leafs, once suggested I get used to capitalizing the *T* in "The" as if *the* elder Richard was some kind of deity. Asked if my assumption was true, Red offhandedly said, "Shit, in my day he was!"

Brother Maurice was regarded as an intense, missile-on-a-mission, rise-to-the-occasion kind of player who asked no quarter and gave absolutely none to friend or foe alike. The Pocket Rocket was literally that, a smaller version of ol' Beady Eyes himself. Henri was a perfect clone, for if intensity, fortitude, dogged determination, and unstinting effort on behalf of the team were suitable indicators, Henri outdistanced his illustrious sibling in every category but goals.

The younger Richard was small but had the chiseled features of a northwestern Ontario CPR rock cut. On or off the ice his square jaw was rarely broken by a smile; more often it was frozen shut like a steel trap. His cheekbones were prominent, swollen, like those of a winning boxer. And while he appeared slight, even overdressed in his uniform, his sloping shoulders capped a solid torso and legs that were able to

52

The Pocket Rocket: "a dour, morose bundle of plastique with a short fuse who seemed to have a weekly allotment of words and expended them with Ebenezer Scrooge abandon."

absorb punishment and still return for more. He was workmanlike, going about his business as if every shift were the deciding factor in making or not making the team. When the call came, he never dodged a toe-to-toe invite, even though there were others less talented who were there to shoulder the load. Most opponents said he required little in the way of help, anyway.

When the Pocket first arrived in 1955, a raw 19-year-old Junior star, there were the usual comparisons, the normal nudge-nudges, those who said his mere presence was due to the influence of the Rocket. That Henri never spent one day in the minors was overlooked. Although he scored 19 goals the first time around in the six-team league, the feat was brushed aside as the result of favoured treatment and great linemates. The fact that he was an integral part of the Stanley Cup win in his rookie season was chalked up to luck. He played 10 games in those playoffs, scoring four goals and four assists. Every player should be so lucky.

Eighteen years later, December 20, 1973, to be exact, I was in the Maple Leaf Gardens press box when the message board atop the north-end, wall-hanger blues flashed word on Henri's 1,000th career point, an assist in an eventual 2–2 tie with the Sabres in Buffalo.

Frank Orr, another experienced hockey writer for the *Star* and a man who could never let an event like this one go by without a pontifical comment, leaned back in his seat and said in his typically whiny, joking voice, "If it wasn't for Pocket's goddamn brother, he would've never made the NHL." Those of us not typing to a deadline nodded sagely and wished we'd said it first.

While diligently searching through my dog-eared dictionary for an unfamiliar term, I came across *incongruous* — "a situation consisting of elements or qualities not properly belonging together." After absorbing this piece of information, a picture flashed to mind. Henri Richard and Eddie Shack. The anglo and franco of the Pop Shoppe.

The TV commercial pairing was tailor-made for the word *incongruous*. First there was Shack, a Tasmanian devil on skates, a wrecking ball on ice, who careened around the NHL like a happy, laughing, 200-pound pinball. Then there was Richard, a dour, morose bundle of plastique with a short fuse, a man who seemed to have a weekly allotment of words and expended them with Ebenezer Scrooge abandon.

There's a story Eddie has told about himself for years to underline the antagonistic rivalry, personally and teamwise, that governed both their lives for a long time. Over the decades hockey has seen many great battles: Leafs and Canadiens, Canada and Russia, Don Cherry and Swedes, John Ferguson and anybody, Alan Eagleson and everybody. Hard-ass, out-and-out, I-hate-your-guts passion.

On a Wednesday night Montreal was visiting the Leafs when a fight broke out — but I'll let Eddie take it from there.

"I'm lookin' around for a small guy. I grab the Pocket. We rassle. I'm pullin' his arms, he's yankin' me around. The fight's over, but I can't get rid of the little bastard. So we're skatin' around like we're dancin' and finally I get pissed off 'cause I can't hit him. We were goin' this way, then that way . . ." Shack demonstrates, jockeying for position with an imaginary foe. "Little Henri would try a punch, then I'd try one, but nothin', nobody, was gettin' nowhere. So I yank him forward and cabonk him with my head. Cut him for six or seven stitches."

Three days later, after the dust settled and the newspapers had a field day over the matter, the Leafs went into Montreal for the return match. As the players left the ice after the warm-up, Shack noticed big brother Maurice sitting directly above the hallway where the Leafs exited to the dressing room. The Rocket looked like his usual self — as if someone had goosed him with a broomstick.

"I'm tryin' to get real close behind [Bert] Olmstead or one of the big guys," Eddie says, "and the Rocket spots me, anyway. He yells, 'Ey, Shack, hit's a good t'ing you never 'it my little brudder wit' dat nose. You would 'ave split 'im in 'alf.'"

Nevertheless, the Pocket Rocket and "Clear the Track" Shack became friends.

Like all hockey players, Henri Richard was at home in the dressing room, the one place that offered protection from injury, management and, for the most part, the media. A dressing room has two sides. The first is where a level of near chivalry exists — men are men, your word is your bond, and "all for one" is a deeply felt commitment. The other side, well, let's just say it can be a place where nothing is sacred, a place where you definitely better fit in.

Dressing room humour is crude, deflating, and generally callous. Small concerns are inflated to gigantic proportions, while minor discrepancies and follies are goosed to new heights of silliness. Personal habits, fetishes, preferences, routines, and rituals are closely examined by experts to see what, if any, routes there are into humour.

No one can evade the spotlight, nor can anyone avoid the abject defeat of seeing a barely noticed indiscretion turned into a major production for the rest of the room to enjoy. Nobody escapes. Not Gordie Howe, not Wayne Gretzky, not Bobby Orr. Not even Henri Richard. But the Pocket was a Hall of Famer when it came to deflecting anything that might undermine his well-being.

A case in point. On October 15, 1970, the Buffalo Sabres hosted the Habs for their first ever home game. Punch Imlach's old buddies from the Toronto media were there, and so was everybody else who counted on the Buffalo social scene. The rink had been a mess in mid-afternoon. The clock had lain on the new logo at centre ice, wires splayed on all four sides while two electricians stood, hard hats in hand, poring over a schematic the size of a Zamboni. White dust wafted iceward from the sweepers and wipers moving through the seats. Undeterred, cleaners sprayed gallons of Windex on newly installed glass panels. Near the upper reaches of one corner another group of workmen bolted down seats with air wrenches. It didn't appear to be an arena getting ready for a game; instead, it looked exactly like what it was — a construction site.

But they got the job done, and at 7:00 p.m. the two teams took a trial spin and a warm-up before retiring to their respective dressing rooms for one last gut check. Back in those days the Canadiens were housed in a room somewhere west of the present visitor's digs, and they had to make their way along a hallway encircling the outer edges of the building, then through an archway to the large doors where the Zamboni gained access to the ice.

Most people in the crowd were used to the American Hockey League Bisons and a dingy, dull, Memorial Auditorium, if they were hockey fans at all. For this NHL debut the Aud was an old lady in new duds and makeup, a Tammy Faye Baker of arenas. New glass, new colour scheme, and the incredible brilliance of the television lights. For the hometown fans it was a sight to see.

By 7:25 p.m. the Montrealers had made their way to the gate area, where crowds of late arrivals were being held back on either side of the pathway by movable barriers and a gaggle of officious ushers. I was in transit to the Sabres' offices but was trapped in the front line as Rogie Vachon hit the ice and a rousing, rumbling cheer sounded from the crowd.

The Canadiens, in their away reds, were an iridescent cerise under the intense TV lights, and the audience, just settling back into their seats for the start of the game, now rose in a standing ovation for the visitors. Suddenly, as I watched the famous and familiar numbers trip by, the chain of Canadiens abruptly stopped. A cameraman, backpedalling in his quest for a better angle, had stumbled and fallen in the entranceway.

I found myself standing at arm's length from towering Jean Beliveau, then Henri, followed by six-foot-something Terry Harper. To the people in the back rows it might have seemed as if there were nothing but space between Beliveau and Harper.

Richard's game face was on, the intense stare riveted forward and to the left. I remember his stolid acceptance of the unexpected halt, because he seemed to be far away, withdrawn, and I wondered what he could be thinking at that moment. I mean, hell, he couldn't be worried. It was only another game on the way to his 10th Stanley Cup.

At the same instant a female concessionaire, cut off between washroom and hot dog counter, found herself almost nose-to-ear from Richard. She peered at him, scrutinizing every feature, while he steadfastly studied Beliveau's left elbow.

"Jeezuz, Marg, he's grey!" she said emphatically to a friend somewhere over her shoulder. The words out of her mouth, she immediately grasped the fact that this was really Henri Richard standing there, not some life-size cardboard cutout. Beginning to blush, she let out a terrified giggle and slapped a self-conscious hand to her mouth. Richard shifted slightly and fixed her with a deadly, eyebrow-shrouded glare.

At exactly the same moment Beliveau smiled regally, while Harper chuckled, his humour antenna picking up major vibrations. Playfully he prodded Richard between the shoulders with a gloved hand, causing the Pocket to abandon his Bela Lugosi impersonation immediately and break into a gap-toothed smile. The woman turned away in red-faced embarrassment.

I knew right then that the smile wasn't for her, but for Harper. Had Henri not smiled, tossed the incident off, indicated it wasn't bothering him, it would have surfaced later in many ways. Such as arriving at your dressing room cubicle to find a jet-black fright wig with a white number 16 stuck on the back. Or opening your equipment bag to find an old dog brush used on a white Russian wolfhound. Or discovering that you've walked through Kennedy International with a sign stuck on the back of your trench coat that reads Grecian Formula — After Only Two Weeks Treatment.

Yes, Henri was very prudent to smile in that split second. Now it was only a minor story, a mere distraction, rather than a coming attraction. Like I said, there ought to be a Hall of Fame for sheer shrewdness. The Pocket would be a charter member.

90-SECOND ALL-STARS

G — **Jacques Plante**

D — **Doug Harvey**

D — **Bobby Orr**

C — **Jean Beliveau**

RW — **Maurice Richard**

LW — **Bobby Hull**

"I hope this team will be satisfactory."

Bobby Hull

Titan of Gold

OR YEARS THE NHL ACTED as if Robert Marvin Hull were an MIA in Laos. His stats were kept up to 1972, then, mysteriously, nothing. They kept active player records for every other pro league — American, Central, even the Eastern — but pretended that the World Hockey Association didn't exist. Therefore, logic dictated that R. M. Hull didn't, either. That always rankled me.

The NHL did the same to Paul Henderson and Frank Mahovlich, for example, yet saw fit to include the WHA statistics of those who returned to the National Hockey League, such as Bernie Parent and Derek Sanderson. With Bobby, it appeared he suddenly went AWOL after a year that saw him rack up his fifth 50-goal season and be named to the All-Star team for the 12th time. To the untrained eye he might have been an Alzheimer victim who had wandered off, or a serious sufferer of amnesia who roamed the streets and hopefully turned up someday having recovered his senses. The *NHL Official Guide* published his record up to the day he "vanished," then ran for seven seasons with a gap that got wider with each passing April.

Naturally, when the leagues merged and the NHL picked up the strongest swimmers (Quebec, Edmonton, Hartford, and Hull's

The Golden Jet: "the NHL should print its own currency for the boys and put RMH's picture on the $1,000 bill."

Winnipeg Jets), Bobby suddenly reappeared, the seven-year vacuum vanished, and an abundant backlog of numbers filled the gap. Briefly the prodigal Jet was golden again.

How did the best hockey league in the world, with very astute businessmen at the helm and lots of money to back up their credentials, get their collective arm twisted into giving comfort to the enemy? Sadly the league traditionally manufactured its own problems on what can only be termed an assembly line basis. Using plantation-owner mentality, ignoring trend indicators, bucking progress, and generally sitting around with their fingers up their collective butts, they waited for someone else to force decisions upon them. And so it was with Bobby Hull.

In a nutshell the WHA, desperate for a centrepiece, shrewdly offered an unheard-of contract, the kind no player had ever dreamed of up to that point in hockey history. Bobby, a businessman himself, told the Blackhawks about the offer, the Hawks ignored the warning, and Robert Marvin took a hike. He got a million-dollar bonus for bringing credibility to the WHA, while the NHL lost at least that much, plus the players who jumped into the pool with Hull. You have to realize that the signing of the Golden Jet made a lot of other players suddenly brave. And rich.

Whenever the name of Bobby Hull comes up, whenever our paths cross, I wonder about the symbol he represented, the greatness thrust upon him, and how his sheer eminence changed the game of hockey forever.

On a day of no particular importance at the Airport Marriott Hotel in Toronto, about 10 years after the final game of his career, he sits behind a table, various coloured pens strewn to one side of his busy hand. Rapidly he inscribes pucks in silver or gold, cards with blue or black; the same goes for sweaters, sticks, pictures, pennants, posters, and programs. The line of autograph hounds snakes along the walls of the room, out the double doors, and down the hallway fronting the large ballroom filled with card sellers and memorabilia freaks.

He's been at it for three hours, the practised, flowing penmanship with a readable signature repeating almost as often as the redundant comments. The most common is: "My first NHL game was when my dad got tickets — Leafs and Blackhawks. I'll never forget it."

Bobby calls one young man's bluff as he writes. "Who won?" he growls, flashing the world-famous grin under the equally famous broken nose.

"You did — 4–2. You got two goals," the autographee blurts almost too fast, the details of that first-ever game an obvious minute-by-minute memory chiselled in stone. The Golden Jet adds a wider, almost sneering grin. It's not arrogance, just a recurrent case of déjà vu.

He talks to everyone, never sets himself above anyone, is always able to level with any level. Friendly, he breaks down apprehension and shyness, the broken nose and gruff voice notwithstanding, posing no threat, disarming men, women, and children equally. The scribbling and patter flow easily after gallons of ink and miles of practice over a career that goes back to autograph seekers who asked for the signature when he was only 13. Back then his mother offered a sage explanation to a question plaguing the teenage hockey star. "Why do they want me to sign my name?" he wondered.

"It's just their way of saying they like you," she answered, then admonished him to be nice to everyone and anyone who took the time to wait for a personal audience.

Mom's advice is still heeded.

While celebrity status is still there, time takes its toll, as well. Some younger members of the lineup, pushed forward by Dad, mouthing a prepared request to the superstar, have no idea who or what the fuss is about. They're into Gretzky, Lemieux, Yzerman. Despite Dad's contradictions, all they see is a guy with a weird, bent finger who advertises power pucks and toupees.

Even if he noticed, it doesn't faze the Golden Jet. "How am I doin'?" he asks, referring to his lineup as compared to one for Gordie Howe down the hall in another private room.

"'Bout 150, 200 to go," observes George Mauro, card show impresario, as he shuttles between rooms, trying to dispense homage and attention in equal amounts to two of the game's leading citizens. Hull and Mauro have already had a disagreement behind the scenes about a rival card show that Hull did a week before today's event. It's the nature of the business.

Later, in the lobby of the hotel, we find ourselves a fivesome — Howe, Hull, Mauro, myself, and the white answer to Charles Barkley, Carl Brewer, who is there to relay developments on the retired players' pension fight.

Brewer sips white wine, while Howe, Mauro, and I have beer; Howe's is nonalcoholic, the rest of us have opted for light beer. Hull nips at a stinger. A business associate of Hull's joins us, and with the conversation turned to reminiscing, I remind Bobby about the time I asked him who the toughest guy he ever met in the NHL was. He nods in recognition and laughs at the story. "Yeah, Chico Maki." I agree, and he continues with the anecdote for the benefit of the others.

"Chico was into horses back then. He was leadin' this mare to the stable when one of the stallions got wind of her and jumps the goddamn fence. Little Chico's hangin' on to the bridle, tryin' to drag the mare out of there, but the stud's tryin' just as hard to jump her." He busts up laughing at the mind's-eye view. "And the horny bastard won't pay any attention at all, so Chico drills him, punches him out like that guy, Mungo in *Blazing Saddles*. He broke his ring finger, for Christ's sake."

"Anyway, he shows up at trainin' camp with this cast, tryin' to keep it quiet, on the QT. He got the trainers to tape it, cut the glove open, you know, cover it up. He'd get shit for it and all that stuff, so they put him out there to check me in the scrimmages. He was on my ass for two days, too, basically playin' one-handed. Never said a word, never complained. He was one tough little bastard."

Then there was the time Bobby broke Harold Ballard's nose. "Ol' Harold is down in his bunker when we're goin' through the warm-up. I guess I came over the red line and let one go. It ticked off something, cleared the glass, and conked Ballard right in the face. I thought I'd killed the old bugger. So when we're comin' off the ice later, Ballard comes up to me and says he wants our picture taken together. Well, we're laughin' an' shit, standin' outside the dressin' room, when Billy Reay comes along, grabs me by the arm, yanks me away, and growls, 'Get in the goddamn room. We don't take pictures with *him*.' He was really pissed off. He hated Ballard for not backin' him up and lettin' Punch Imlach can him back in 1958. Harold was left standin' there, lookin' like a raccoon, two shiners, nose the size of a beer bottle."

Needless to say, it's a popular story at our table. But later, after Bobby returns from a business discussion with Mauro, the mood changes.

Like anybody, Bobby can slip into an attitude, one that's surly and a touch challenging and disconcerting to those nearby. He can be opinionated with a hard edge and, relying on his position, notoriety, and obvious station in the game, there are moments when he will brook no contrary evidence or suggestions.

When he returns from his meeting with Mauro, I'm telling Howe and Brewer about the professor I heard on a local radio program who said the game of hockey was better now than at any time in the past, despite the watering-down of the league itself. The talk show guest cited four areas where differences between the players of the past and today were obvious, at least to him.

"Like what?" Hull asks testily after being brought up-to-date.

"Well, for instance," I venture, "he said the player of today is bigger, heavier, that he's more — "

"Aw, come on, they are like fuck!" Bobby interjects, snorting. "Think they got any bigger than we were?" he asks derisively, waving a hand that encompasses the table.

"He said it was a fact, that from a nutritional standpoint and past records the players today, as a group — "

"Get outta here," Bobby interrupts again, shaking his head.

"Okay," I say, taking another tack. "He said the players today are better conditioned."

"No way. That's crap. Just because they don't work in the summer like we used to doesn't mean they work out all year, either."

"Well, he went on to say they were better coached," I offer.

"Better coached?" Bobby's face becomes the very picture of incredulity. "Why?"

"He said today they have specialty coaches, goaltender coaches, coaches in the press box, more than one coach on the bench. He said it was normal practice nowadays to see an NHL team with three-man coaching staffs, plus he mentioned the minor hockey coaching certification deal, the university and college programs, the game videos, all the — "

"All the bullshit" is all Bobby comes up with. I look around at Howe, who rolls his eyes and takes a sip of his nonalcoholic beer.

"Okay, okay, he also said the player today was better equipped. You gotta give him that, Bobby. Shit, the skates alone, the helmets, the redesign of almost every piece . . ."

"They wear too goddamn much equipment" is his defence. And I figure it's time to move along and let these old vets discuss their lost pension rights, because regardless of what's said, it's going to go against Bobby's grain this afternoon. Maybe this is his way of getting rid of me.

Which may not be too far off the mark. After making my goodbyes and an exit, I run into the still-disgruntled Mauro in the hotel hallway. He tells me that when he left Bobby, the Golden Jet suggested, "Why don't you take Brewitt with you?"

Still, even after being told about this little side play, my evaluation of Bobby didn't, and hasn't, changed. Like anyone, he's entitled to choose his friends, business partners, and those who appeal to him as a social guest or a drinking buddy.

The only way I've ever known Bobby Hull is as a congenial host, or guest, an interesting and informative travelling partner, and someone, in short, who is generous to a fault. The one thing you have to accept when you're in his company is that he's a presence, a piece of Canadiana, an international star, and a luminary of the highest order. However, the fact that he can get a tad crusty from time to time is only normal. What the hell? Nobody said he was perfect, with the possible exception of brother Dennis, who happens to be the Golden Jet's biggest fan to this day. But if Bobby isn't perfect, at least he's sincere.

On a dinner-speaking date in Guelph Dennis and Bobby were the headline guests, along with myself as a fill-in for a ballplayer who had dropped out at the last moment. During the cocktail party prior to the dinner, I had mentioned I was trying to rent a boat for a one-week Lake Ontario cruise my wife and I had been considering. Out of the blue Bobby said, "You can have mine for nothing." Then he went on to describe a 34-foot Chris-Craft cabin cruiser, adding that the mechanics had gone over it during the winter, and with the exception of a bit of opening-day cleaning, it was ready to go.

I assumed he would forget, that he had only made the offer in the spirit of the evening, but I was wrong. When I called a month or so later, he remembered, even wondered if I was going to call, and then said the offer still stood. My wife and I packed up our gear, drove to the marina in Deseronto, stayed overnight on the boat after a session of elbow grease, sailed down the shore, and put in a week at Confederation Basin in downtown Kingston.

On our return we sailed the boat to Bobby's waterfront home on the Bay of Quinte. During our two-day stay with the Hulls, I had the opportunity to spend some time in the den, an addition to the original house overlooking the bay. If anything, the room said more about the man than all the descriptions and mini-biographies voiced and written I had ever come across.

I've always prided myself in not being overwhelmed in the presence of celebrities, whether they be from sports, show business, or politics. I look on such an encounter as a chance to observe, and I'm forever conscious of committing to memory little facets and moments. Invariably I find the "stars" to be ordinary people in every other sense, trying to accept their notoriety in one field despite everyone else's attempt to put them on a pedestal. Maybe it's my personality that allows me to accept celebrities as regular guys, or perhaps it's the innumerable opportunities to be with and around them that allows my nonchalance to show. Whatever the reason, it wasn't until I had a moment to sit in Bobby's rec room alone for a moment that I experienced an eerie sense of history, of excellence and accomplishment. For perhaps the first time in any celebrity association I was inwardly saying, *"Wow!"*

Small silver miniatures stand out on brickwork, nooks, and crannies. The Hart Trophy, the Art Ross scoring cups, the Lady Byng, All-Star game mementos, an Avco Cup from the WHA. Oddly enough, when I look for the lone 1961 Stanley Cup reproduction, it's among the missing. The walls are home to plaques and certificates, inductions into the Hockey Hall of Fame and the Canadian Sports Hall of Fame. The Order of Canada medal, looking very plain and commonplace despite its prestige, reclines in a satin-lined case on a shelf. Another wall holds the framed cover of *Time* magazine. Not many Canadians have made that first page. Then there's a Jantzen swimwear ad from *Sports Illustrated,* with Bobby, Frank Gifford, and another athlete whose name now escapes me, cheesecaking under Hawaiian palms. Only a few photos have survived the cut, one with brother Dennis in Chicago, another with son Brett at the University of Minnesota. Sticks, silvered and engraved, some of old-fashioned wood with the signature curved blade, run up a corner like ladder rungs.

Most intriguing, though, is a line of endless pucks encircling the room like wainscoting. Little engraved plaques tell of a winning goal here, a hat trick there, a 50th, a 52nd, 54th, then a 58th. How about a 77th! A chain of pucks in one room whereas some players just have their first, and last, not even enough for a decent set of bookends.

Even the gifts of fans are strewn around — a hockey doll, a Winnipeg Jets hooked rug, with perhaps some unknown importance attached to it. There are a host of baubles, trinkets, ornately printed tributes, and doodads of lesser awards. Everywhere I look there's a piece of nostalgia, recognition, and merit.

When Bobby returns, I sit at the well-stocked bar and watch the muscular forearms blend a couple of more drinks. It's at that moment that I get the strange feeling of recognition for the talent, greatness, and enormity of what this guy has brought to arenas around the world of hockey. But there's something wrong with this picture, and then it finally dawns on me as I note with surprise that the main attraction in the room isn't hockey. The showcase is the bricked, floodlit wall surrounding the fireplace, where the mantel is crowded with blue and red ribbons, photos, and titles for . . . the bulls.

Acknowledged as one of the country's leading authorities on livestock and their breeding, Bobby Hull is a recognized expert to the point where his opinion, and his bulls, are sought after in the marketplace. Despite the preponderance of hockey souvenirs, regardless of the history and accomplishment on the surrounding three walls, the stars of the show are the tributes to the bulls, to the bloodlines and ancestry of world-class cattle breeding, his posthockey vocation, his present-day passion.

As I sip my Bloody Caesar amid all the trappings of the game, I get a momentary glimpse of what it must be like to be a hockey deity, and the heavy burden it must bring. It made me think about how many times I've sat with hockey journalists, fans, scouts, coaches, GMs, active and retired players, listening to arguments into the wee hours of the morning, going through prodigious amounts of drink, and ticking off a litany of good and valid reasons why this player or another changed the game of hockey.

They'd cite Bernie Geoffrion, who took the fledgling slap shot to "Boom Boom" heights. Stan Mikita and the accidental broken stick in a practice that became the forerunner of every goaltender's worst nightmare — the curved stick. Bobby Orr, combining the talents of an Eddie Shore, Doug Harvey, and a touch of Pierre Pilote into a package that lifted the position of defenceman into the space age. Jacques Plante, who defied convention and critics to become the prototype and forerunner of every modern goaltender from Vladislav Tretiak to Patrick Roy, from Bernie Parent to Ed Belfour. And then there was Wayne Gretzky, but even the Great One has to take a back seat to the man who led the way.

For without Hull's grit, those iron muscles and the will to match, the courage to fly in the face of the status quo, the nerve to sail uncharted territory, there would have been no viable WHA, no other league for Gretzky to turn to, no bargaining chip for the others who followed to play off against. All the roads lead back to Bobby Hull. Forget the agents; the Golden Jet's the man the newest millionaires in hockey owe a debt of gratitude.

Leaving the Marriott card show that June day in the early nineties, I said to myself, It's okay if he's opinionated about allowing fighting, about neglecting the smaller man in the game, two subjects that go against his grain. I recalled his fight with the Hockey Hall of Fame when he threatened to take his sticks and other gear out of the exhibits if they dared to charge the public. So, I reasoned, it was perfectly all right for him to disagree with what some candy-ass university professor said concerning the height and weight of present-day players, or for him to take a tunnel-vision pride in the boys of winter during his era, and in his own considerable accomplishments. Who else has earned more right to stand on his position? Who else struck a harder blow for the players? Who took on a hockey's old-boy network and made them dance to another drummer?

In my humble opinion the National Hockey League Players Association, now that it's gained a lofty foothold on the NHL ladder, should use some of that clout to declare a Bobby Hull Day, maybe play its own version of a Bobby Hull Game, with the proceeds going to the retired players' legal expense fund. In fact, even though I believe Eric Lindros thinks he's a leader in the field of sports/labour relations, he should doff his helmet in the direction of the Golden Jet and offer a thank-you, too.

Reaching the car that day, I was reminded of a conversation I had in a coffee shop at the Edmonton airport. My tablemates were Chico Maki, goaltender Marv Edwards, and Pat Stapleton. "Who had the harder shot, Dennis or Bobby?" I asked, having worn out every other means of chitchat.

"Harder or heavier?" grunted Maki, Bobby's roomie for many years.

"What the hell's the difference if the puck's goin' 103 or 108?" Stapleton groused, and we considered the facts momentarily until we gave up and shrugged.

"How did you play Bobby when you had to go one-on-one?" I asked Edwards, who would surely know.

"Jeeeeezus," he said, running a toothpick from one side of his mouth to the other. "I used to come out to cut down the angle, make sure my legs were together, and hope to hell he scored." We all snickered at the logic in the remark.

Change the game?

The NHL should print its own currency for the boys and put RMH's picture on the $1,000 bill.

90-SECOND ALL-STARS

G — **Glenn Hall**
D — **Bobby Orr**
D — **Doug Harvey**
C — **Stan Mikita**
RW — **Gordie Howe**
LW — **Ted Lindsay**
"Either way it's pretty hard to top these six."

George "Punch" Imlach

Pugnacity in a Fedora

N THOSE EARLY DAYS before the Buffalo Sabres became an
on-ice entity, a year and a half of work was being crammed
into eight months. Everyone had a job to do, and no one had
time to delve into the other person's area. My job was to make certain
the Sabres had a first-class publication, nothing more, nothing less.
And since I ran the same kind of operation for the Leafs, I had to shuttle constantly between Toronto and Buffalo. The biggest problem was
convincing advertisers that this indeed was the NHL, which meant old
ad rates used for the AHL Bisons no longer applied. The second diffi-
culty was the need to upgrade the advertising from parochial to national. The sell wasn't easy, and resistance to change, and rates, was
strong. There were times when my work consisted of nothing more
than local telephone calls, downtown sales pitches, and office meetings
with ad agencies. On those occasions when a car was unnecessary I
would either fly to Buffalo, a puddle jump of 17 minutes, or arrange to
drive down with George "Punch" Imlach. We did it as often as our
schedules allowed. I believe he made the effort to leave the 401–27
junction, our pickup station, simply for the company, because both of
us made the trip to Buffalo alone more than enough in those first
months of 1970.

Punch Imlach: "an ability to combine the aged with neophytes, the castoff with the crewman, blending the two like a chef with a magic Cuisinart."

Now it was May and the guessing game was on concerning the first draft for the Buffalo Sabres come June, and the Toronto media was more excited than they had been for a couple of years. Punch was back, and their job would be more interesting, and easier.

When Imlach drove, he let it all hang out. As one former ashen-faced passenger had remarked after a brief 40-minute jaunt from Maple Leaf Gardens to the Peterborough Arena, driving with Punch was considered "low-level flying," or as another pasty-faced pundit put it, "rapid transit." He didn't motor from point A to point B — he attacked.

To combat stress I would often burrow into a paper and read aloud as a substitute for conversation. On those occasions my only inkling of other traffic would be the rise and fall of straining engines as we passed everything in sight. Mario Andretti would have been proud. On that particular day a Frank Orr feature in the *Toronto Star* caught my attention. He was comparing attributes of the acknowledged one-two picks — Gilbert Perreault and Dale Tallon — in the amateur draft, a subject Imlach had commented on only by saying that either pick would be a cornerstone of the player's new team, whether it was Vancouver or Buffalo. Or as Imlach used to say in private — "La-La-Land and Hamilton South."

Orr wrote that Perreault's forte was his flashy, considerable offensive skills, particularly his puck handling. In Tallon's defence he cited defence, the fact that the Noranda native was a tough guy as well as able to play two positions — versatile to a fault. And there were allusions to the fact that Perreault was going to be Lady Byng's steady date, taking very few penalty minutes and shying away from the heavy going, whereas Tallon could be up for Linebacker of the Year. The implication was veiled, but clear. Was the Montreal Junior going to lose his touch in the NHL's law of the jungle, while Tallon fitted in like a pit bull with a sore ass? Orr painted a picture of Perreault graduating from a dancercize school; Tallon, on the other hand, was a scarred veteran of Australian Rules Football.

I read the entire article to Punch, knowing full well he had read it himself in the morning. Then I put it down in time to witness our vehicle nose past a Corvette, dive down a lane between semis, then emerge on the top side again, passing a row of yellow school buses. I quickly returned the paper to an upright position for my own well-being. "He says it's a tough call," I said, my way of eliciting an opinion. Imlach merely pursed his lips, pushed back the ever-present hat, revealing more forehead, and adjusted the sun visor to compensate for the lack of brim.

"Have you made up your mind, Coach?" I asked, using the title we'd been hearing a lot when Imlach met with Buffalo civic figures and prospective season ticket holders. In case you haven't noticed, Americans accord coaches the same respect reserved for senators, congressmen, big cops, men of the cloth, and bank managers.

"Jesus Christ, Ross, what the hell do *you* think?" he demanded, glancing over at me and shaking his head, an indication that I had been spending too much time in the pool.

"So what's it gonna be?" I tried again, knowing full well I was fishing without a lure.

"You think I'm gonna listen to bullshit — defence against offence and all that other good stuff? No goddamn way! I gotta sell hockey down here," he insisted, jabbing a finger toward a Bridge to the Falls sign zipping by overhead. "I don't need anybody to try and stop goals. Shit, I need somebody to put the fuckers in. Perreault, not the Marlie son of a bitch. Perreault's the guy who's gonna sell the fucking game to Buffalo. I'll get some other bastards to check for him, hold his fuckin' hand if the boys get too rough. Besides," he allowed with a bit less vitriol, even a hint of a sideways smile, "I don't think our young Frenchman's gonna need any looking after." He made the statement positively, as if mental possession was nine-tenths of a draft choice.

Giving me a minute to digest this pointed position, he glanced over at me again. "Now, I guess you know enough to keep a lid on this, right? It ain't for public consumption until the minute I announce our choice. Got it?"

I could only nod.

"You never know. I might get one or the other, but if I get 'the other,' I don't want him pissed off at us because I played him down. Besides, those assholes in Vancouver are probably second-guessing the shit out of themselves, wonderin' what the hell I'm gonna do. Wouldn't it be just goddamn great if they get first pick, grab Tallon, because of something I said, and I wind up with Perreault, anyway? Wouldn't that be a kick in the balls?" He laughed and shook his head at the wonder of it all, this mind game, this armchair quarterbacking.

In the days to come Imlach would hear the question asked again and again, and he studiously praised both players, even made influential cases for Reggie Leach and Rick MacLeish, who would go third and fourth respectively come June 9.

He loved the constant give-and-take of the business, especially the managing part. The bartering, the constant phone calls, the evaluation of talent, not so much what a player had done somewhere else, but what he could do under the wing of Imlach. He had displayed a penchant for wringing the last drop of hockey out of old-timers and retreads in Toronto, his years there marked by an ability to combine the aged with neophytes, the castoff with the crewman, blending the two like a chef with a magic Cuisinart. In Toronto, with its wealth of players and farm system of pros and juniors, his credit card had no limit. In Buffalo he didn't even have a billfold.

Undeterred, he put together bits and pieces, like a reclusive miser collecting string, calling back former Leafs and experienced ex-opponents. Dick Duff, Ed Shack, Don Marshall, Phil Goyette, Reggie Fleming, goaltenders Roger Crozier and Joe Daley were some of the friends and former foes who came to roost. But his best acquisition came in the form of John Andersen, who left the Oakland Seals almost the moment Imlach reached an agreement with the Sabres. It was Andersen, the super-scout, who had done so well with Imlach's Leafs and would now do the same with Punch's Sabres. Aside from the stroke of pure luck on the over-and-under wheel when Gil Perreault came to Buffalo, Andersen was responsible for those who followed — Rick Martin, Craig Ramsay, Jim Schoenfeld, Larry Carriere, Lee Fogolin, Danny Gare, Bob Sauve, Ric Seiling, Larry Playfair, Tony McKegney, players who made significant contributions.

Only once, in 1973, did scouting take a holiday. The first two rounds landed Morris Titanic from the Sudbury Wolves and Jean Landry out of the Quebec City Remparts. Titanic, plagued by injuries and bad timing, suited up for only 19 Sabre games over two seasons before departing the scene. Landry would never wear the crossed swords of Buffalo, nor any other jersey in the NHL. But the amateur draft is a crapshoot at best, and it was in the evaluation of other people's talents that Andersen dovetailed with Imlach and made his biggest contributions. The ability to gauge how a player would adjust to Buffalo was something of utmost importance, and in that respect Andersen always served his master well.

The first Buffalo NHL team was a mishmash of shopworn vets and wrinkle-free kids. Typical of the infirm, the unwanted, or the unprotected bodies who found their way to the first training camp were defencemen Doug Barrie and Al Hamilton. Barrie, a scrappy, five-foot-nine 175-pounder, was lifted from Pittsburgh by way of Baltimore. Hamilton, at six-one and 200 pounds, was a smooth-skating puck handler, an offensive power play specialist plucked from the clutches of the New York Rangers. Their personalities were as disparate as their sizes, and each in his own way was a cross for Imlach to bear.

Barrie had the misfortune to have a shipment of his sticks go astray and eventually turn up in Boston rather than Buffalo. Having to eke out a career, he carefully guarded his remaining right-hand stick until one night, during a game, it broke. Hurtling past the bench, he grabbed at the first lumber offered only to discover that it was a leftie. Seconds later he was victimized by a bad pass off the blade of his replacement stick, resulting in a goal. Hamilton himself picks up the story.

"Punch blew up as we hit the bench," he recalls in a voice that reminds me of Marlon Brando's Godfather. "'What the fuck were yuh doin' out there?' he yelled. Dougie and I just put our heads down. I mean, what the hell else could you do? But Punch kept it up. 'Yuh got shit fer brains?' he snapped, glaring at Doug.

"Ol' Dougie slowly turned around, held up the stick, and said, 'You can't play correctly without the proper utensils.'

"You shoulda seen Punch. He almost had a shit fit. He pushed his hat back a mile and walked up and down behind the bench with his hands on his hips, muttering, 'Fuckin' asshole reads too much.' Dougie ignored him, but the rest of us were just pissin' ourselves laughing."

To Imlach, as the title of his autobiography suggests, hockey was a battle, and the Barrie incident was small potatoes, an aggravation that came with the job. One morning, sitting in his office, he told me about how he was finally lured out of what was probably an enforced retirement. At the time he was writing a well-read column for the *Toronto Sun,* hosting his own TV show, and otherwise collecting money from his wise investments.

"I had lots of coaching offers," he told me, "but that's not what I wanted. It was either gonna be general manager or GM/coach. Besides, I could pick my spots, didn't have to go to goddamn work, you know. Money wasn't a problem. The writing was nice, kept me involved, then I get this phone call from Buffalo — Seymour Knox. Would I speak to him about a job? Simple as that. They wanted a GM/coach. Hey, it wasn't my place to tell them what they needed. I just answered the goddamn questions straight. First friggin' thing I told 'em face-to-face was that they paid too much money. No bullshit! And they better be prepared to get some bang for their buck. I guess they liked what they heard, because they offered me the job."

I believe it was the man's candour in these kinds of situations that marked his appeal. He had a proven track record to hold up to scrutiny whenever the need arose. He was a straight talker in a world of fence sitters. And I suspect he came across as the genuine goods when meeting team owners. Going back to when I first met the man, I had already had some preconceived notions. From a distance I thought he was vain, arrogant, and overbearing, given to opinionated self-importance, not to mention an overconfident evaluation of his real or imagined talents. And he had a whiny, sharp voice, the kind that cuts through the eardrums, which didn't help his case, either.

As I got to know him, I realized his public and private sides were two different pictures. When I look back, I see that he was only a transition between Howie Meeker and Don Cherry. In those days he was not only the guy who said it like it was, but he did it with the flair, colour, and insight that was lacking in all others. He was a writer's dream, a coach who wore his game face even on open days of the schedule. You always knew where you stood with Punch, and the feeling was mutual.

He liked you or he didn't, you were on his side or against him. Just like the public perception of him, there were no grey areas.

In his office during those early Buffalo days he had a sign facing his desk that spelled out BEAT TORONTO in foot-high letters. It was there for everyone to see — no cover-ups for visitors, no apologies to peacemakers, no olive branches for bleeding hearts.

"That's right," he told me the day the sign went up. "It's my objective to be able to take it down someday, to stick it down their goddamn throats." At that point the finger drumming would start, for if there was one thing Punch was best at, it was holding a grudge. The man bore a grudge like a carrier pigeon — tirelessly and in a straight line to the ultimate payback. "I wanna beat the old man [Ballard]. I wanna beat those bastards and finish ahead of them in the standings. And when I do, when I get ahead of those assholes, well, I'll have proved my point, shoved it up their asses. I guess I'm kind of a prick that way, but goddamn it, it's what gets me going. My wife said I was nuts takin' the job, and I suppose when I beat the fuckin' Leafs, well, I'll just find somethin' else, some other goddamn challenge. It's the way I am, I suppose."

After only three seasons, the Sabres finished fourth and went to the playoffs, while the Leafs limped along in sixth. In its fifth season Buffalo went all the way to the final, losing to the defending Stanley Cup–champion Philadelphia Flyers in six games. Punch was right. He was still a driven man.

To my way of thinking the job he did in Toronto, phase one, was remarkable, gratifying, and to say the obvious, the last time a Leaf fan had the chance to walk around with a song on his or her lips until very recently, 1993 to be exact. Punch was the man, the leader of the pack, the unquestioned major domo. But what he did in Buffalo was miraculous, an incredible feat of wizardy unmatched by anyone before or since.

However, ultimately, genius reaches a point where changes are made with the times or the genius quickly fades, and so it was with Punch Imlach. Ending the Buffalo chapter of his career in 1978, he again returned to Toronto on the whim of his old adversary, Harold Ballard, for an ill-fated stint as the Leaf GM once again. As before, he didn't need the job, didn't need the aggravation, but the gauntlet was too enticing not to be picked up. By now Punch had become almost prehistoric, trying the same draconian methods he had used back in the sixties. No one could tell him that the hockey world had changed forever. No one could make him aware that expansion, an era he had participated in, and the advent of the WHA, were the death knell of treating players with a "take it or leave it" attitude.

The old Punch was revealed to me over coffee in the Hot Stove Club in 1979 when I offhandedly inquired about the prospects of another year of the Molson ProStars, a collection of Leafs, ex-Leafs, and a sprinkling of others I organized to play charity fastball every summer. We only scheduled seven games a year, finishing by the first week of August in order to allow as much time as possible to prepare for hockey in September. The team was a popular attraction throughout Ontario, and one of the rare public relations moves I ever saw from the Leafs in those days.

When Jim Gregory was GM, there was never a hint of a problem. Gregory took up the issue with Ballard, along with some pressure from Molson's, and because it was originally Darryl Sittler's way of getting the team together in the off-season, something he felt was needed to foster togetherness, we had no glitches. But once Punch returned to the scene it was rumoured the team was history.

When I politely and properly asked Imlach if he was going to have any objection to our fastball team, he immediately bristled. "Goddamn right! We don't pay these bastards to go out prancin' around no ball fields. And I don't give a shit about Molson's," he added emphatically. It eventually came down to the problem being "Sittler's fuckin' brainstorm," and the fact that "no goddamn hockey player is gonna tell me how to run *my* hockey club." That was the end of the conversation. I felt discretion and retreat were the best ways to combat his agitation. We did play that year, reluctantly sanctioned by Imlach, but it was never the same, nor was Sittler. The ball team was just a small concern, but Sittler and Imlach were on a collision course, and soon Punch began dismantling the Leafs, jettisoning those he considered free spirits. It was his last, sad kick at the can.

One analogy he drew for me on one of those long-ago drives to Buffalo stuck with me then, and still does today. I was complaining about the job, the constant wrangling and resistance by advertisers, by printers, by bean counters. I jokingly said all he had to do was make sure he had some bodies to fill uniforms on opening night, whereas all I might have is something resembling an A & P Wednesday food flier by October.

"Don't be so goddamn soft on these people," he singsonged to me. "Stick to yer guns. It ain't gonna get any easier next year. Besides, I know you think our jobs are different, but they're not. We're both governed by the bottom line. I gotta put asses in seats, you gotta cover the cost of the magazine. You don't get the advertising, and I don't get people to the rink, we're both out on the street with our goddamn flies open. To get to the bottom line, wins and losses, money in the till, you have to build a winning team. A winning team is everything."

Of course, he was right from a business standpoint, but that was then and Punch's now came when he returned to Toronto. There is no bottom line in Hogtown. The seats are sold and have been since the late forties. The only way to generate more money is to put a seat in every available square foot of remaining space and raise ticket prices. Ballard did that one to death.

Toronto was the only NHL city where lacklustre teams could be shoved onto the ice for 25 years and not only be tolerated but still turn a profit. In any other locale the fans, the people who pay the piper, would have shunned the Gardens like a morgue. The team called the Maple Leafs wasn't a priority in Toronto, only the bottom line.

At one stage the powers that be were on the right track, but it only became a killing field for ownership. Punch was given a free hand, more than Jim Gregory before him and Gerry McNamara after. He let ego get in the way of a common goal. He forgot the human element, the players you have to have to win, to go out night after night and do the job. He forgot one of his own most valued qualities — loyalty.

In the end he even abandoned his own sage advice. Not about wins and losses. In Imlach's last pathetic go-around the team limped in and out of the playoffs. Not money in the till, nor the bottom line. That was Ballard's area, and he policed it like a drill sergeant. No, Punch forgot that "building a winning team . . . is everything."

Bill Sweeney

Search-and-
Destroy Centre

I T'S UNUSUAL THAT BILL SWEENEY is in this book. All the other people I've written about I know on a first-name basis, or at least we've been together at a dinner or a golf tournament. Once, briefly, tersely, I was within speaking distance of Bill Sweeney, yet I still have a vivid memory of that meeting.

Oh, I had heard about him often, about the talent, about the crazy escapades. In hockey circles he was a legendary figure, even among people who were considered legends themselves. Bill Sweeney was a man on a search-and-destroy mission for his entire career.

There are many ex-players out there uttering the time-worn phrase "born too soon" with justification. There are a lot of areas they're entitled to gripe about. Pension is one. Expansion and the chance to make some real money are two more. They languished in the bushes while owners and managers either kept them from other teams desperate for help or buried them in hockey limbo on the whim of a petulant kingpin or coach. They bemoan the fact that they never had the freedom nor the bargaining power of the ones who came later. They grind their teeth at a fate that denied them salaries trailing enough zeroes to resemble the national debt. And, more than once, I've heard old-timers rate former minor league stars, sometimes obscure names from the past, in a latter-day shadow draft, an imagined selection of the best talent and where it would go if . . .

The list is long. Willie Marshall, Dick Gamble, Ray Gariepy, the Glovers, Jim Anderson, Dave Amadio, Phil Maloney, Guyle Fielder, Brian Kilrea, and certainly the ubiquitous Don "Grapes" Cherry.

Bill Sweeney was a career "if." A large number of his peers feel if he were coming up now, instead of turning pro back in the late fifties when hockey serfdom was at its peak, he would have been snapped up in the first or second round of today's amateur draft.

He starred for the Guelph Biltmores, the same training ground Andy Bathgate, Harry Howell, and the irascible Eddie Shack also worked for in Junior. In fact, Sweeney, Shack, and a winger named Brian Webber were a high-scoring trio for the Biltmores before Shack and Sweeney were assigned by the Rangers to the AHL Providence Reds.

In his first season Sweeney rang up 31 goals and 46 assists over a full 70 games to finish as AHL rookie of the year. Shack had an acceptable first outing at 16 goals and 18 assists, more so because he only dressed for 35 games. But it was Eddie who got the call and left for the Big Apple to begin 17 NHL seasons, where he helped earn four Stanley Cups in a career that was only marred by a couple of short diversions to the minors. Sweeney, on the other end of the hockey tunnel, laboured in the boonies for another 11 years, with only a brief four-game stint with New York. Yet he put up consistent point totals, including three consecutive league-leading 100-plus-point years from 1960 to 1963, long before century seasons were fashionable.

The official knock on Sweeney was his skating, or so they said. The hockey pooh-bahs also cited his size as a detriment. Compared to Shack's six-foot-one, 195-pound variety of exuberant enthusiasm, Sweeney was slight, borderline average, and ordinary at five-ten and 165 pounds. As for foot speed, if he couldn't skate, he could sure as hell run on his Tacks. The numbers he put up were too good to be posted by a broomball player, therefore the fact that the man had a touch around the net was obvious. Size? No one ever questioned his grit despite his shortcomings in height and weight.

To hear the boys tell it, he could have played in the NHL, and the facts surrounding why he wasn't given a chance aren't clear except for one glaring fault: Bill Sweeney drank to excess. He wasn't the first to have the problem nor would he be the last.

Don Cherry, a career minor leaguer himself and a friend of Sweeney's, emphatically says, "It's a shame he never got the opportunity in those early years. He woulda turned himself around. I know it. I know he woulda done whatever it took if he'd gotten the chance." Grapes then cites Sweeney's qualities — his toughness in the slot area and his ability to get the puck to good wingers. "They say he couldn't skate, but the guy wasn't afraid to come all the way back to his own end and get the damn puck, either," Cherry mutters. "Yeah, he was a bit of a rebel," he adds, chuckling at some memory, "and he didn't take to restrictions, either. Jeez, the last thing the coaches and GMs in that day and age needed to hear and see was a smartass. Unfortunately, despite his talent, Billy *was* a smartass. But he could help a team. He coulda helped the damn Rangers."

Ed Shack is of the same opinion. "He didn't skate real good, you know? I mean, he could skate, but he didn't look nice. But, shit," Shackie says, rolling his eyes, "he coulda played in the NHL."

Bill White was a teammate in Springfield, a place respectfully referred to by ex-Indians as "Devil's Island," a snide reference to Eddie Shore, the eccentric, tyrannical owner and closet coach of the team. White's sentence in Springfield was five years, while Sweeney spent eight. "Swiner [another nickname] was a scratch golfer, very competitive. If he walked into a bar and there were darts, even if he never played before, by the end of the evening he'd be strapping everyone's ass. It didn't matter — shuffleboard, basketball, pool, you name it. He could master anything. On the ice he was the same way. You rarely saw Billy knocked off his skates — very solid, very tough, and a brilliant centre. Hell, he had moves along the lines of Stan Mikita. He'd swoop in over the blue line, make that little turn, the fake-and-delay, then slip a seeing-eye pass through to Bruce Klein. Just beautiful to watch. Yep, give Swine a shot at the NHL, a season, and I believe life would have been different for him."

In a lighter vein White recalls the days of their servitude together in Springfield. There were some who would wager Sweeney "played better pissed than most guys did straight up." There were tales about him dozing off for a few winks at face-offs, nodding off on the bench, or not remembering entire games, which simply put him in the company of Howie Young, Jim McKenny, and Derek Sanderson, to name a few who experienced blackouts in their careers. White remembers one oft-repeated scene in particular from his days in the Massachusetts city. "He was pretty good about it. He'd get tanked and call for someone to pick him up. Usually it was me and somebody else who went over to McCarthy's. I'd drive while the other guy ferried Swine's car home. You had to cross a narrow two-lane bridge over the Connecticut River to get to Bill's place. There was one night, near Christmas, when he called around midnight, but I was already in bed. I passed and told him to call somebody else. Said I was too tired, you know, too comfortable to get up and get dressed. Next day at practice he arrives in the parking lot with the car scraped fender to fender down the passenger side. Strips of chrome trim and crap were hanging off the doors, the mirror was flattened, the aerial looked like a question mark. All I said was 'Bridge?' All he said was 'Drove home myself, thanks.'"

The stories were numerous, outrageous, borderline ridiculous. The retelling became historical fact rather than embroidered irresponsibility, merely the riotous carryings-on of a good-time Charlie, a guy who didn't know, or care, about the price tag. Truly one of the boys.

There was the time he got up to close the bedroom window of his second-story apartment and somehow managed to fall out nude, only to wake up in the parking lot. On another occasion, concerning a New York tryout the year the Rangers trained in Europe, Sweeney allegedly took the team bus for a jaunt through downtown streets somewhere in Switzerland, while the waiting team and management cooled their heels in a hotel lobby.

Rumours, half-truths, hearsay? Whatever the case, the drinking was beginning to catch up with him, something that wasn't lost on GMs and coaches, the people who dealt careers around like cards in a stud poker game.

Three straight scoring championships were the apex before a slow but steady fading of skills. The year prior to the NHL expansion in 1967–68 to 12 teams Sweeney scored only 16 goals, adding 50 assists in 65 games. The edges were getting frayed, the routine was becoming stale, and the reputation preceded him at every turn.

By 1968 Bill Sweeney had reached the end, playing a game in Memphis, 15 in Vancouver, and only nine in Springfield. In 1969, at the age of 32, he dressed for a token 10 games in Rochester, left without registering a point, and dropped out of pro hockey altogether.

That same year Shackie was finishing up his 11th NHL season, his second with the Bruins, and was soon on his way to L.A., where he joined Bill White, already a fixture on the Kings' blue line, and Dale Rolfe, another Springfield alumnus who had been sprung for good behaviour. Meanwhile Cherry was finishing up his playing career, too, but his posthockey star would rise while Sweeney's sank farther and farther.

Back in the early 1980s I walked into The Manor, a Guelph landmark tavern perched on a slight rise overlooking the then new Highway 6. The place eventually became a strip joint that dealt out X-rated lunches, but on this mid-afternoon day it was simply a dark, dismal, barely inhabited shelter from the September warmth and sunshine. I was there to meet Gord Smeaton, a Labatt's salesman. We had to talk about one of the Original Six games on our winter schedule. Only four unrelated patrons were strewn around the battered right-angled bar, and as my eyes grew accustomed to the gloom, I realized my neighbour on the nearest stool was Bill Sweeney. At least I thought that's who it was, relying on recollection of photos and an in-person identification by Pit Martin when we spoke at a sports celebrity dinner in Guelph two years earlier.

Hesitating, trying to make sure I had my memory screwed on tight, I eventually felt confident enough to speak to the man who stared steadfastly at two draft glasses, one full, one half gone. "Excuse me, you're Bill Sweeney, right?"

He turned his head slightly to find the source of vocal irritation, then eyeballed me vacantly. The look stretched and lingered absently for several seconds. I thought he wasn't going to answer at all until he returned his attention to the beers and finally said dully, "Yeah." The tone left the question "So what?" unsaid. I didn't realize it then, but that was the first and last time he would look at me.

In order to establish a reason for my forward behaviour I made a case by association. "I was with Ed Shack just yesterday. We were at a dinner in Woodbridge. He was talking about the Biltmores. You used to play with Shackie, didn't you?"

Sweeney never looked up. He just snorted and let his gaze drift over to the lone square of light lancing through a window down the hall. It stood out like a beacon, the only reminder in the entire joint of a world outside.

"You got it backward, pal," he said with some sarcasm. "Eddie Shack used to play with *me.*"

Chastised into silence, I stared at the bottles behind the bar and waited for Gordie, while Sweeney, hunched over on his stool, sipped the two drafts to their inevitable bottoms. The man never said another word, nor did I. He just sat there, half turned away. His attitude struck me as bitter, smart-assed, too. But maybe in this case, I thought, he was justified.

When I read many years later about his passing, I went to the *NHL Official Guide* and looked up his final NHL record. Was it out of curiosity, a tug of regret? Or was it simply a small touch of respect?

Four games, one goal, no assists, one point.

What a goddamn shame.

Don Cherry

Dandy of Steel

THERE ARE NO GREY AREAS with Don "Grapes" Cherry. You are either with him or against him.

This was the same mantle worn by others such as Punch Imlach, Scotty Bowman, John Ferguson, and Harold Ballard. On or off, black or white, love 'em or leave 'em, they are either arrogant, opinionated, hard-hearted, insufferable assholes, or good ol' boys with a touch of misunderstood genius. Anytime I do an interview with someone connected to the game, I slide in a standard question, using at least one of those four names, and ask for a personal observation in three words or less. Rarely do I ever hear "don't have an opinion." Some people add several four-letter words to the three already allowed.

But in Cherry's case there's a strong feeling of support, and in television success lies in whether the fans will watch. Fortunately he has a lot more boosters than detractors, especially among hockey fans, the people who really count.

Is Don believable? Is bungee-cord diving stupid? Of course the public believes him. Who else tells us about the "muckers" in the game, the guys who follow the Fred Shero theme of "going straight to the man with the puck and arrive in a bad mood!" Who else has

The dandy at rest: Don Cherry at home with Blue.

successfully bucked the system and wears his own clothes rather than those wussy blue blazers that seem to be one-piece coveralls with Velcro fasteners in the back. Who else has the patience to listen to Ron MacLean bring up the lead topic each night? And who else has the courage to say he was wrong on the few occasions such an event occurs.

I know people who only tune in for "Coach's Corner," passing on the actual game. Why? Because he tells it like it is. He says what we as viewers want to hear. He takes us behind the scenes, onto the ice, and into the corners where it's dangerous. He gives opinions like no one else ever has and backs it up with confidence. When Grapes gives us the big thumbs-up, you can take it to the bank.

So here's someone who has parlayed a six-year NHL coaching career and the self-deprecating humour of his own hard-hat and safety-boots playing days into a business. And a nice little business it is, combining print and television ads, a radio talk show, a bottomless barrel of videos, a syndicated TV show, and a chain of restaurant/bars.

Cherry's Mississauga eatery is located at the base of an office tower in Square One, a large complex that has become the centre of the universe for the place we call home. It is the halfway point between the main shopping plaza and Oz, which is what the natives refer to as City Hall.

The city's political incubator looks like something out of Dorothy and Totoland, beautiful inside, but outside a testimonial to what architects can do with a jumbo Lego set, a few beers, and your money. Supposedly it won some design awards, but I always thought they must have been for cartooning. Looking out the front door of Cherry's Grapevine, you can see the trademark minaret, bell tower, Meccano clock stand, or whatever prefab title you wish to hang on the structure.

The place was officially opened by the Duke and Duchess of York, Prince Andrew and Sarah Ferguson. Remember them? And as fortune would have it, I wanted to do a community newspaper column about the event at the same time I had already begun a piece about Don's place. I couldn't resist the temptation to put the two together. Sort of their royalty, and ours:

Royal watching. It's everywhere. Like acid rain.

Only a few days have passed since the D & D of Y visited our city, but it seems like a long time ago.

Anyway, I was in Don Cherry's newest eating establishment the other day and the subject of the royal couple came up. Well, sort of. Once inside, I jokingly asked if Andy had dropped in, seeing as how he was right next door.

"Van Hellemond? A referee wouldn't come into my place unescorted," Cherry said, shocked that I would presume such a thing.

"No," I corrected. "Andy and Fergie."

"John Ferguson was here?" he said, eyes widening with greater surprise.

Before I could begin to straighten the situation out, Shirt & Tie #1 at the corner of the bar, obviously a regular, said it for me. "He's referring to the Duke and Duchess of York. Y'know, Prince Andrew."

"Well, why didn't he say so?" the mildly offended proprietor snorted.

A brief but lively discussion followed, proving that royalty watching, amid this photographic collection of missing teeth, clenched fists, blood, sweat, and even a few tears, was alive and well.

"Wait a minute," the flustered Cherry said. "Is this guy a duke or a prince?"

Shirt & Tie #3 said, "C'mon, you should be familiar with the man. You wear suits just like his."

With a withering stare the coach said, "Wrong. *He* wears suits like *mine!*" Case closed.

It was duly explained over the next five minutes what the royal visit was all about, and that it was now history since the D & D were currently out west on a canoeing trip.

"You mean you people are worried about a guy who'd take his wife to Medicine Hat on their anniversary? You really care what he says about our City Hall?" Then he cocked his head toward me and said out of the side of his mouth, "This duke, he ain't a Swede, is he?"

It never happened that way, of course, but it might have.

Cherry's aversion to Europeans has been a public posture for years. He derides Swedes, Russians, Czechs, and anyone else playing or considering playing in the NHL, with the same disdain and dismissal they, in his eyes, deserve. He will dispute and argue against any player from outside the wonderful world of visorless, clean-cut, face-first-checking Canadians. He claims these interlopers take jobs away from homeboys and usurp awards like the Calder Trophy from ruddy-cheeked, runny-nosed, frozen-toed Canadians who have done their time in outdoor rinks. He is simply against free trade within hockey.

His staunch, unwavering bias was best illustrated the day he and Brian Williams of CBC fame were hosting the World Junior Championships. It was the memorable and noteworthy bench-clearing dustup between the Canucks and Russians.

A righteous, mortified Williams deplored the fighting, labelling it disgusting, embarrassing, shameful, and other words to that effect. An obviously agitated and just as righteous Cherry alternately stared at the camera in simmering impatience or glared at Williams in disbelief. Their on-camera disagreement graduated to a near-shouting match before the producer could cut to a handy, "We'll be back after this word from our sponsors." Williams picks up the story.

"Anyone who thinks he wasn't angry, that he was doing it as a setup, was badly mistaken. Including me!"

From Don's side the reaction was neither contrived nor staged. "Jeez, he's sittin' there, wavin' that pencil around, sayin' he's devastated, that it's a black mark on the game of hockey. He's never seen such a display. He's takin' the Russkies side an' everythink. But, Jeez, he kept it up, goin' on and on about ten goddamn times, an' here's me gettin' hotter and hotter."

By the time the break for commercials arrived, Williams realized Cherry's anger was real. Confused and wary, if nothing else, he moved away from the seething ex-coach. When the director asked them to sit closer for the camera, Cherry said with force, "Better not. I might get my hands on the little bastard's throat and never let go."

It was an outtake that never made the tube. Even if it had, the uninformed might have read showbiz hype into it, but it was real anger from Cherry and real regret from Brian. As Williams tells it now, with a nervous laugh, it was a close call.

The fact is, the Russians started the melee right in front of a Finnish referee who had demonstrated no control over either team. But, to be honest, there were iniquities on both sides. However, if Williams thought he was speaking for the audience when he lamented the event, he was wrong. Instead of Cherry coming off as the coast-to-coast heavy, it was Williams who received the brunt of negative opinion.

Which brings me to the next point in the mass appeal of Don Cherry. Again, in another newspaper column, I observed he was more often right than wrong, probably in the high 80 percent range with his prognostications. In addition, the way he put his case reflected knowledge, insight, and understanding. The fact that he didn't articulate the language like a college professor was immaterial, certainly not a hinderance. If anything, it was a plus. In my opinion he spoke like most of the people in Schreiber, Napanee, Weyburn, and Sydney. He was simply one of the crowd, talking to the crowd.

How did he get that way? He didn't *get* that way. He is that way.

Despite the fancy suits, shirts, ties, and cuff links, Don is a lunchpailer, a construction guy, someone who came home every summer from another season in the minors. The very best thing about Grapes is that, as his income and tailors changed, he hasn't. Underneath the double-breasted suits and a neck encased in six-inch-high shirt collars is the same guy who put in 15 seasons as a pro, but only one game in the NHL — a single Stanley cup tilt. The rest of the record reads zero across the page.

He wore the jerseys of nine different minor league teams over all those seasons, some of them twice. Not an easy life, not a life conducive to greatness. And that's what the fans understand. He's a grinder, a paid-up member of the club.

Back when he was breaking into television under the guidance of Gerry Patterson and the support of *Hockey Night in Canada*'s Ralph Mellanby, he was already established as a character. He was bigger than life and able to maintain his status as a star. He had been surrounded by Bobby Orr, Phil Esposito, and Gerry Cheevers, each in his own way a dominant personality, and he survived. Although he took the Bruins to four first-place finishes in five years and the Stanley Cup final three times, he was dumped, as all coaches are eventually discarded.

Yet despite the disappointment of not playing in the NHL and the ignominy of being released by the Colorado Rockies after only one year as coach, his indomitable personality led him to stardom on television. Showmanship, daring, tongue-in-cheek bravado, and a flair for the dramatically ridiculous were the qualities that captured the hearts of the people. The fact that he spoke like a rube was belied by the natural on-camera sense of performance he brought to the show.

The first time I saw him up close and working was in a converted Hamilton theatre, the set of Channel 11's *Grapevine* series. I watched as the fake bar was set up, the corny locker backdrop was rolled into position behind the interview chairs, the fake bartender was primped, and the curious were ushered to tables. A preoccupied Cherry ran through some stage directions with the floor manager. He looked a bit out of place back then amid cue cards and the theatrical settings. Those were the days when writers would loosely script a show, a line of thinking for him to follow. After the discussion with the production team, he headed for "makeup." I next saw him in front of a floor-length mirror, making adjustments to tie and suspenders. He was deadly serious, lost in thought, distant and focused. As I recall, the three guests that evening were Scotty Bowman, a mallard-necked kid named Gretzky, and a referee whose name escapes me.

He did all three interviews with barely a hitch. However, I still remember the strain showing at the end of each show, and again at the beginning of each wardrobe change. But despite the trepidations, he was funny, inventive, and listened to answers, unlike a lot of so-called accomplished interviewers. Instinctively he knew when to jump in with a neat segue whenever the pace sagged, whenever the need arose. At the time he was a veritable novice, but he was already a consummate professional.

Many years later I sat in on another taping. The setting was the bar in Mississauga. No more contrived sets, walk-throughs, or briefings. The guest was Bobby Orr.

This time there were no cue cards that I could see, no plot line in evidence, no support roles by other people, and except for producer Frank Dienardis's instructions to those in attendance, it was nothing more than two old friends chatting about hockey, with each man in turn playing the foil for the other.

That's the way people perceive Don Cherry — garrulous, flamboyant, fun-loving and, most of all, interesting. Take away the posturing, remove the gruff exterior and feigned indignation he uses on television, and you have a happy guy who would just as soon rehash the old days or last night's game — take your pick. It won't matter, because he'll have an ironclad assessment of either one. Sure, he's opinionated, but what the hell? He does have valid opinions.

If you want to see him change into a softer-spoken, more considerate person, get him talking about the people he calls "career minor leaguers." He loves to talk about the players who laboured all those years in Rochester and Seattle, in Kingston and Cleveland, in Victoria and Providence. There were a lot of them — Willie Marshall, Dick Gamble, Ron Attwell, Cec and Ed Hoekstra, Brian Kilrea, and Bill Sweeney.

"Sweeney would have been there, no sweat," Cherry reflects. "They said he couldn't skate, but he could get you the puck. He could stand the heavy goin', no problem. Brian Kilrea, too. Never saw Killer lose a face-off. Dick Gamble, Jeez, he woulda been a 70-goal man now, comin' in from the wing with that wrist shot of his."

Typically one of his proudest moments was the night the big boys came to town. The parent Stanley Cup–winning Leafs skated into Rochester to play the farmhands in a preseason game.

"I'll tell ya. That was a night I'll never forget. They come into our building, a sellout, and we waxed 'em — 8–1 or somethink like that. Yeah, right in front of Stafford and Harold. Punch was behind the bench, face about a mile long." He chuckles at the memory. "We had *that* good a team, no kiddin'," he adds, as if I'll doubt him. We both get a second laugh, thinking about what the Leaf practice probably looked like the next day. He basks in the reflection. Justice has been served.

I believe it was this early adversity, the constant striving to succeed, the uncertainty of coupling hockey with the raising of a family that gave Cherry his special quality. It allowed him to let his personality thrive on the good things that have happened, the notoriety, the business success. And, as lofty as his position is now, he still isn't above appreciating some dressing room humour at his own expense.

I relate to him how the Labatt's Original Six team was playing on the East Coast, finishing early enough to catch the *Grapevine* show back at the hotel. Cherry filled the screen, pinstripes and all, along with a shot of Blue, the most famous bull terrier in the world. Jimmy Pappin, a Rochester teammate of Don's in the 1960s, watched the show briefly, turned, and said with a laugh and a snort, "Shit, I knew him when he wore a kilt and had a goddamn poodle."

"Hey," Cherry says, laughing, "I did have a poodle and I always wore a kilt. What the hell? I was a drummer in a pipe band for over 20 years. Even these days I like to wear a kilt every now and then," he adds with a chuckle. Then he shrugs and grins. "But I gotta pick my spots. Yuh know how it goes."

90-SECOND ALL-STARS

G — **Gerry Cheevers**

D — **Bobby Orr**

D — **Larry Robinson**

C — **Wayne Gretzky**

RW — **Guy Lafleur**

LW — **John Bucyk**

"Even I coulda won with these guys."

Phil Esposito

Fury in the Slot

HILE WATCHING THE 1992 amateur draft on TSN, I absently observed the soon-retiring John Ziegler smile his way through his swan song in front of the hard-nosed legions of GMs, coaches, and scouts seated at the 24 tables scattered around the Montreal Forum floor. Along with the assembled draftees, families, fan clubs, and visiting Russians and Czechs about to become rich, I listened to Ziegler's smarmy welcome, which conjured up visions of Arnold Schwarzenegger briefing the tots in *Kindergarten Cop.* But the pizzazz didn't stop there. Next came Brian O'Neill, the NHL's executive vice president, who gave an absolutely riveting rendition of the draft rules. It was as if someone from NASA's Mission Control were announcing the blowup of the latest shuttle launch. So much for show business.

The only interest I had in the telecast was in who Phil Esposito was going to select as the first ever Tampa Bay Lightning player. Espo's luck had prevailed again, and he owned the first selection overall. Knowing him and his sense of the dramatic, I figured the choice would set the tone for the rest of the draft, providing topic, theme, and substance to the media for hours, if not days, to come.

Classic hockey: Team Canada's Phil Esposito moving in on the Soviet Union's Vladislav Tretiak during the fabled 1972 Summit Series.

My mind went into neutral as the camera panned over the logoed table signs. All I could see was silver hair, broken noses, the new teeth and old scars of the hockey faces of the past now sitting in judgement on the new crop of hopeful stars of the future. I conjured up a vision of Espo, funereal in a grey suit, looking more like a Mafia don than Al Pacino on his best day, brother Tony at his side, wearing a mask and weaving left and right. They would bring down the house with the news that the Lightning had secured the services of Eric Lindros. All it took was Tampa's draft choices through 2005, the Indian River grape-fruit groves, the rights to George Steinbrenner, and all the sushi the Quebec Nordiques could eat ad nauseum. As a disturbing sidebar, I couldn't help but wonder if Marcel Aubut might go for such a deal.

Phil did arrive in a grey suit, flanked by brother Tony on the wing, albeit without his mask. But before making the dramatic announce-ment the entire production was hanging on, Espo took the time to give thanks to Ziegler for his years of service. The statement got the luke-warm applause it deserved. After all, these people came to make money, not attend a burial.

I had to smile, though, because once again Esposito was calling the tune. He was so sincere that it was hard for me to determine whether he was serious or merely putting us on. He's like that, you know. And I couldn't help thinking about all the people who had openly told me he would never make it in Tampa. Now here he was with the first pick in the 1992 draft. It looked good on him, and in the end he put his money on a young Czech defenceman named Roman Hamrlik.

Fortune, luck, fate, all have played a large part in Phil Esposito's life, with more on the plus side than the minus. But it was never easy.

His hockey career began, like most northerners, on outdoor ice and was capped when Sault Sainte Marie won the All-Ontario Juvenile championship.

Juvenile! Now there's a term from the evolution of hockey. Nowadays, if a kid hasn't caught the eyes of the Junior bird dogs by the age of 15, he's usually scheduled to play his remaining hockey at 1:00 a.m. in an undersized uniform at some four-rink complex in the suburbs.

After the Soo, Espo found his way to Sarnia Junior B, playing as a chubby five-foot something who skated badly but had a deft scoring touch. The following year he grew a few inches, leaned out a bit, and stepped up to the St. Catharines Blackhawks. St. Kitts had previously turned out Hawks such as Pierre Pilote, Bobby Hull, Stan Mikita, Chico Maki, Wayne Hillman, Ab McDonald, and Pat Stapleton. Even at this late stage of his development, Esposito fully intended to follow their lead. And he did.

At the first training camp in Chicago in 1962 he was touted as the up-and-coming replacement for crusty Bill "Red" Hay. Phil knew it. He read the papers.

"He was a mean son of a bitch. First scrimmage, we face-off together, so I skated right up and said, 'Hi, Red.' He never answered. When the puck was dropped, he didn't even try for the draw, just brought his stick up and jabbed me in the jock. Hard, yeah, and all he said, was, 'You ain't taking my job, rookie.' Taught me a lesson. I guess he was reading the papers, too."

Hay would hold on to a centre spot until the end of the 1966–67 season, but by then Esposito had put in three full seasons with the Hawks, establishing himself as a potential scoring threat. His future in Chicago was assured, or so he thought. After the 1966–67 season, the Blackhawks decided Pit Martin was the centre they needed to get the puck to Bobby Hull. In May a preexpansion trade sent Esposito, Fred Stanfield, and Ken Hodge to the Bruins for Martin, goalie Jack Norris, and defenceman Gilles Marotte. Norris would play a total of six games for Chicago, Marotte would put in two seasons before going down the road to L.A., and Martin would eventually head to Vancouver and close out a fine 17-year career.

Except for the initial shock of being traded, something that is a part of the game for all but a few who make the NHL, Esposito and his emerging talents were in the right place at the right time to take advantage of the Bruins' era in the seventies. He was a part of two Stanley Cups and nailed down eight All-Star selections, two MVP awards, and five scoring championships.

For Espo's critics there was always the Bobby Orr factor. They said anybody could win or put up numbers on the power play with the gifted Orr. It sure as hell didn't hurt, and Esposito was the first to admit it.

For seven years, leading up to the mid-seventies, if it wasn't Espo on top of the point parade, it was Orr. In five of those seasons they were one-two. Without question they were the greatest scoring duo on one team, peers and rivals of the greats — Mikita and Hull, Howe and Lindsay, Gretzky and whoever.

Yet everyone has a single event that has a profound effect on his life. For Phil Esposito Team Canada was a date with destiny.

In 1972 Espo would establish himself as a leader without equal, a super-catalyst who over one historic month would drive players from different teams, backgrounds, and attitudes to pull together, sacrifice, play a notch higher, and turn back the Russians in the face of incredible pressure. Of the players and qualified observers I've talked to concerning the Summit Series, all, without exception, point to Esposito as the reason the team won.

According to Dennis Hull, at the outset of the Team Canada training camp in Toronto, Phil told the other hopefuls in the dressing room that he could be expected to get two points per game. No waffling, no bravado, simply a fact. Then, taking in the room with an all-encompassing wave, he said that with the firepower sitting around the room, and their goaltending, nothing could stop them from winning.

Phil's point total in eight games was three short of his target, but it's interesting to note how he compiled the 13 points and the tournament scoring lead. In game one in Montreal he opened the scoring, then, like the rest of the team and an overconfident country, watched the Russians put on a humiliating show. The final score: Russians 7, Canadians 3.

The saga kicked off the same way in Toronto. Like a poker player with a betting hand, Espo once again contributed the opener, then assisted on Peter Mahovlich's incredible shorthanded marker in a 4–1 victory. In Winnipeg he assisted on J. P. Parise's opening tally and got another assist on the goal that should have put the game out of reach for the Soviets. However, that wasn't in the cards, and the two teams finished tied at four and were deadlocked in the series 1–1–1.

On the West Coast, in Vancouver, Phil contributed two assists in the crushing 5–3 loss. From all firsthand reports the televised tongue-lashing he delivered to the Canadian public following the game revealed two things: first, frustration, due to their own poor play, and the booing of the equally frustrated Vancouver fans; second, fanatical determination. Esposito stood there with Johnny Esaw, exasperation and embarrassment written all over his sweat-drenched face. He was stung, hurt, and although Team Canada felt abandoned by all of us, he knew their only hope lay within themselves and the two weeks they had left to get their act together.

I don't think it ever occurred to Espo that they would fail. The personal pain and humiliation in Vancouver only boosted him another rung. In hindsight it was predictable that he wouldn't accept this treatment, this designation of his and his teammates' talent. Everything, absolutely everything, was now on the line. He simply, brazenly, articulated the situation to all of us and made Canadians look at themselves as no politician could ever do.

On reaching Mother Russia Phil was shut out in the 5–4 Team Canada loss. More aggravation. In the sixth game, feeling the strain and the checking blanket the Soviets had assigned to him, he was horse-collared again. Even his double minor in the first period, plus a major penalty in the third, only highlighted the intensity that powered the Canucks to a 3–2 victory. As a team, they weren't going to take any more crap from referees or Russians.

In game seven, as if to make up for his previous petulant performance, Espo popped in the first two Canadian goals and garnered two more bitterly antagonistic penalties, while leading the good guys to a 4–3 win. Now the stage was set.

In the eighth and final game he opened the Canadian scoring for the fourth time, bringing Canada even at 1–1, then led the charge to the edge-of-the-seat comeback, scoring again in the third and assisting on both of Canada's final two goals, including the Paul Henderson winner. A four-point finale. Game, set, and match.

Most people have seen the winning goal several times. Some of us, hundreds of times. Henderson slides into the end boards in a heap, then scrambles to his feet in time to pick up a stray rebound. He fires once on the move, picks up his own rebound, and puts it home. Yvan Cournoyer and the national fireworks follow.

The actions leading up to Henderson's effort are rarely shown, but when the full sequence is aired, it shows Esposito corralling a loose puck in traffic near the left face-off spot and, without looking, snapping a forehand that Tretiak was forced to play. The shot was in time to give Henderson the stray rebound.

Fluke, luck, sheer desperation, said the Esposito detractors. But that's the way he'd been doing it all his life, with that extra sense, the hair-trigger response to a given situation, the ability to know where all the players were on the ice at all times. Regardless, it was the play that made *the play* happen.

And, through all the gut checks, head games, politics, wrangling, and browbeating, Esposito did it without Orr. Through no fault of Orr's, of course. His knee had taken him out of the series. And it's safe to assume that had we seen Orr's considerable presence throughout the eight games, there wouldn't have been any need for last-minute heroics. Even so, he was there at the end — disabled maybe, but there just the same. As for Espo's performance that day in Moscow, any misgivings about the size of his heart, his competitive fire, and his great leadership qualities should have been laid to rest for good.

Still, the thing that stuck with me the most about the man was the late-night flailing he gave the country at large in Vancouver. Aside from being a beautiful piece of television history, that was the night Team Canada came together and developed a team spirit nothing could destroy — not the backbiting by the Canadian public, the name-calling of the Swedish press, nor the loss of the first game in Russia.

I bring this up because the only way you can offend Phil Esposito is not to have the same enthusiasm he has for a project or idea he believes in. Supremely tenacious, he's confident in his abilities, and yours, too, if you're with him. Three examples particularly come to mind. Two are large and one is only a small consideration, but they all indicate the character of the man.

When Phil was suddenly traded by Harry Sinden from the Bruins to the Rangers in 1975, he felt betrayed. The swap followed a discussion Espo and Harry had in which Phil was told he would finish his career as a Bruin. Two days later he was on his way to New York, where he played for the better part of six seasons, then coached or managed — take your pick — for another three. But never during that period did he trust Harry Sinden again. He told me that in 1991 during a speaking tour of Ontario.

The second incident, the small one, concerned him and me. We had been booked to speak in Nova Scotia. The deal was made, the travel arrangements were confirmed and faxed to the Lightning office, and we had talked a couple of times on the phone about his choice of material. Phil flew from Tampa to Toronto's Pearson International, arriving about 10:45 a.m. Durwood Merrill, the American League umpire and our third man on the trip, was slated to arrive from Dallas at about 1:00 p.m. We had arranged to meet, like golfers on the tee, at Terminal 2 for our 2:30 flight to Moncton.

I was on the run that Wednesday morning, making the usual arrangements to be out of town for five days, and when I returned to my office, the message machine was blinking. The sound of heavy breathing was the first thing I heard, next a garbled airline announcement, then Espo.

"Roscoe, it's me, Phil. It's 11 o'clock. I'm at the fucking Toronto airport. Don't even know which fucking terminal I'm in. I'm loaded down with fucking bags. I have no fucking idea where I'm going. Where the fuck are you? Roscoe, this really sucks, man. I'll be waiting in the fucking airport. Roscoe, here I am talking to a fucking answering machine. Where the fuck are you? Byeeeee!"

My office is in my home, has been since I left Buffalo back in the mid-seventies, and to say I was only perturbed about the message was not to know me at all.

Steamed, I threw my suit bag and carryon together, left for the airport long before I intended to, and arrived at Terminal 2 at noon. Luggage in hand, I plodded from one end to the other and through the gate into Terminal 3, where Mr. Esposito had arrived, but I couldn't find him. Retracing my path back through the sparsely populated hall-ways, I finally spotted him coming toward me. He, too, was carrying a week's supply of luggage.

"Hey, Roscoe," he greeted me happily as I angrily hurled my unfolded suit bag onto an empty bench along the wall. "Whatsa mat-ter? You pissed?" He looked disappointed. "Shit, I've been walking all over the goddamn place looking for you."

"Don't you ever call my house again and use that kind of language. I have a family that listens for my messages and I don't appreciate the crap I just heard from *you*." I pointed my finger menacingly at him while he was still a couple of steps away. My face was probably white or red — I can't remember which — but the change in him was immediate.

"Hey, I'm sorry," he said softly. "Shit, I didn't know. Hey, I'm sorry, but I didn't have any itinerary."

"I sent you all that goddamn information," I protested, still angry as I sweated in my trench coat from the march I had endured with con-frontation uppermost in my mind.

"Hey, shit, I'm sorry, okay?" he repeated, putting his hands together like a football referee signalling to push off.

He appeared genuinely concerned, and I recall saying to myself, What the hell? Let it lie. The tone changed, we exchanged pleasantries, and then we went for coffee while we waited for Durwood. Later, Merrill never knew we had a disagreement, nor did anyone else.

The point of this little incident is: when Espo's wrong, he admits it. When you stand up for yourself and you're right, he has no problem backing off. With some other people it's a matter of saving face. Conversely, when Phil's right, look out! He's got a one-track mind, and if he believes strongly in something, never bet against him.

The third example happened when Phil, Durwood, myself, and Duff Montgomerie, our driver and genial sidekick/host for the Nova Scotia Sports and Recreation Ministry, were motoring between Amherst and Truro, our next stop on the tour. I had prodded Phil into talking about his days in the front office of New York.

It was obvious he didn't like the corporate management team run-ning the finances of the Ranger organization back then. It was interesting for me, and illuminating for Merrill and Montgomerie, to be in on some privileged information.

"You know," he said at one point, "I talked with Sather [Edmonton GM, Glen Sather] about getting Gretzky to New York in '86 or '87, whatever, and our goddamn bean counters put the skids to that idea. Then, listen to this shit, I went after Messier, too, and the same fucking thing. You know what they said? 'We don't need asses in seats. We already have them. What we need is a Stanley Cup, and we think we can get one with the bodies we have here now.' Can you fuckin' believe it? I said, 'Those guys won four of the goddamn things already. What do you think they're gonna do if we get them here — oversell the fucking place?' Jeez. So what happens? Gretzky goes to L.A. and Messier goes to New York. Go figure."

Later the talk came around to Team Canada '72 when Durwood asked innocently how important it was to win the series. We three Canadians looked at one another as best we could in the moving car, either in shock or ready to laugh. We must have come to the same conclusion simultaneously. Living eight months of the year rambling the baseball circuit, then living the balance in Hooks, Texas, didn't require Merrill to endure any derision concerning this particular question. So we let it pass, but Phil made it right, anyway.

"Ol' buddy," Espo said to Durwood, "I'm not a violent guy. Ask Roscoe. Ask anybody, okay? But if someone had told me, 'Phil, the only way you can win this thing is to go out and kill one of those Russians,' I would have."

As I turned in my seat to look at Phil, surprise written on my face, he reached over and put his hand on my shoulder. "Ross, you *know* I would have," he said emphatically with those baleful dark eyes and the no-nonsense look of a man reliving a harrowing combat mission. Everybody was quiet, especially me when I recalled my earlier finger-menacing assault in the Toronto airport.

I told him he should use the line in his speech.

And he did.

Still does.

I believe him, too.

90-SECOND ALL-STARS

G — **Tony Esposito** *". . . my brother was the most competitive goalie in the world."*

D — **Bobby Orr** *". . . best defenceman ever."*

D — **Denis Potvin** *". . . second-best defenceman ever."*

C — **Wayne Gretzky** *". . . there's no question, the greatest."*

RW — **Mike Bossy** *". . . he's gonna score ... simple."*

LW — **Bobby Hull** *". . . he's gonna get a goal if you need it."*

"By the way, who's gonna get the puck off these guys, anyway?"

Bill White

Mr. Oh, Yeah

A S I'M LEAVING the Canadian Legion at Islington and Bloor in Etobicoke, Bob the bartender quietly asks, "Was that Bill White you were sitting with?" I nod, and he mirrors my reply, as if to say he'd known the answer all along. Nothing else is asked, or offered, which is typical.

Bill and I had sat in the lounge just back of the pool tables, talking about old acquaintances over the clacking of balls and the merciless heckling of the players. We had exchanged information on who was where nowadays, and no one had interrupted us for an autograph, nobody had stopped by to review or profess their undying support for Team Canada '72. I believe that's because Bill White is someone who fits into the "almost" category. They "almost" know who he is but aren't sure from where, or when, and they're reluctant to approach. We used to call this kind of player an "Oh, Yeah." Someone would ask, then say, "Oh, Yeah . . . I thought I knew him." Bill "almost" looks like a hockey player, but in appearance he's more along the lines of a cop on his day off, one of those detectives who investigate white-collar crimes. That being the case, who wants to stumble into an interrogation?

At first glance there's nothing remarkable about Bill, with one possible exception. On the ice he looked much taller than he actually was. Angular,

Bill White (left) *poke-checks Rick Martin:* "*he could wrestle with the biggest centres or drape himself all over the small ones like a construction scaffold.*"

he didn't seem to fit into his uniform, as if he'd been equipped over the counter by an army quartermaster with no sense of aerodynamics. In action White was a mixed bag of contradictions. His compact skating style was a cross between "stride and glide" that was fluid but never appeared to move his large frame quickly enough, although he was always there, in the road, blocking the way. He used his skates well, smothering loose pucks in the corner, and had unusually large, beefy hands at the end of a reach bordering on illegal. He was inordinately strong and was workmanlike in the corners and in front of the net where he could wrestle with the biggest centres or drape himself all over the small ones like a construction scaffold. He was a deft passer and had no problem jumping into the offensive rush. At his best weight, 200 pounds, he was spread sparsely over a lean frame, but he packed a punishing check when the opportunity merited, and with his reach, size, and skating style, he seemed to be in several places at once. Understandably he was a coach's dream, and in the realm of defencemen he was simply an outstanding example of how to play the game most efficiently, and effectively.

Bill's conduct off the ice is similar in that he's quiet and unassuming, socially correct, polite to the letter, gracious when and where it's required, attentive to conversation and surroundings, yet still able to maintain an aura of unpretentious acceptance of his station in life. He has a wit resembling the best martini, dry and stimulating, and his appreciation for humour is masked behind an inscrutable facade of sincerity. More than once his cohorts on the ice, masters of the put-down and the send-up, have been blown away by a White one-liner. And yet he's a master of self-effacement.

One of those rare people who can say they were born and raised in Toronto, he played his Junior with the Marlboros, where his teammates included Bob Nevin, Wally Boyer, Jim Pappin, Carl Brewer, plus goaltending brothers Ken and Len Broderick. As a Marlboro, he once watched the Leafs prepare for a new season and observed a crotchety, caustic Conn Smythe greet all veterans and rookies with a ritual pre-season handshake. The year before he turned pro, Bill overheard a disgruntled Smythe remark, "The boys are taking it too damn easy in the summer. There isn't one good, firm handshake in the whole lot." When it came his turn to enter the professional ranks, he, too, got his chance to shake hands with the "Major."

"I gave him my best, made his eyes bulge out. I thought, what the hell, if he judges players by their grip, they won't be cuttin' me first."

But he was shipped out for a brief stint with Sudbury of the Eastern Professional Hockey League, then to Rochester for the balance of his first season and all of the next. In his third pro year he was part of a five-for-one trade that sent White and four other Rochester Americans to Springfield for Kent Douglas, the AHL's top defenceman, who would go on to be the NHL rookie of the year and win a Stanley Cup. On the other end of the exchange White came under the tutelage of Eddie Shore, part genius, part Dr. Strangelove. To be kind, the regimen was different. Shore was known to produce highly disciplined hockey players who were overjoyed when they finally got out of Springfield.

Predictably Bill reflects on his five winters with Shore as "illuminating, yes, very informative," which is White's way of dusting off a hectic and sometimes wacky period in his hockey career.

They were turbulent years, and later beneficial, in an era when those inside an NHL minor league system had a tough time cracking the parent club lineup, and those outside a system, such as Springfield, had it even rougher. Shore's practices were run like accounting seminars — how to skate and shoot, give and go, think and react, plus the theory, the when, why, and wherefore of the game. He was an eccentric taskmaster, a whimsical puppeteer, and a fanatical believer in his own methods and systems. He governed his players' lives with a whistle, although he wasn't listed as the coach. Among the skaters who went through his prep school it was said that a life-size cardboard cutout might as well have been propped behind the bench as a coach, because it was Shore who ran the team with an iron hand.

"Most times we would only scrimmage for 10 to 15 seconds between whistles," White explains. "Eddie'd be out there instructing — drop the puck, whistle again, go through something else with a different guy. It was never-ending, continual, nothing was ever quite right to him. Plus there were the skating drills, crossovers, duck walks. He had this thing about skating in a squat, your ass about knee-high, especially defencemen. He used to call it 'taking a shit in the woods.' The best practitioner of the style was Ted Harris — at least he was my all-time favourite. Sometimes we'd be just gettin' rolling and Eddie would toot the whistle. 'Mr. White, how would you like to run that by us once more? You're not skating properly.' And we'd have to go through it again, except this time I'd have to skate with my head up, back straight, knees bent, ass sticking out like somebody had just yanked my chair away. He could be a real pain, literally. I used to have to leave the top two eyelets of my skates undone, almost like shoes, because I'd get this pressure buildup on the top of my instep. It looked like the front of my ankle had swallowed a golf ball. Never got rid of it until I went to the NHL."

As White's term with Springfield reached its fifth year, he and Shore attained a level of mutual respect. Entering the 1966 training camp and having discussed what he thought was a reasonable raise, Bill arrived at the arena for an appointment to sign his contract. Shore, an avid golfer, was putting on the rug. White's contract lay on the desk. Shore absently intoned, "Sign it," then stroked a ten-footer.

"It doesn't have the salary written in," White said, looking over the document.

"Don't you trust me, Billy?" Shore asked innocently, lining up the next shot.

After a momentary hesitation, White signed and left the office. "See you on the ice," Shore mumbled, continuing to practise. White received the raise.

Grudging respect and trust aside, the year got back to normal as the season progressed. Two-a-day practices were commonplace, mandatory for the "Black Aces," the players out of the regular lineup, in the doghouse, destined for the shit list, or coming back from injuries. These poor unfortunates were on two-a-days when the team was out of town.

Even if you were dressing for games, there was a three-level players' bench in the Springfield arena, and rare on-ice appearances would relegate a player to a spot known throughout the AHL as "the top shelf."

In his last year with the Indians White took to chewing tobacco at practice. Spitting, an athlete's prerogative, became an entirely new game on a surface of white ice. Shore, a fussy, nitpicking arena operator in addition to his manager, coaching, and resident counsellor duties, quickly noted the source of the markings, skated up, and said, "Mr. White, if I see you spitting on the ice again, you will be fined 25 hard-earned dollars for every goddamn spot I find." White's habit was kicked immediately.

Shore, an independent operator and a law unto himself, enjoyed his dictatorial role, advising players on medical matters, prescribing nutrition and system-cleansing agents from time to time, even assigning members of the "Black Aces" to menial chores around the arena when they weren't on the ice. But by the midway mark of the 1966–67 season the winds of change began to blow.

Despite a 7–1 victory in Quebec City, centre Brian Kilrea, White, and defence partner Dale Rolfe were suspended without pay for "indifferent play" by Shore. Starkly underlining the flimsy, ridiculous allegation, Kilrea had collected a pair of goals to go with two assists. White and Rolfe had two assists each. It was the proverbial straw.

"We called up Al Eagleson," White allows, "said we were prepared to go on strike if necessary, in fact, were wildcatting now, and if he was interested in our situation, to come on down to Springfield." White adds that Shore stuck to his guns, but the players were prepared to go all the way.

Eagleson arrived for his first legal kick at hockey's fat cat. The issue was resolved, but it was only the tip of the iceberg and signalled the beginning of the end of Shore's tyrannical rule and the kick-start of the present players' association. It was the first player rebellion to result in a sizable crack in hockey's armour.

White was rescued by NHL expansion and elevated to the Los Angeles Kings along with Rolfe and Kilrea. His two and a half seasons in L.A. established his reputation for steady, consistent play in both ends of the ice. The teachings of Eddie Shore were apparent, at least to Kings coach Red Kelly, who said, "You can always tell a Shore-coached defenceman. They're so mobile, so aware of where they're supposed to be at all times."

The admiration society came to an end when Kelly moved on to Pittsburgh in 1969, and Larry Regan added the coaching job to his GM role. White believed he and Regan had a deal worked out at training camp, but by mid-season it became apparent the deal wasn't going through, ostensibly because Regan might not have checked with owner Jack Kent Cooke. White figured a deal was a deal and bridled at settling for less. After all, a player who stood up to the redoubtable Shore wasn't about to be cowed by a regular guy like Regan, or a balky owner, so he sat out for a few weeks, asking for a trade. The teams named were Montreal, where a deal was within a whisper of being done, along with overtures from Boston and Chicago. But in the end it was off to the Blackhawks in late February, where a whole new world opened up for White. Billy Reay was the man behind the bench in Chicago.

"He was unlike any coach I had ever had before," White says. "He treated us like men, people capable of responsibility. It was different," he tells me with a shake of his head and a smile that implies wonderment. His first defence partner was the lightning-quick Doug Mohns, then he paired with Pat Stapleton, and they became as famous a twosome in Chicago as Pierre Pilote and Elmer Vasko had before. They were named to the second All-Star team in 1971–72, and White would eventually be selected two more times.

Their play didn't go unnoticed, and the five-eight, stocky Stapleton and the six-one, rangy White would be a solid tandem on the Team Canada '72 blue line. On arrival at the training camp at Maple Leaf Gardens, White recalls how naive the entire team was concerning the Russians.

"I think we all believed it was gonna be a breeze. Just looking at our team in practice was intimidating, to me, anyway. I remember one writer asking me what I thought the prospect was for the series, and I said something like, 'If we win eight straight, we'll be the only ones who'll know. I never believed it would develop into a crisis — you know, us or them — and I definitely never thought we, or the whole country, would be so wrapped up in it."

The two Hawks sat out the opening loss, but they would dress for the remaining seven games of the series, capped by White ghosting through the Soviet defenders into the slot and scoring a critical third goal to tie the crucial eighth game.

Having been burned on his first quote, he was reluctant to coin another, but did comment years later on Pete Mahovlich's memorable shorthanded goal at Maple Leaf Gardens. "Good thing Pete ran into the crossbar, or he woulda gone all the way out the back of the Gardens onto Wood Street." By his own admission the series with the Soviets was the biggest thrill of his career and the best team he ever played on.

That day in the Legion the dry wit had surfaced when Bill delved into his memory of a September 20 years earlier.

"I flirted with danger on a daily basis," he mused, deadpan, stroking his chin and gazing into the upper reaches of the Legion display cases. "Yeah, you have to have nerves of steel to play this game." After saying that, he launched into a description of what danger was all about.

On the flight from Russia to Czechoslovakia the drinks flowed and nostalgia mixed with the rituals of athletes winding down, overwhelming everyone. Avowed enemies over the regular NHL season backslapped and exchanged heartfelt platitudes with one another. Respect for all abounded, friendships had been forged, endurance under incredible odds had been vindicated — they were the remaining survivors of a battle, the returning veterans of a war. Then came the awful realization that except for a couple of meaningless exhibition games with the Czechs, this magic carpet ride was over. It was an all-consuming depression coming after gallons of expended adrenaline. For some it was too much, and melancholia scuttled even the staunchest of the group at one time or another.

As they winged their way to Prague, White, on one of his patrols down the aisle, caught John Ferguson in a lonely, reflective moment, a bit teary, eyes glistening. Their glances met, but only for a few seconds. Ferguson looked quickly away, reached for a tissue, and guardedly wiped at his ample nose.

"As I passed," Bill told me, "I patted John on the shoulder and said, 'Don't worry, Ferg. I'll never tell anyone I saw you crying.' Then I hotfooted down to the rear of the plane before he could get his seat belt undone and grab hold of me. Now that's flirting with danger."

Two weeks later Bill and I run across each other again in a neighbourhood bar called The Office. Billy is on a stool at the bar, watching a TV set with bad reception at the back of the room, an oversize draft glass ensconced in one large hand. After the pleasantries, I re-create for him a scene Dennis Hull had related to me about the Team Canada practice in Toronto following the first crushing loss.

Sinden and Ferguson gathered the players in a circle at the end of the workout. This was a perplexed crew that had just been humiliated, and the wrath of the press and the fans was still under a lid of shock. These were tough times that required tough minds. After Sinden conducted a one-sided discussion, he looked around the group, some on one knee, others leaning, their chins resting on gloved hands balanced on the tops of their sticks. "Anyone have anything else to add?" the coach asked.

To almost everyone's surprise a voice piped up from the back row — White's. "Well, guys, there's two ways to look at this." Then, as the group waited, the silence and anticipation growing more agonizing by the second, Billy turned and skated away through the gate leading to the dressing room. The release of tension in the form of groans and laughter followed him off the ice.

"That's my Billy. Whadda funny son of a bitch," a proud Dennis had said at the end of our conversation.

And, as White gingerly uncoils his large frame from the stool — a concession to a bad back — he leaves The Office the way he probably came in. Without fanfare.

The bartender, a "Billy" himself, comes over to ask, "Who was that guy?"

"Bill White," I say.

"Oh, yeah. I knew it was somebody," he says, turning away to rinse some more glasses.

90-SECOND ALL-STARS

G — **Gerry Cheevers** "... *toughest guy in a pinch.*"

D — **Doug Harvey** "... *like a music conductor on the point.*"

D — **Jean Guy Talbot** "... *he'd stay home and mind the store.*"

C — **Stan Mikita** "... *toughest, most skilled centre.*"

RW — **Gordie Howe** "... *a nightmare to keep in check.*"

LW — **Bobby Hull** "... *greatest left winger ever.*"

Tony Esposito

Cobra in the Crease

I NEVER HAD A FIRST INTRODUCTION to Tony Esposito. We simply eased into a face-to-face meeting in late January 1992 at Toronto's Pearson International, Terminal 1. Tony was arriving from Tampa, while I was waiting with a car so I could drive us to a speaking engagement. The next seven days covered St. Thomas, London, Wallaceburg, Toronto, Buffalo, Toronto again, Thunder Bay, then home to Tampa. Our prior relationship was a slow process of passing messages back and forth through brother Phil, leading to telephone conversations where we made our arrangements, and finally to this first road trip together. We had talked so often, so regularly, that it seemed we already knew each other. In the short span of a week he dispelled every opinion and rumour I had ever heard come down the pipeline about Tony O.

It's not as if I wasn't familiar with the stories about the Chicago Hall of Famer. I had occasion to run across him during my time at Maple Leaf Gardens and in Buffalo. At practice he was foreboding and fierce, snarling at errant high shots and sloppy defencemen. Like a lot of first-string goalies, he would work casually or reluctantly. Game-day skates aren't a goaltender's top priority. However, nothing changed when the evening rolled around. During a game, he could be

115

Tony Esposito without the mask: "weaving from side to side, like a cobra in a basket."

heard berating his teammates, foul-mouthed and demanding, the tone never far from insulting.

After a practice or a game, he was sullenly consistent. When he left the dressing room, usually alone, I often saw him carrying the signature Coke can, his coat open, his shoulders locked in a permanent hunch, as if he'd been frozen in mid-shrug. He always appeared determined to make it out of the arena without talking to anyone or signing anything. A loner, in short.

I was exposed firsthand to this strange brand of PR when I elected to wait in the Buffalo Auditorium hallway one Thursday morning, intent on getting an interview. Passing on other Hawks on their way back to the hotel, I was finally rewarded with the sight of my subject, coat and scarf streaming behind his stepped-up pace. As I pushed myself off the wall to make an introduction, he simply said, "Sorry." Then, throwing back his head, he took a long pull on a Coke and left me to talk to myself. I can still remember the feeling of resentment as I stood there with my tape recorder, thinking, No one is *that* far up the ladder. Later, after hearing some of the derisive remarks tossed off about him by other people, I would catch myself smiling inwardly, somewhat vindicated in my earlier impression of the man.

But 18 months further on I saw, what for me, was one of the finest moments in goaltending by the same Tony Esposito. The date was September 4, 1972, and the Russians had severely damaged Canada's hockey reputation with a stunning, crushing win in Montreal two nights earlier. The bubble had burst and condescension had been wiped off Canadian faces coast-to-coast. The snide remarks of the hockey knowledgeable were buried and hopefully forgotten. Needless to say, I was one of the knowledgeable who had suddenly developed severe amnesia.

Back in those Buffalo days my favourite watering holes were Coles on Elmwood Avenue and a smaller neighbourhood bar under the unassuming name of The Place. My connection with the Sabre organization at the time automatically gave me a status very few of my barmates could equal. When I was inevitably asked how I saw the upcoming Summit Series, I would pause for effect, then emphatically state that "The Russkies might, I repeat, *might,* tie a game, but they will not win one." I went through this statement, complete with pause for effect, in both establishments. I also suggested that it would be good to record this profound prediction so they could remember where they had heard it first. Of course, somebody forgot to relay the message to the Soviets, as I was reminded many times over the ensuing months and years.

There were questions to be asked, and everyone from the bag boy at the A & P to Lloyd Robertson was asking. Ken Dryden. Overrated? The defence. Weak? The forwards. Not tough enough? Was Team Canada woefully out of condition beside the barely sweating Reds? The story raged across the country's sports pages. The bandwagon was empty.

Pat Stapleton and Bill White took over from Rod Seiling and Don Awrey. Serge Savard suited up alongside Guy Lapointe for his first tilt. Stan Mikita, Wayne Cashman, J. P. Parise, and Bill Goldsworthy would add some tough asses and bad attitudes to the front end. Tony replaced Dryden.

Ultimately the pressure of the second matchup would fall on Tony, and to say he came up big would be an understatement. Standing through the interminable Russian anthem made me appreciate the brevity of our own, but it didn't take away from the electric buzz of apprehension in the crowd that evening. I couldn't help but wonder about the Canadian players, and especially about Tony O. It wouldn't be the first time overanticipation and tension had turned a fine-tuned athlete into a lead-legged uncoordinated lump, and I wondered if the pressure had gotten to Esposito and left him like a man in a dream running through sand. At about the midway point of the opening period all of Canada received the answer. In retrospect, after all these years, I still firmly believe it was the play that eventually won the series for the Canucks.

A Brad Park penalty left the Canadians shorthanded. Kharlamov rocketed past the defence and made a move to the short side, but Tony, moving to his right, snaked a foot to the goalpost and trapped the puck for the save. Kharlamov was so sure about the goal that he raised his arms overhead in celebration as he circled behind the Canadian net. I can still see Esposito getting back onto his feet, housecleaning the crease, looking up at the clock, nonchalant and relaxed, as if to say to Kharlamov and his mates, "A routine save. I do it all the time, asshole."

To me, scrunched into my corner seat in the golds, it was the omen, the lift Canada needed to go the extra step. With all due respect to the greatest shorthanded goal I ever saw, the incredible and memorable dipsy-doodle by Pete Mahovlich to salt the game away in the third, it was Tony O, under crushing stress, with a whole nation biting its nails in front of TV sets and looking over his shoulder in Maple Leaf Gardens, who was the big story. I remember being on my feet at the end of the game with the other 16,000-plus, saying to myself, "You keep playing like that and you can ignore me forever."

A few years later I was working the American Airlines–NHL Players Association golf tournament at Glen Abbey when I had occasion to observe Tony up close and personal. He was being unceremoniously delayed at the clubhouse door by a security guard who was only doing his job.

"I'm Tony Esposito. You ever see a fucking hockey game?" he fumed.

My explanation to the guard and Tony's subsequent passage into the building brought two similar responses from each man.

"Fuckin' jerk!" Esposito tossed off, no thanks offered or intended as he hunchbacked his way downstairs to the media room.

"Whadda dickhead!" I heard the guard say later, relating the scene for another rent-a-sentry.

I don't believe it occurred to Tony that his face wasn't as known or as accepted as his brother's. The anonymity was simply the result of wearing a mask for his entire career, a mask that he sported almost every moment he was on the ice, even during the national anthem and the pregame and postgame skates to the dressing room. In the 1980s there was a U.S. commercial that showed ex-Ranger netminders John Davidson, Gilles Villemure, and a few others all in masks. Then Tony walks in and says, "Hi, guys!"

Davidson immediately asks, "Who's that?" At that point Tony slips on his famous mask and Davidson yells, "Tony . . . Tony Esposito," to the cheers of the other goalies.

In recalling the incident with the security guard I always remember how appropriate that commercial would have been in explaining to

Tony the predicament of the guard. For on this occasion, casually dressed, he was without a mask or any other form of ID. Tony doesn't play golf, never has, and doesn't look the part, either. He was there as a player rep from the Blackhawks, one of Al Eagleson's group. He wafted in and out of both the golf location and Skyline Hotel like a spectre, a ghost moving from one site to the other without seeming to travel with anyone else. A lone loner.

It was all part of the mystique, or part of the intolerance. From opponents I heard a number of blistering four-letter descriptions of Tony, while others weren't much more charitable in their name-calling. Inevitably the cursing was followed by "Ask anyone who played with him."

So I did. One former Hawk, asked for a one-word description, thought for a moment, then said, "Sour." Over the years it would be safe to say that Tony wasn't held in high regard socially, as a teammate or opponent, by those who went through Chicago's dressing room doors on either side of the hall. Most considered him opinionated, arrogant, self-indulgent and, worst of all, "not a team player." The last remark was a bit hard to believe, since the very challenge of goaltending is to keep the other team from scoring, the job most other players do in tandem with their defence partners or linemates, and in the best scenario, all together as a unit. Yet, as the saying goes, goalies stand alone; they're the last stop before the red light. The goaltender's position, given the pressure of the job, is bound to have a major share of flakes, weirdos, and people who march to a different drummer.

Most GMs consider the moods, unathletic builds, and behaviour of goalies the cost of doing business in the NHL. They know full well that bad teams have won with great goaltending. Conversely a great team can fall by the wayside with bad goaltending. So, if you're fortunate to have a good netminder, you suffer through the piques and valleys, so to speak.

Through 16 seasons Tony Esposito rubbed many people, for and against, the wrong way. He alienated teammates, opponents, management, and the media, but none of them could argue with his talent, or numbers. And so he was grudgingly accepted, just as any top-calibre player will be. It wasn't until he left the game that his private side began to catch up to his public side. Make no mistake, he was still grating and just as outspoken. There were those who said it was a family trait.

So, after our first formal head-on meeting at Pearson International, our mini-tour of Ontario was anything but unpleasant. He was gracious with fans and understanding with fouled-up arrangements and delays. In London, after a Junior game, he purposely took the time to wait and talk with the Knights' goalie so that he could pass along pointers and observations he had made while watching the butterfly style of the youngster that evening.

Over the miles between sites he told me he rarely talked about hockey, and he was right. We touched on fishing, his cottage on the Wisconsin shore of Lake Michigan, life in Florida, his succession of vintage cars, and the ones he regretted giving up. We talked about our hometowns, Thunder Bay and Sault Sainte Marie, and his degree from Michigan Tech. Eventually, though, we got around to the Tampa Bay Lightning.

Perhaps my reflections on the birth of the Sabres and the troubles the team had gone through struck a chord with him. Obviously it was a comparable situation to the one he and Phil faced in Tampa Bay. As we headed down the Queen Elizabeth Way to Buffalo, he began sharing a wealth of stories.

"You know, I didn't retire because of injuries, age, or anything physical," he said suddenly, as if I had asked a question. We had been talking about the number of games he had worked, and he explained how he would have played 80 if they had let him.

"I felt good, but I just couldn't take the aggra," he said, flipping a hand in resignation. "Coaches and players would look at me and figure I had been there so long I must be a pipeline to the front office. I just got tired of the rumours. Shit, I was the player rep for so damn long, on the other side, so how the hell could I be a pipeline?"

Then, in a better mood for having said that much, he talked about the innovations he brought to the game, but missed capitalizing on. Once, victimized by a shot that barely touched his glove hand, he read the rules and found out that only the maximum width of the glove was indicated, not the shape. So he added webbing from the thumb to the wrist protector. "Never patented it," he said to the car window.

Taking a shot to the face, he almost suffered severe eye damage despite the protection of the mask. He again went to the trainers' room and fashioned the mesh eye cover that evolved into the most popular mask worn by today's practitioners. "Never patented that, either," he offered.

Hit in the throat and almost losing use of his vocal cords, he went to the drawing board once more and came up with a protector for that vulnerable spot. Needless to say, he never took the time to chase it down from a business standpoint. It was simply survival in a painful game.

But he saved the best for last. Tired of the occasional puck that found its way through the "five-hole," the popular term for the area between a goaltender's legs, he decided to stem the criticism often directed at those who practised the butterfly style and were sometimes victimized by the small opening between the legs as they sank to the spread-legged position.

"I asked my wife if she could get some of the elastic panelling used for women's maternity skirts, which she found at a fabric outlet. I got a triangular piece, about eight inches deep, and had her sew it into the seams between the pant legs. The elastic was black, the pants were black. When I dropped down, nobody noticed. I wore it for a few games, no problem, but when the Canadiens came in one night, I dropped and stopped a screen shot from Serge Savard. It caught the panel perfectly and snapped back out almost to the goddamn blue line. That's when they started asking questions." He laughed. "Never patented that one, for sure," he snuffled into the ever-present Coke can.

But the one anecdote that said a lot about the Tony Esposito I was getting to know was the story about playing for another Canadian team in the World Championship held in Germany. The Blackhawks had made a quick exit in the playoff round, early enough to garner him an invitation. He was put into his first game the day after his arrival.

As usual, to those who have observed him during the national anthem, he stood in the goal crease, masked, weaving from side to side, like a cobra in a basket. This trademark characteristic obviously caught the eyes of the tournament officials, and they suspected the worst. A goalie on drugs. Following the game, he was whisked away and escorted to the testing room. At that point he didn't think anything was unusual, since a player was always selected from each team for the exam.

"They told me I had to supply a urine sample in the presence of an official, and if I wanted anything to drink to facilitate the test, just say the word. So I had a couple of soft drinks, you know, something to get me goin', and I managed to get a little bit for them. Next goddamn game, the identical routine. I'm out there bobbin' and weavin' through the anthems, and this same son of a bitch grabs me comin' off the ice again. I mean, what the hell? These are supposed to be random tests, so how the fuck can I get picked twice, huh?

"Now I'm mad, really pissed off. They ask for a sample. I say, 'Look at me. I just played a game, I'm soaked to the ass with sweat, I look like I just ran through a goddamn car wash, and I haven't got any piss to spare.' I got all my gear on, drippin' wet, musta lost 10 pounds in the game, and this dumb shit wants me to whiz in the bottle. Gimme a break. I almost lost it I was so cheesed off at the whole stupid drill.

"Then they ask me if I want anything to drink. I start thinkin' it over and decide, 'Hey, I want beer. Yeah, beer,' so they bring me one of those quarts and I downed it. Two more quarts later they were looking at their damn watches, gettin' antsy, when I finally gave them a sample. Almost a goddamn pailful. You shoulda seen me. I still had my stuff on, still in my skates, I'm half in the bag . . . Jeez, I did some weavin' for them on my way back to the dressing room, I'll tell ya." And he chortled at the window again.

The incident simply said, "Don't rattle my chain." It said he liked to grate people who grated him. He never even mentioned the score of either game, the wins or losses, only the iniquity of going through back-to-back dope tests.

I couldn't help wonder if most people had missed the point with Tony. Maybe the fact that he didn't suffer fools, important fools or others, was a bad rap. Maybe he just preferred people at arm's length. And, I thought, perhaps the people who disliked him for his temperament, the ones who were victims of his trenchant comments, were those who tried to get too close.

He had been back at the Tampa office for a few days when he called to say how much he had enjoyed the trip. I, in turn, asked how things were going with brother Phil, and he said, "Perfect, couldn't be better. We're fightin' like cats and dogs. It's great!"

He laughed into the handset, and I could almost see the can of Coke.

90-SECOND ALL-STARS

G — **Glenn Hall**

D — **Bobby Orr**

D — **Larry Robinson**

C — **Stan Mikita**

RW — **Gordie Howe**

LW — **Bobby Hull**

"Too tough to pick just six, but these guys aren't bad."

Vic Hadfield

A World of
Hurt and Pain

HURT AND PAIN APPEAR to be siblings, but there's a subtle difference. They're more like cousins. Hurt and pain have degrees of intensity, like hurricanes. Hurt is hurt, and pain, well, pain is a fact. There's no brushing pain aside, no covering it up. Anyone who has been there can tell you that a lot of pain is involved with being an athlete. Hockey players endure the everyday, regular dangers, but they also face the added hazards and perils of frozen pucks, skates, sticks, boards, and glass, all of which are capable of ending a career.

To be a hockey player is to know the hot, numbing smack of a puck and the stabbing pain following a stick to the face, with the subsequent removal of a few of your favourite teeth. You haven't lived until you can experience the unforgettable, stomach-churning fire when a knee can't absorb a body check, or the crippling crunch of a snakelike slapshot off the toe or ankle. The expected macho response is to get back in there as quickly as medical science will allow and face it all over again, something almost as mindless as bungee jumping, sky diving, or rodeo bull riding. Obviously the longer you play, the more risks you take. Injuries will occur because, just like Christmas, they are inevitable. Only the reward isn't pleasant. Far from it.

125

New York captain Vic Hadfield: hurt and pain personified. Roger Crozier is the goalie.

Therefore, if you compare Vic Hadfield with his NHL rap sheet, you realize the man, the stats, the terms *hurt* and *pain,* are bound to be one and the same.

Sitting in the sunlit coffee shop of the country club Vic manages northwest of Toronto, I can see plenty of evidence that hockey has taken its toll. He still looks the part of an ex-hockey player, even a shade toward an ex-tight end, and you sense, amid the precise decorum on all sides, that here sits a man who thrived on what is arguably sport's most violent game.

The golf course is called Huntington, and it's private and as removed from hockey as you can get. Everything is neat and tidy, the staff are polite, the nongolfers lounge around the impossibly blue pool, and there's a cross section of businessmen not doing business as they hiss past in white golf carts. In the background the faraway hum of construction equipment builds mounds and swales that will eventually resemble new golf holes. There's not much in the way of pain here unless you pull something trying to force a six iron up to a three.

But the reminders sit across the restaurant table.

The nose is the first giveaway, almost a dead ringer for Bobby Hull's. It's not bent, merely "suppressed," to use a term I once overheard a former welterweight champ use. His name was Carmen Basilio, and he made no apologies for his features.

On this day we're sitting with Dennis Hull, a former adversary and old acquaintance of Vic's, with a four-year age advantage. They played their Junior in St. Catharines, albeit not at the same time. Hadfield would have been a Blackhawk, too, except that Chicago decided a big 20-year-old, first-year left winger with only five goals could be hidden on their Buffalo AHL team. The Hawks had picked up Todd Sloan from the Leafs and, because of the numbers game, left Hadfield out in the open. Muzz Patrick made sure Vic became a Ranger.

After two abortive attempts to settle in with New York, he stuck to the wall in 1963–64. He was no great shakes on the scoring front, but he gained the attention of the entire league by leading in penalty minutes with 151. His goal scoring was consistently in the teens for the first four seasons, but in the next four he graduated to the twenties. He made all the usual sacrifices, expended all the prerequisite effort, and learned when and when not to push the limit. Like all players who tuck 11 seasons under their belt, he tried and tested, lived and learned, and suddenly it was all there, a whole package called Vic Hadfield. The 1971–72 season was what the pros refer to as a "career year."

In that season he and his mates, centre Jean Ratelle and right winger Rod Gilbert formed a line that scored 139 goals, with Vic ringing up the magic 500. The New York press dubbed them the GAG line (Goal-a-Game), and all three would be elected All-Stars.

But the personal success didn't come without an accumulation of pain. Knees took on the first telltale wobbles and shoulders separated, not to mention the assorted cuts and contusions that are the general fare of life in the game. There was the night against Chicago when Vic was cruising through the goal crease and, screened from the play, took teammate Dale Rolfe's slap shot in the face, an incident captured by a New York photographer with a motor-drive camera. A sequence of ten pictures shows Rolfe's windup, the flight of the puck to impact, and the stricken Hadfield dropping to the ice. Keith Magnuson, the Blackhawk toughie, close enough to know a bad injury when he saw it, is captured standing over Hadfield and waving to the New York trainer even before the play was finished.

Not surprisingly, Vic didn't return to that Sunday night game, but typically, with Monday off and missing practice on Tuesday, he was ready for the Rangers' next game on Wednesday night. If anything, the incident is a testament to toughness, to not playing the game for the rah-rah value or the limelight. This is the underside of what it's like in professional hockey, the side the fans rarely see or attach any value to when they wait, pen and autograph book in hand. How the star got there, or stays there, isn't important to them. Only the players.

For myself, I'll always remember a Saturday game in Toronto. It was at the end of the 1971–72 season, and Hadfield had 49 goals with only this game and a home tilt against Montreal on Sunday to get the 50th. Boston was cooled out and in the barn atop the East Division. New York could finish no worse than second, Montreal was a solid third, and the Leafs were a solid fourth. A nothing game for all but Hadfield.

During the third period, Jim McKenny took umbrage at some phantom stickwork by Hadfield and stopped abruptly to fling his gloves off. He took a wild roundhouse at the startled Ranger, then ducked under any possible retaliation, grabbing on to Hadfield's legs. One punch landed in the brief altercation — Hadfield's fist bouncing off McKenny's knee-high head — before the linesmen arrived to quell the superbout. McKenny arose, more red-faced than usual, to the cheers of the fans following his first known fight since a grade three punch-up at recess. Hadfield was obliged to retire to the dressing room with a dislocated thumb, now in an inverted position halfway up his forearm.

There are two reasons why I recall the event. First, a whole generation of Leaf sufferers had never seen Jim "Howie" McKenny "jab-jab-stick-and-move," regardless of the short duration, with anybody, let alone a league-endorsed hard-ass like Hadfield. To me, it was a singular act of blind courage, or even blinder stupidity.

Second, considering the result of Jimmy's foray into the "sweet science," it was almost a foregone conclusion along press row that Hadfield's detoured thumb had cancelled the chase for his 50th. In fact, the concern among the New York media was that he might not be available for the critical playoffs, only a few days away.

After the game, McKenny, ever the comic and never one to let the opportunity for backhanded humour slip away, approached his wife, Christine, who was waiting near the Wood Street exit of the Gardens. With a straight face he said, "Sorry, but I have to report to the police station."

His wife blanched and asked the inevitable, "Why?" within earshot of the rest of us.

"The cops say I have to register these as lethal weapons," he told her with total sincerity as he held out his offending fists amid a crescendo of guffaws and wry chuckles.

It was no laughing matter for Hadfield, however. Still, with his usual grit, he had his injured thumb taped parallel to his index finger, then jammed both into his glove and got his 50th goal in a 6–5 loss to Montreal at home in the final game of the season. The Rangers went all the way to the Stanley Cup final against Boston, bowing out in six.

In the early summer of 1972 GM Emile "the Cat" Francis offered Hadfield a new, lucrative contract with the Rangers, and the years of hard work and dedication saw him reach the upper echelon of the NHL. His team was no longer the also-rans they used to be, and the future was bright. In hockey it doesn't get much better than that, and he literally had the world by the ass.

Then came Team Canada, and hurt, as opposed to pain.

There are those who can rightfully argue that the NHL's best players didn't show up in Toronto for the opening workouts. That's an uncontested moot point. While no one would be cut, not all could play, which was obvious, a fact of life and mathematics.

The formidable GAG line had every reason to believe they had as good a chance as anyone, certainly more than some players. They were a slick threesome, used to one another's moves, and capable of scoring every time they stepped onto the ice. They were all early 30-somethings, experienced, playoff-toughened veterans who had much to offer Team Canada.

They would suit up as a unit in the opening loss, just as they would sit out as a threesome in the redeeming win in Toronto two nights later. It was the last time in that fateful September they would be together. Ratelle played solo in game three, then watched as Hadfield and Gilbert again dressed in a loss in Vancouver.

Somewhere between Phil Esposito's national tongue-lashing and the first game in Russia the gap widened between Hadfield and the coaching staff of Sinden and Ferguson. Hadfield never played again and eventually left Russia in what was reported as a "desertion." The term *quitter* was tossed around, and Sinden, in his book, said that the eventual four returnees (Hadfield, Rick Martin, Josh Guevremont, and Gil Perreault) "jumped overboard like rats that didn't want to drown with the ship." To be realistic, Team Canada '72 had more politics coursing through it than the Meech Lake Conference. There was Triple E back then, too — Eagleson, ego, and equivocation — and more than enough of each.

Vic Hadfield, deep down, believed he could play, indeed, insisted he had been told at the outset he would play, felt he deserved to play, and when he was told point-blank that he wouldn't be playing, figured he had been betrayed and chose to withdraw his services. At home in New York there was support for his position. A lot of general managers, Emile Francis and Buffalo's Punch Imlach front and centre, grudgingly paid lip service to their owners' wishes, but privately they couldn't care less about Hadfield's "desertion." It was the same for Team Canada's nonstatus players, and at one time there were rumblings of as many as a dozen who were ready to haul ass. Only three appeared in the hotel lobby the morning of the showdown. Back when the group had swollen to more than 10, it was suggested Eagleson could hold a press conference to pave the way to a smooth exit for the returnees. That was back when things were amicable on the surface. The suspicion remains that after late-hour lobbying, soul-searching, and peer pressure, the 12 became three and those three left Russia, thinking the proposed press conference would still take place. It never did, and they arrived home as lepers.

In light of what Vic had been told, his reasons for leaving the team seemed rational and practical. "I had just signed a new contract. Emile was up my ass to get back, anyway. I felt my loyalty was to my NHL team, a new season, and another chance at the Cup. I had nothing to contribute, according to them [Sinden and Ferguson]. Why should I hang around for another week? I mean, Jesus, the rest of us didn't even have a chance to practise anymore — not enough ice time or facilities."

In his defence, grouping him with some of the kids (Dionne and Tallon) as Sinden did at the time to defend Hadfield's nonplay, was slightly unfair. It's doubtful they would have cracked the lineup except for spot duty or a change of program. And, as far as the nonplaying veterans went, Hadfield's numbers were better than those of Goldsworthy, Berenson, or Redmond. The only player who could speak with the same chagrin over not playing was the incomparable Stan Mikita, and if nothing else, Mikita could look forward to the exhibition games in his native Czechoslovakia, following the Russian tour.

In defence of Sinden, Ferguson, and Eagleson, maybe Vic's style of play wasn't in keeping with what had to be done to stifle the Soviets, and then there were the unbending attitudes all round. It probably came down to personalities and a chin-first assumption by Hadfield that he should be on the active list. He couldn't accept overt or covert reasons for his demotion. In his eyes it was injustice plain and simple. The upshot was that Hadfield, as the first declared dropout, wore the biggest monkey on his return.

The "long" of it was that Hadfield, unsatisfied, pride stung, reputation sullied in his own eyes, chose to leave as his last act of choice. The "short" was that Canada won. Regardless of politics, egos, favouritism, ass-kissing, good guys and bad guys, real or fabricated slights, all became irrelevant. The eighth-game win made the right people right, the wrong guys only second-guessers.

A lot of hockey has been played since 1972. Hadfield stayed two more seasons with New York, never attaining the 50-goal height again. He then moved to Pittsburgh for two full seasons, the first a creditable 31-goal year, and in the second, at the age of 36, he still contributed 30 goals for the Penguins. But by 1976–77 season injuries diminished his playing time, resulting in only nine games on the card and a mere two assists. The time clock had punched out another career after 16 years in the NHL.

While Dennis and I prepare a cart for our 18 holes, I notice the talk from Vic is mostly about golf, with a touch of Lindros, how Bobby is, and what this course will look like in a year. There is nothing ventured or asked about Team Canada, nor reunions and events surrounding the 20th anniversary. After a 1,000-game career, I suppose two spins around the ice with the Russians don't amount to much.

Later, on the seventh tee, as Dennis and I wait for a group of tycoons in front of us who have spent most of the day hitting out of the bush and from behind trees, I bring up the topic, the fact that nothing has been said about the 1972 team.

"Do you get the feeling it still rankles him?" I ask by way of an opening.

Dennis starts to answer, but pauses, then squints into the sun-drenched fairway. "You know, I'll bet you've never heard one guy on Team Canada criticize Vic, Rick, or anybody about that episode."

I have to admit, after some pausing of my own, that it's true, I've never heard any complaints, only those I've read by Sinden and, subsequently, Eagleson. I tell Dennis that their remarks had been less like explanations than attempts to "set the record straight," with a lot of the setting straight slanted to make the teller of the tale look good.

"Do you know why none of the players ever criticized Vic or the others?" Dennis asked, selecting a long iron from the bag.

I shake my head.

"Because, except for some dumb circumstances, like the WHA thing, some of us might never have been invited. Except for some injuries, a few more might not have been asked to come out. And, just like gambling, some of us were lucky, some weren't, but we all knew it could have been one of us instead of them. It could have easily been me instead of Vic. Shit, we all wanted to play. Vic could have played, and all of us understood that."

Later, when we finish the game, I catch a glimpse of Hadfield, slope-shouldered à la Gordon Howe, T-shirt, shorts, and sneakers, just in from the back 40, walking across the parking lot and heading for his office in the main clubhouse. I note the slight hitch in his step. The right knee. That's *pain,* I think silently.

Team Canada '72 was *hurt.*

90-SECOND ALL-STARS

G — **Ed Giacomin** *". . . handled the puck so well, always controlled it."*

D — **Bobby Orr** *". . . nobody ran the game like he did."*

D — **Brad Park** *". . . another two-way player who could hit."*

C — **Phil Esposito**

RW — **Gordie Howe**

LW — **Bobby Hull**

"Three goals in 90 seconds wouldn't be impossible."

Rick Martin

French Connection
in Buffalo

IT'S BEEN SEVERAL YEARS since I last saw Rick Martin, and I have to rummage through my memory banks to come up with a tournament at some Golden Horseshoe country club. I seem to recall Rick on the practice range, smacking one clean iron shot after another as befits a scratch golfer. That had to be 10 years earlier, I reckon.

This time we arrange to meet in Buffalo. I arrive early, driving in from Toronto directly to the Boulevard Mall, a shopping centre made up of every store you've ever seen from Santa Rosa to Boston to Mississauga. Mainly it's an indoor home for kids in Nike pumps, oversize jackets, and back-to-front baseball caps. I hotfoot directly to the only beer dispensary, Fridays, as if I've got radar, a character trait that's served me well over a lifetime of nonshopping. The place has a large step-up square bar surrounded by window tables and a crew of waiters and waitresses, all of whom are weighed down by personal collections of pins and badges attached to their aprons, shirts, and suspenders. My waitress sports a Buffalo Bills, Superbowl '91 badge the size of a hubcap. It's mounted on a cowboy hat whose chin strap is cinched tight to keep the lid on.

After I get my schooner, I stare over the rim of the frosted glass into the bright sunshine outside and wonder if Rick's changed much in the

Rick Martin on the bench after a shift: "the guy was a scoring machine, and the Sabres couldn't wait to unveil him to the public."

time gone by. I remind myself to be cautiously optimistic concerning appearances. Grey hair, lack of grey hair, jowls, paunches, wrinkles, and creases are acceptable. After all, there are some cultures that consider them distinguished. Yeah, right, I think, to hell with the pubescent hordes in tiger skin baggies and never-ending Roots sweats. And who was Vuarnet, anyway?

Once again the young woman, too bubbly and happy to be an experienced waitress, pops up in my face, catching me by surprise. I order another beer by reflex and hark back to the second amateur draft of the Sabres, the year Punch Imlach gloated inwardly, realizing he had plucked another gem out of the Junior grab bag in the person of Richard Martin. Picking from the fifth position, Punch had only hoped Martin would be available.

The foregone conclusions went one-two. Guy Lafleur to Montreal, Marcel Dionne to Detroit. Then came the agonizing part. Josh Guevremont to Vancouver. Whoop-dee-doo! Gene Carr to St. Louis — bingo!

As the draft approached, we heard a lot about Rick Martin, and there was a lot to hear, and compare. A member of the same Montreal Canadien Juniors where Gil Perreault was forged, he shattered Brian Cullen's OHA Major A goal-scoring record with 71 markers. It was said his 51 assists came mostly from teammates pouncing on rebounds and loose pucks after a Martin rocket. The guy was a scoring machine, and the Sabre brass couldn't wait to unveil him to the public. His vital stats said five-eleven, 170 pounds, but I have to admit I thought we'd been misled, because in real life he looks shorter, more compact.

I recall Imlach's suppressed glee at getting lucky in the draft again. Punch was the superstitious kind and placed a lot of stock in lucky routines, clothes, and hats. He went out of his way to court Lady Luck, then when she arrived, he got whiny and self-satisfied, treating the old gal like a promiscuous auntie. A few days after the draft, over a drink, Punch once more was shaking his head and wearing an arrogant grin, almost a smirk, as he extolled the talents of Martin.

I lightly ragged him. "I know you always wanted a Ree-shard, but this one is Mar-tah, not 'On-ree," I told him in my best Montreal put-on.

"Brewitt," he said, starting the name out high and ending on a low note, "I'll bet you $50." Then he leaned over to dip into a pocket for some up-front, whip-out cash. "Shit, make it a $100. Take any part of a $100." And he tossed an American C-note carelessly onto the table. "This kid Martin will be the Calder winner. You can take any other rookie, *any* other goddamn rookie."

I took Lafleur.

No money ever changed hands at the end of the season, though. Ken Dryden, who Imlach claimed "wasn't a rookie in the first place but a stringy son of a bitch who played 26 games last year, for Christ's sake," took the trophy, but Punch never let me forget that Martin was the runner-up. Furthermore, Imlach added, "The balloting was probably goddamn rigged because those bastards don't want us to have back-to-back Calder winners," whoever the *bastards* were.

At the first training camp we all watched with approval while Martin displayed a shot rivalling the best in the league. On opening night he was there, number 7, and he didn't disappoint the fans or the brass. His first shot on the Pittsburgh goal was from just outside the blue line. None of us could say whether it was definitely on the net — it was that close — but the glove was torn off Jimmy Rutherford's hand, a portent of what we could expect the rest of the year. Gil Perreault's record of 38 rookie goals was short-lived, completely shattered, when the Sabres' new top gun put up 44.

Although his career only spanned nine full seasons and two knee-injured partials at the end, it was eventful. He saw lots of change in his Buffalo tenure, playing for no less than seven different coaches. Imlach led things off, then Joe Crozier, Floyd Smith, Marcel Pronovost, Billy Inglis, Scotty Bowman, and even, briefly, "Captain Video," Roger Neilson. From the outset he would score more goals than assists in each of the next nine seasons with the exception of 1977–1978, sagging (by an ordinary player's standards) to 28 goals and 35 assists. He had back-to-back 52-goal seasons, just missing the 50-goal plateau in the third with 49, and in four consecutive years he was named an All-Star. What's more, the chance of a lifetime followed his spectacular rookie beginning when he received the call to Team

Canada '72; his potent stick would be a replacement for that of a boyhood idol, the WHA-ineligible Bobby Hull.

Bubbles swings by again, breaking my reverie, and I order a third beer, glance at my watch, and absently wonder if Rick has quit trying to make people's eyes water when he shakes their hands. That's one of the things I recall most often — the hand strength. I don't have long to consider the problem, though, because just then he walks into the restaurant.

The only thing missing from the early seventies are the oversize sideburns. Fit and trim, suntanned, casually dressed, the familiar slight bow in the legs, and an unlit cigar in one hand, he peers side to side into the gloom, but before he can make his way up the stairway I hear a surprised voice say, "Rico!" Turning, I see that the voice has come from a man in a wheelchair at a table window. Martin looks over, his face breaking into a smile of recognition, and he goes over to shake hands and talk for a bit.

Is it going to be like this all day? I wonder, second-guessing the choice of a meeting place. The man in the wheelchair looks overjoyed at the chance encounter, and when Martin thumbs behind him, indicating his meeting with me, they part with a touching hug. Rick and I shake hands firmly, and I ask him who the man is.

"A guy who used to go to all the games, a good fan, a nice guy," he says, waving once again at the departing wheelchair.

We get right into golf games, turn to updates on other players, and eventually move into a rehash of those early days in Buffalo. I recreate the story about the Calder Trophy bet, and the discussion naturally leads to his relationship with the main ogre, Imlach.

"I had a lot of respect for Punch," he tells me, taking a puff on a cigar that clears out all eavesdroppers except one, a Suit & Tie seated behind Rick at the bar who pretends to read his unfolded paper. "He was good at psyching me up a notch. All I can say about him is that he gave you the benefit of the doubt, tried to understand your style, gave you lots of rope, and let you run. He was two guys really. He could be a pal for life, and if you had his loyalty, you could take it to the bank. Or you could be on his shit list forever." Rick gives a perfunctory nod, takes another puff, then coughs over a funny memory.

"My rookie year we went into Vancouver a day early. I didn't know it, but my initiation wasn't gonna be shavin' or shit like that. I guess 'cause I was doin' so good, the veterans — Tracy Pratt, Al Hamilton, Don Luce, those guys — decided to get me in Punch's bad books. So we went out for a few beers after dinner, and Hammy says we were going to stay out after the 1:00 a.m. curfew. Fuck Punch and his hours 'n shit. Screw him, you know, get an attitude on. We close the place and take a cab back about 2:00. They leave me to pay the fare, rookie punishment, I guess, and bugger off real quick into the side entrance to the hotel.

"What a dummy I was!" he laughs into his cigar hand. "They musta called Imlach before we left the bar, because when I come through the door, there he is — hat, suit, and tie, hands on his hips, and he starts in about me being a rookie, that I'm obviously dumb and 'can't tell the fuckin' time' because I'm an hour late. He says, 'Or maybe we ain't payin' you enough money to afford a goddamn watch.' Anyway, it's gonna cost me $500.

"Now I'm standing there shittin' my pants. I don't want to be on his list of dopes, and I already suspect I've been set up, but Punch, just to show you how he was, says, 'Look, it's yer first offence, so I'm gonna give you a chance to recoup your money. If you can give me a good show tonight, since *it is a fuckin' game day,* I'll forget the fine.'

"Jeezuz, that night I went out and got a hat trick and one assist. We tie the Canucks 4–4. Punch takes me aside at the airport and says, 'Okay, kid, I'll pass on the fine, but if I ever catch you again, it'll be $1,000.' See, he always wanted to have something on you." Rick chuckles at that memory, and the Suit & Tie jiggles right along with us.

"Yeah, Punch was good," Rick continues. "You know, he used to bring all the players in one at a time after a season to get their ideas on what happened, what the player thought could help, that kind of stuff. Me and him spent three hours one day, three fuckin' hours! It was after we lost out to Philadelphia. I told him it wasn't [Bernie] Parent. It was the goddamn intimidation. And he listened to what you felt was the problem. Yeah, I always found Imlach tough, but fair, and loyal."

LAST MINUTE OF PLAY

I ask if it's true that Imlach busted up the French Connection (Martin, Perreault, and Rene Robert), or was it personal differences that caused the split.

"Rumours, all bullshit and rumours. It wasn't the three of us. Hell, we always got along, and it wasn't Punch, at least not for any negative reason. Shit, it was plain and simple. The other teams we're front-end loading against our line. Every time we went to Montreal I could expect to see [Bob] Gainey or Jimmy Roberts, sometimes Mario Tremblay, for the whole fuckin' night. In Atlanta it'd be Lew Morrison. In Pittsburgh Jean Pronovost. It was a matter of splitting us up for the team's best offence. Hell, when I got my first 50, it was with Lucey [Don Luce] and Rammer [Craig Ramsay]. Another time I was with Pete McNab and [Brian] "Spinner" Spencer, and we got 24 goals in 22 games. Yeah, it had bugger all to do with us, or Punch. It was just sound hockey." Suit & Tie is all ears as he nods his agreement to the want ads.

Together we relive Tim Horton's fatal auto tragedy and the black armband game in late February 1973.

"Timmy, whadda guy!" Martin enthuses. "You know what I seen him do once?" He puts down his cigar and takes on a pose that suggests he's going to wrestle sumo-style. "You know, he wasn't the kind of guy you'd wanna fuck with, believe me. We're playin' the Flyers and some shit starts. Timmy looks around and spots the Hammer [Dave Schultz] muscling his way into it. Tim grabs Schultzie, flips him, puts him on his back, and says, 'Whadda y'gonna do now, sonny?' I could hardly believe how easily he manhandled the guy. Fuck, he was 42 at the time." Suit & Tie really likes that one.

Finally we reach Team Canada '72 when the dream of a rookie became a bad memory about a kid who ran afoul of the coach, Harry Sinden. Rick never played in the four Canadian games, but dressed for one of the exhibition games in Sweden. The inactivity began to unnerve him. Martin had quickly become known as a fun lover and practical joker, a guy capable of putting on other rookies and veterans alike. As a nonactive player-in-waiting, he had coined a visual catchphrase among the more adventurous kindred spirits of the Canadian team. Sitting on the bench during a practice, he stuck his hand up, like a schoolboy with the right answer, and begged plaintively, "Harry, can I play now?" That soon became a signature move for pine polishers like Stan Mikita, Dennis Hull, Marcel Dionne, Dale Tallon, and the other miscreants on the team. He further outlived his welcome when, out on the town one night in Stockholm, Sinden advised Martin as they were leaving the same establishment that, since Rick was 10 minutes from the hotel and it was 11:25 p.m., he had missed the curfew of 11:30. "I was with five other guys and we were leaving, too. Harry only saw the ones he wanted to see," Rick grouses.

It didn't get any better the next day after practice. To the delight of the whole team, he was caught in mid-impersonation of Sinden. It was a kid's prank, but an inadvertent coffin nail. When the team for the Russian games was announced, he was another player who opted to return to his NHL club and, like Hadfield, he felt there were no hard feelings. "Later Sinden wrote a book [*Hockey Showdown*] and called me 'a defector,' said I told him I wanted to get in shape for the regular season. That's not what I said at all. I was getting feelers from Punch, just like some of the other guys were getting from their teams. Hey, the message was, 'If you're not playing and you have no chance of playing, get your ass back here. We need you.' The fact is, I was in great shape, worked my ass off. Hell, I was a 21-year-old rookie. Why the fuck *wouldn't* I be in good shape?

"Naw," he says, waving his cigar, his hazel eyes sparking with intensity, "he was full of shit. When we left, it was with the understanding that Eagleson was going to hold a press conference, explaining things. Instead, when I landed at Halifax airport, all I got was a dozen news guys in my face, wanting to know why I 'deserted.' I never deserted anything, any team, in my life. If I didn't have much good to say about Sinden before, I sure as hell don't have any respect for him now.

"Get this one. First time we play the Bruins after the Russians, one of their players — Nope," he says abruptly, holding up a cautionary hand, "I'm not gonna name him. He's still in hockey, and so is Sinden. This player comes up to me before the game and says, 'Keep your

head up tonight, Rico. We're supposed to make life miserable for you.'
I asked the guy what else Sinden could pull to make it worse — shoot
my fuckin' dog? The next year, at the All-Star game, Harry couldn't
go face-to-face with me, couldn't even look me in the eye, ducked me
every chance. To this day I got no use for Sinden."

I feel it's time to change the subject, figuring I'm only riling Martin
and upsetting Suit & Tie, who's irritably snatching at a fashion section
page. Then I proceed to put both feet in by bringing up visions of
Scotty Bowman. The talk goes all right at first, but soon degenerates
like a Wayne Gretzky disc.

"Scotty, Jeez, when you ask about breaking things up . . . The day
he was named coach and GM Rene Robert said, 'I'm outta here, gone,
history.' He felt that way because, you know how Scotty used to yap at
everybody on the ice, calling guys names and pissin' them off, well, he
used to call Rene chickenshit, floater, hot dog, stuff like that. So Rene
called him 'platehead.' You know about Bowman's old head injury,
eh?" I nod my awareness of the injury that ended Bowman's own
hockey career. Suit & Tie looks puzzled as he stares at some recipes
for broccoli.

"New Year's Eve," Martin continues, unaware of the consternation
behind him, "we're in Montreal and it's Rene's birthday. In the papers
Bowman says he's got a present for Robert, a loss, but we win 7–3 or
somethin'. Rene gets a hat trick, and after the third, he skates over to
the Montreal bench and says, 'Here's a present for *you,* platehead,' and
he tosses the puck into the bench. Scotty went nuts, scramblin' around
the floor, looking for the puck. When he gets it, he comes up firing at
Rene, who's skatin' away. Nuts, you know, wacko.

"He used to yack all the time. Shit, Tiger Williams conked him with
his stick in Vancouver, remember? Tiger got suspended. Musta been
the NHLPA's [NHL Players Association] most popular suspension of
the year. But Bowman got even when he arrived in Buffalo. Rene was
right. We didn't even make it through training camp in '79. Scotty
packed him up first week in October and shipped his ass to Colorado."
A long pause ensues as Rick takes a pull on his beer. "Got me out of
Buffalo, too, the next year when I got injured."

I had been told by mutual acquaintances that Rick was a bitter guy these days, partly because of incidents like his Team Canada experiences, once with Sinden, once with Bowman in 1976. Then there was the knee injury and a trade to Los Angeles, which led to the end of his career and a tangled lawsuit for compensation. Named in the suit were L.A., the Sabres, Bowman, and the doctors. The suit was initiated in 1982 and, as we talk in the bar, is still dragging through the system. According to Rick, the legal wrangles have prevented him from becoming a coach or special instructor, either in Buffalo, where he still resides, or anywhere else for that matter. The futility of it has occurred to him but still leaves him cold. He feels he has a lot to offer young players, and I don't doubt he longs for the opportunity to pass along his considerable scoring philosophy and expertise. But, like the lawsuit, that will take time.

All of his memories aren't gloomy today. One of his better moments came the night he had dinner with Bobby Hull, his boyhood idol and Team Canada '76 teammate.

"It was great. We talked and laughed for a couple of hours, and he gave me a great tip. He said I was going to be speared, hacked, boarded, and hooked to death if I didn't get a message across. He said it would happen every year, with every crop of new guys coming up. He said, 'Next time they foul you, when you come up the ice, blast one at 'em. Shoot at their goddamn head. Let them know you aren't going to stand still for any more crap. Scare the livin' shit out of them.' So we're playing Pittsburgh, and Eddie Van Impe has always been in my face over the years. I come trampin' down the wing, and he's standing on the blue line, big fat face hangin' out, and I drill one just to the side of his head. Musta went in to the crowd about 15 rows up. But Van Impe doesn't get it. Next shift we had to throw the puck in, anyway, and I did it again, this time about jock-high, a little to the left. Still no reaction. Then, when we're leaving the ice at the end of the period, I say to one of their players, 'Tell that asshole I can't keep missin' at this range.' He musta clued in, because after the game he says to me, 'Kid, you got a lotta balls.'" Suit & Tie likes that one, too.

When we get ready to leave Fridays later on in the afternoon, I ask Rick to rate himself, to comment on his career. Ever serious, he takes out a new cigar and leans back for a moment. "I developed my own abilities. I didn't need a coach to motivate me. I was motivated on my own. I knew how to score." He snickers at the immodest remark. "I mean, I was aware the openings for a pass or a shot are only there for an instant. I was always very aware of that, and I had good hands, you know. I could take advantage of that fraction. I had a lot of drive, a lot of pride in my game. Pound for pound I was one of the strongest guys in the league, and I was tough."

He nods to himself, mirroring Suit & Tie's agreement. "But I know one thing. I'd trade my 50-goal years, my All-Star selections, for one Stanley Cup," he says wistfully, a touch of regret in his voice.

90-SECOND ALL-STARS

G — **Tony Esposito** *". . . he stoned me the most."*

D — **Bobby Orr** *". . . a great athlete who could go both ways, always looking ahead."*

D — **Larry Robinson** *". . . solid, almost impossible to get around."*

C — **Marcel Dionne** *". . . amazing, played like a juggler handling 36 balls — incredible stick."*

RW — **Mike Bossy** *". . . best right wing scorer I ever saw."*

LW — **Bobby Hull** *". . . he played the game at another level."*

The Knoxes

First-class Sabres in
a Blue-collar Town

THE BUFFALO SABRES TENTATIVELY became members of the National Hockey League on December 1, 1969. It was a conditional franchise, a minefield of contrary considerations involving the on-again, off-again financial shenanigans of the Oakland Seals. The Knox brothers — Seymour III and Northrup — and their associates in the Niagara Frontier Hockey Corporation were on the hook for a million dollars. It was a tangled, complicated arrangement whereby they would refloat the sinking Bay Area franchise from a distance of 3,000 miles in return for either an agreement to move the team to Buffalo the following season or be guaranteed the next franchise in a further expansion of the NHL. The "deal" was a legal can of worms.

That wasn't how the Knoxes had planned it, parachuting behind the lines, elbowing their way into the bandwagon. Rather, they had intended to enter through the front door with a bit of fanfare. However, after four years of frustrating, guerrilla-style lobbying and perilous footslogging through boardroom booby traps, the brothers Knox were grateful for small favours.

They had originally made an ill-fated application in 1965 for the first expansion in 1967 and were assured they would be included in the final six, only to be left out, replaced by a city (St. Louis) without a local group remotely interested in or even asking for a franchise. It was the maximum snub, unless you clued in to the Norris–Wirtz ownership of an empty, fading St. Louis Arena and the nebulous rationale of Jim Norris, the Chicago Blackhawk owner and influential governor of the NHL. In the mid-sixties the Knoxes weren't quite so cynical.

The Norris disdain for Buffalo ran the gamut from petty name-calling to unrealistic, self-serving resentment. Back when wheeling and dealing in commodities and real estate were the lifeblood of the Norris empire, Jim Norris lost two million dollars in an abortive Buffalo grain elevator deal. He attributed the setback to a civic politician, and all through the Knoxes' persistent knocking on hockey's penthouse door, he doggedly repeated, "Buffalo will never get into the league as long as I'm around." He continually referred to Buffalo as being a "bush town," adding sullenly that it had "a terrible airport, too." Norris proved correct in his prediction. He passed away before the Sabres became NHL lodge members.

By late January 1970 John Whalen, my boss at Maple Leaf Sports Productions, had gained us an audience with the Sabre hierarchy to pitch them on doing some business. After all, we ran a successful promotion, advertising, publication, and marketing concern in the Big Smoke. Why not Buffalo? Besides, the Sabres had just sworn in our old pal Punch Imlach as head honcho, and he could vouch for us.

The first exploratory meeting was held in the Sabres' offices, and after the groundwork was outlined, Whalen left the ensuing details of a working arrangement to me. Eventually the deal was sealed over a luncheon at Seymour's home. It was April. The only tangible sign of the Buffalo Sabres was a logo, some rich people, a quotable GM/coach, and a few hired hands.

The Knox residence on Nottingham Terrace brought back scenes of my time spent in the Royal Theatre back in Fort William as a kid. Had the home been located on a hill, framed by lightning and pouring rain, it would have been a dead ringer for one of those eerie aeries in a Boris Karloff movie, the ones that made ten-year-olds bolt past laneways, ominous, unlit doorways, and empty lots on dark winter nights. The house was old, grey, and palatial. A courtyard fronting a carriage house had parking for more cars than you'd normally find at a liquor store on Friday night at closing time.

I can't recall whether I punched a buzzer or hefted a knocker, but an oaken door the size of a bus shelter opened, and there stood Seymour in a golf cardigan, casual slacks, and sagging woolly socks piled over loafers. I remember his garb because of my surprise — it was so out of character. I had never seen him in anything but a blue, sometimes grey, suit. Occasionally he would sport one of what seemed to be an endless string of single-breasted navy blazers which, over the next four years, I became convinced was his one and only jacket.

Punch was already there, hands in pockets, standing in a side ante-room, maybe a library, although I don't remember any books being present, only furniture with a limitless line of cross-stitched pillows and cushions. Apparently Jean Knox was into needlework.

Our host offered us a prelunch drink, and we agreed on rye and water. Knox left the room, returned a moment later with a quart of Canadian Club, wiped a substantial layer of dust off the bottle, and said, "This'll have to do," as if he were offering us mountain moonshine from a backyard still. Punch and I quickly peeked at each other. The flickering glance was to let me know a reference to the dust wouldn't be smart in this case. In an educational telephone briefing the day before Imlach had cautioned me about the Knox sense of humour. "More moderate than perhaps you're used to. Definitely not locker room, not pool hall, if you get my drift. These people aren't Smythe and Ballard," he admonished, making the point perfectly clear.

Our business discussion was merely confirmation and acceptance of our proposal. While we didn't get all the things we wanted, we did get our foot in the door with the Sabres' publication and the sale of print advertising. The general shoptalk out of the way, we were invited to lunch, and to my surprise we were taken to a bright and cheery solarium projecting off the back of the house, totally un-Karloff, definitely not scary. We sat at a large glass-and-wrought-iron table, bare of everything but plates and cutlery. A big maid trundled in, obviously unimpressed with the guests and seemingly sullen over this weekend visit. She proceeded to clatter the lunch onto the table, and we began to clank, clink, tinkle, ping, and bink our way through the meal, too noisy to talk easily. Finally Seymour asked us, "Jean just bought this table set. What do you think of it?"

Putting down a fork, I offered up an opinion, just as Punch was taking a swallow of his soup.

"Well, the first thing I noticed was that if the guy across from you scratches himself, you can see what he's scratching."

Imlach coughed through the mouthful of soup, grabbed for a napkin, and glared sideways in my direction. Knox only hummed a "hmm," then gradually let a smile that grew bigger and bigger cross his face. "The situation never occurred to me" was all he said, still smiling. Punch merely appeared peevish.

Yes, I suppose I was overstepping the line, but the incident points to a comparison and provides an insight into the brothers who spearheaded the move to bring major league hockey to a blue-collar town.

Northrup or Norty, the younger of the two, was a former college goaltender at Yale and a world champion in court tennis for 10 years. In fact, he retired undefeated, then was captain of the U.S. polo team twice. Norty is outgoing, feisty, given to impatience, competitive bordering on combative and, most of all, gives off an aura of energy.

Seymour, on the other hand, appears imperturbable, can muster a smile through almost any trial or tribulation, and even shakes hands with those who work against him. He's analytical and faultlessly diplomatic.

They were brought up civic-minded and fiercely loyal to Buffalo, even though their wealthy station in the community allowed travel and sojourns in family enclaves in North Carolina and Florida. After college, they followed their father's lead and became involved in banking, the local art scene, and various business interests, which included a chance foray into an NHL franchise. If anything, the hockey wars catapulted them into a more exclusive club than they had ever dreamed of joining, a club where your prospective partners led you down the garden path and tested your mettle to the fullest. In their four-year rollercoaster ride to bring the Sabres to ice, they suffered innumerable setbacks, side trips, and near misses. They were bumped off stride many times, outmanoeuvred in the way foxy, jealous old pros have always taught brash, idealistic rookies a lesson. Even their family business background, their careful schooling in the wiles of commerce and ivory-tower negotiations never prepared them for the rough-and-tumble tag team punch-ups in pro hockey. Every now and then, finding themselves at another dead end, they were told to "hang in there." And they did.

The Knoxes' pursuit of an NHL franchise says something about character and tenacity, about determination to see an idea through. They paid the piper and outlasted the naysayers. It was brotherly support that bulwarked the entire group, their one-on-one open-minded personalities taking them above two-faced rhetoric and misinformation. They complemented each other. Where Seymour was prone to take things at a calmer, more measured pace, Norty was blunt and to the point when pressed. While Seymour took matters a practical step at a time, Norty tended to approach by the most direct route.

Therefore, it was no surprise when Norty, typically out of the blue, asked me, "Have you ever written a book?" The year was 1971, and the answer, of course, was no. At that time, out of necessity, I was writing more and more articles in the hockey magazines but had the luxury of choosing my own subjects. One of my Buffalo efforts was a piece on the Sabres' first offices, a second-floor rabbit warren of cubicles on Niagara Circle in the downtown core. The story was a tongue-in-cheek poke at the Mickey Mouse beginnings, the tacky forerunner of the slicker, opulent-by-comparison digs to come at the renovated Auditorium. Norty liked the story. In fact, he eventually had it framed and hung in his office.

When he inquired about my becoming an author, it wasn't the first time I had considered the possibility, and I have to admit the idea intrigued me. But even back then I wasn't so naive as to believe books came from a couple of beers and a few catchy anecdotes tossed over a table to a captive audience.

"Do you really think you have a story?" I challenged. He suggested a meeting to discuss the project with Seymour, team attorney Bob Swados, who played a major role, and himself, allowing me to be the judge.

To say the brothers were diplomatic and competitive, to imply that their taste in comedy didn't include sophomoric or *Animal House* appeal, wasn't to suggest a sense of humour was missing entirely.

While Norty's personality and earthier vocabulary allowed more lee-way, neither one was above a good laugh at their own expense.

When we met for the initial interview concerning the book, Norty, at his brother's prodding, told the tale of Seymour's St. Louis trip to take a firsthand look at a successful expansion franchise. Taking notes, he dutifully observed the frequent use of the Blues' logo and their colour scheme. Blue, white, and gold were rampant, from the carpeting to the walls, from the stadium seating to the concession stands. But the cap-per came in the washrooms.

"The colours carried over through the corridors and onto the wash-room walls, but . . ." Norty paused and chuckled. "But when Seymour saw the blue water in the white urinals —" by now he was snorting fit-fully "— he was really impressed." We all had a howl while Seymour tearfully tried to explain how inspired he'd been with the sheer audacity of the idea before realizing it was simply industrial-strength Tidy Bowl.

Four years later, in 1975, the result was *A Spin of the Wheel*. The title referred to a garish, battered, over-and-under gaming wheel rolled into Montreal's Queen Elizabeth Hotel ballroom. It was the NHL's considered method to determine who would select first — Vancouver or Buffalo — in the 1970 amateur draft. The contraption looked like an old hooker at a high school prom, but Imlach's luck prevailed to deliv-er the Sabres' firstborn, Gil Perreault.

By the end of the 1973–74 season I had left the Sabres' organization and returned full-time to Toronto, yet still kept close ties and contacts in Buffalo. I recall the frequent good-natured telephone urgings of Norty concerning the unfinished manuscript, even when snags arose and cre-ativity just wasn't there. The fact that he had handpicked me to write the story, even though he knew plenty of capable people who were proven hockey writers with a lot of background on the Sabre situation, was never lost on me. It shored up my resolution to finish the job and reflects the way the Knoxes stick with members of their "team."

If any one moment underlined the point, it was a little sidelight that took place at the very first Sabre exhibition game, a tilt against the New York Rangers in Peterborough. The arena was sold-out, primarily by the influx of Buffalo people. I cruised the walkways leading to the ice and patrolled the four corners of the arena, occasionally taking a look at the game, primarily concerned with my photographers as they peered through viewfinders at rinkside and tried to shoot Perreault for the elusive cover of the first Sabre magazine. As the second period started, it was obvious that the lighting in the building was a major problem. I was looking through the glass, lost in thought, contemplating a staged shot for the next morning, when I sensed someone standing beside me. It was Seymour. Furtively he said, "Here you go," and glanced downward between us. As I followed his lead, I could see that he held something in his hand. On closer observation I recognized a piece of rolled material with little Sabre logos — a tie.

Remember back in the seventies when ties were wide, real wide? In fact, it was almost impossible, if you were stylish, to drip anything on your shirtfront. The tie I was being offered was the kind you found in profusion at any Buffalo bar or social function. It was an inch and a half wide.

Seymour, arm still at his side, rotated his wrist, palm outward, and said, "Take it, but don't say where you got it."

Revolving my hand, I took the tie like a spy in a Bogart film and said, "Don't worry. I won't!"

Fashion aside, it was the thought. Here was the chairman of the board and president, inundated with requests for such a sought-after memento, making sure that I, an "outside consultant" at the best stretch, was looked after. Although I never forgot the gesture, the very next day I gave the scarce-as-hen's-teeth neckpiece to Trey Coley, a Buffalo print salesman and friend who wore it religiously.

That's the way I remember being treated by the Knoxes — first-class. I was always invited to year-end team parties and club golf tournaments, and they never failed to give me the same trinkets and gifts as other staff and players.

Over the many years that followed nothing changed, and if I needed further confirmation that a sense of humour pulsed under the collective Knox persona, it came on a one-night trip Tony Esposito and I took to a Sabre game. Between periods I dropped into the directors' lounge to say hello and visit, as I had been instructed to do anytime I was in town. We chatted, and I brought Seymour up-to-date on what I'd been doing, mentioning that I was writing a novel focusing on a young Maple Leaf player. The story line was spread over six games of a Stanley Cup semifinal between — who else? — Buffalo and Toronto. "Science fiction to the core," I joked.

Suddenly perking up, Seymour held up his hand in mid-laugh and urgently asked, "Do we win?"

"Yes," I answered, puzzled and a little reluctant to give away the complete plot.

"Awright," he stage-whispered, pushing and pulling a fist in a passable imitation of Wayne Gretzky celebrating yet another goal. "Gawd, Howie," he exulted with a laugh to Howard Saperston, another of the original board members in the sixties. "We finally won something." Then he launched himself around the room, regaling and relaying the fictional semifinal victory to the other Sabre faithful.

On the drive back to Toronto the next day I realized that Seymour and Norty were the best of the relatively few professional team owners I knew on a first-name basis. I mentally wished them a quick Stanley Cup.

After over 20 years of answering the bell, hope and humour still have a priority. So, for all the crap they've weathered, and for all those long-suffering, good ol' Sabre fans, I hope they have a June to remember someday soon. They deserve one.

90-SECOND ALL-STARS

G — **Terry Sawchuk**

D — **Bobby Orr**

D — **Tim Horton**

C — **Wayne Gretzky**

RW — **Gordie Howe**

LW — **Bobby Hull**

"A great team . . . how can you beat it?"

Yvan Cournoyer

Roadrunner in Red, White, and Blue

WHEN HE WASN'T OUTFITTED in his Montreal Canadiens uniform, Yvan Cournoyer was a bit of a shock. At least to me. Or maybe it wasn't my fault, because my first sighting of him, sans equipment, was in August. It was hot, and it was 1972. He walked down Carlton along the front of Maple Leaf Gardens where Team Canada hunkered down in the Leaf dressing room, getting ready for a laugher against the Russians.

Toronto was an odd place to see him in. He was coming off his best goal-scoring season ever and was at the midpoint of his career. In Montreal he would have drawn a crowd, but out here in the sunshine, in civvies, in the heat of August, he was just another unknown pedestrian making his way toward Yonge Street.

My surprise wasn't in the instant of recognition, but came from his physique. He was tanned, stocky, muscular, and had the confident walk of a man at peace with his lot in life. Out of curiosity I recall turning to watch him walk away, and for the first time didn't see him as being short or diminutive, words sports writers frequently used to describe him. *Fast* was another they often employed.

So this was the "Roadrunner," the one who was going to show the Soviets what the word *speed* was all about. To me he looked

Yvan Cournoyer, the Roadrunner, in full flight: "a triggerman, a pure goal popper whose scores and assists were never far apart."

innocuous, unassuming, pleasant, and about as far away from the typical hockey player as you could get. He also had a cherubic face, which was another misleading visual. A weight lifter, yes, a bodybuilder, of course, but a hockey player? This guy? No way, because in a T-shirt and jeans he was one compact hombre.

To be fair, lining up night after night with teammates such as Jean Beliveau, Serge Savard, Guy Lapointe, and the brothers Mahovlich would make anyone sporting a vertical of only five-seven look diminutive. I have to admit that the times I had seen him up close in his oversize red, white, and blue sweater he looked like a mailbox on skates, just about perfect elbowing height for the rest of the league. But that day, on the streets of Toronto, I had the distinct impression he didn't wear any equipment under his team jersey.

Fifteen years later I walked into his Dorval restaurant with another ex-Canadien, Al "Junior" Langlois. Cournoyer joined us at a table after the rush of the lunch crowd. Two-storied, the place was large, and business was brisk.

Our conversation came round to the beginnings of the appropriately named Club 12, and he told us about the building problems. There was a bylaw prohibiting people, like himself, from being the official contractor and jobbing out the actual trades work and construction. But he knew what he wanted, knew exactly how the finished product should look, and refused to relinquish his job/superintendent role. Rather than give up the position, he paid a fine in the thousands of dollars to supervise his own job.

"I know where h'every stud, h'every h'lectric junction box, h'every nail h'is," he said, looking around the interior with a respectful nod.

That said something about him, about his pride of accomplishment.

On this day he didn't look much different than I remembered him back in 1972. Yes, he had lost some muscle mass, but at least he hadn't replaced it with bulk fat. I sensed he had a self-appreciation of the transition from player to businessman, from Roadrunner to restauranteur. Despite the continual interruptions that required his attention, he was relaxed and in control of the generally hectic pace. I recall thinking that compared to the speed and danger of his hockey-playing days, the action around him in his restaurant must seem tame.

As he switched from French to English, discussing details with staff, searching for the right word with Langlois, or speaking directly to me, the only unilingual one in the group, he managed to carry on three different topics without increasing one iota the tempo of his words or the tone of his voice.

I questioned him about the traces of flour and a sticky substance that appeared to be a spatter of chocolate on his shirt sleeve. He admitted that it was his habit to come in early and bake Black Forest cakes. My look of disbelief must have been obvious.

"Yeah, I bake a lot. Go t'ru a lot of shirt, too," he insisted with a slow, warm grin.

The coy smile hides a lot of other accomplishments. In fact, it's difficult to associate the man with his record. He was a tough right winger who only spent a mere seven games in the American Hockey League before joining the Habs for 16 seasons and enough Stanley Cup rings to cover all his fingers. He had been brought along carefully, like many rookies talented enough to break into the Montreal dressing room. Spot duty, power plays, and full-court presses were his lot with a team deep in talent. Merely having played with the Habs brought you instant recognition anywhere else in the NHL.

He was a triggerman, a pure goal popper whose scores and assists were never far apart — 428 and 435 respectively during regular season play and 64 and 63 in postseason. He was a closer, a finisher, a water spider who could shoot BBs past the best goaltenders in the world. He played all eight games in the 1972 Canada–Soviet Union series and, typically, scored three goals and made two assists. He was a player who blew past rival defencemen, a guy who could accelerate with a single stride, a veritable time bomb for the opposition, ready to explode offensively at any given moment in a game.

Yvan was one of those players that TV failed to capture effectively. You had to see him in person to appreciate the speed and ability. I have no better example of firsthand appreciation than the night in Toronto he took a blue-line-to-blue-line pass from Brad Park, simply opened up the afterburners, and swooped in on Vladislav Tretiak alone, making it 2–0 Canada. When he circled and came out over the Russian blue line to the arms of his waiting teammates, Tretiak was still digging the puck out of the net.

Yet in 1987 the mild manner, hesitating forays into English, and intent way he listened to every cross-table remark didn't fit the image, the memories of those days when he was a great player on a great Montreal team.

Two years later I returned to Club 12, this time in the company of Red Storey, the laugh-a-minute, everything's-great referee who had picked me up at the downtown Forum and regaled me all the way out to Dorval with the usual reminiscences about life in the NHL. Red never changed, and neither had Yvan. He was behind the draft taps when we came in, smiling, obviously at home in the bustle of the service bar and hum of the luncheon crowd.

When Yvan joined us, it was beginning to slow down, but we were interrupted by an incessant flow of patrons looking for autographs, while staff members constantly proffered menus, place mats, and paper flotsam and jetsam from pockets and purses on behalf of their customers. There were more than enough interruptions for pictures, too, from tentative, red-faced women and bashful, embarrassed, full-grown men.

Yvan would do more than cooperate. He'd get up from the table, go behind the bar to the draft taps, the awestruck customers in tow, and pose for a picture with *madame* and *monsieur* that one of his waiters would take. When he returned after the sixth or tenth time, I asked if he ever became tired of the routine.

"Tired?" He looked up, momentarily puzzled. "I never get tired. Dat's why I'm 'ere h'every day when I'm not out of town. Dey expect of me, you know. Dey come from h'all over da place, h'everywhere."

The words were chosen carefully, and I sensed that he wasn't being cocky or arrogant. Yvan signed another place mat, asked the waiter where the people were sitting, and left us again to deliver the autograph in person. He chatted with them in French for several minutes, shook hands around the table, including those of two young boys of about 10, and waved as he left and walked back to our table.

"See, dere from Plessisville. Dat's far, eh? Da two boys, play 'ockey, but ah don t'ink dey know me." He flashed the boyish grin and shrugged, pointing to a few threads of grey hair.

Just then a bolder couple came forward with a request for pictures. The woman was all atwitter and placed both arms around Yvan's neck, draft taps to the side. In the next photo the gentleman shook Yvan's hand, then they both posed for a shot in which they drew beer from the taps. Finally there were smiles, a babble of *français* to my anglo ears, then a wide-eyed explosion of laughter and handshakes all over again.

"From H'Edmunston, New Brunswick," Yvan supplied to my unspoken question when he returned to our table. "Dey been 'ere for t'ree games already dis year. Dey got tickets for 'artford tonight." He looked back at them as they happily watched the Polaroids bloom, then rubbed his eyes and squinted.

"Flash spots?" I questioned.

He nodded and smiled away any concerns. "H'every day. H'it's da 'ardest part, you know — da lights." When I asked again if the extra duty ever wore thin on him, he said candidly and carefully, "For a long time da fans dey make me a better player, and now I'm in business, dey make me again, you see? I owe dem h'everything, and dey h'expect to see me 'ere. My name is on da sign, eh? So I'm here for dem to see, and I will do da picture, da signing . . . it's not too much."

Those remarks always come to mind whenever the talk includes Yvan Cournoyer. Despite the limitations of language, regardless of the hubbub around him, I've always marvelled at the simplicity and eloquence of the explanation, the graciousness of the consideration, and the classiness of the thought. The Roadrunner still dazzles.

90-SECOND ALL-STARS

G — **Johnny Bower**

D — **Bobby Orr**

D — **Guy Lapointe**

C — **Henri Richard**

RW — **Gordie Howe**

LW — **Bobby Hull**

"So many good player I 'ad on my team — Lafleur, Savard, Robinson, Beliveau, Mahovlich, yes, and Dryden. So many, but John Bower gave me da most problem."

Mike Palmateer

Goalie on a Trapeze

THE GRIN IS JUST UNDER THE SURFACE, indicating a guy who knows the punch line but likes the joke, anyway. To say the pale eyes twinkle would be a stretch, but they definitely have a glint of mischief. His walk still has a bit of a swagger, a "what the hell" boy sway that says the fun isn't far off.

Back in his playing days a Toronto writer said he was a leprechaun in goal pads. Others, not as charitable, said he was a brash, overrated, overconfident flake who carried a chip on his shoulder.

There were nights when his play resembled one of the Flying Wallendas trying to regain balance on the high wire, times when he put on more miles than his defencemen, moments when he'd make a Ray Bolgeresque save and rebound to his feet like one of those bottom-weighted punching bags, exhilarated, ready and willing for the next attack. Yet, more than once, superconfidence gave way to subdued humiliation, as it does with all professional players, especially goalies. Under the stylish mask, after certain games, the twinkle would leave his eyes and the near grin would be long gone, but only briefly because, to Mike, goaltending was an adventure, a trip that some people could only get out of a bottle or a drugstore.

159

Mike Palmateer keeping Sabre Jim Lorentz at arm's length: "he was colourful, cocky and, considering his size, crazy."

He was exciting, daring, and always played on the edge. He was colourful, cantankerous, cocky and, considering his size, crazy. The people who paid the cash knew they were getting their money's worth. Up in the greys, where the real fans hunker down, he was a bona fide hero, one of their own.

Even though he was virtually under the noses of the Leaf brass and scouts from the age of 12, playing right through the Marlboro system from Peewee to a Memorial Cup, he was Toronto's fifth pick in the 1974 amateur draft and the 85th player chosen overall. His raw talent didn't receive the value his short but eventful eight-year career would eventually underline.

The Leafs finished fourth in their division in 1973–74 and selected 13th in the first round. Jack Valiquette, the OHL's leading scorer from Sault Sainte Marie, was the first to get the call, Dave "Tiger" Williams was chosen in the second round, then came Per Arne Alexandersson and Peter Driscoll, household names to be sure. If that doesn't make you wonder about the science of scouting, keep in mind that three other goaltenders were selected ahead of Palmateer, too. Pete LoPresti went 42nd to Minnesota, while Jim Warden and Bruce Aberhart went 75th and 80th. Although Palmateer spent two seasons in the minors sharpening his game, he eventually went on to outnumber and outplay LoPresti in every category. Warden and Aberhart never saw an NHL game from the crease.

Mike also became one of Trivial Pursuit's toughest answers. The question? "What goaltender posted shutouts in the International Hockey League, the Central Hockey League, the American Hockey League, and the NHL?" Whoever wrote the question was cruel. Cottagers, trapped indoors by rain, cold, or boring hosts would mutter, "Who cares?" The twist to the query was the fact that Iron Mike had been sent down for his one-and-only trip to the AHL to do some fine-tuning after his return to the Leafs from Washington. In his second game he collected the shutout to complete the cycle and was promptly elevated to the big club again.

Despite the fact that he played behind Leaf teams that never crawled higher than third in their division, and a Washington club that only saw fifth place, he left the game at the age of 30 with a winning percentage and 17 shutouts. He also exited with knees resembling targets at a biathlon range. Like many near-crippling injuries, it was an accumulation of wear and tear, leading to a total of 14 surgical procedures, three on the left and 11 on the right.

Sitting now behind a desk at ReMax in the burgeoning town of Aurora, north of Toronto, he appears close to his playing weight of 170. A touch of grey is beginning to peek through the reddish hair, but the barely hidden grin is still there and the casual manner is reflected in the way he tilts his chair back dangerously, propping a foot against the desktop for leverage.

Above and behind Palmateer is a framed colour illustration, not of him making a save as you might expect, but out of his crease corralling a loose puck and getting ready to fire it out of danger. Typical.

When asked if the comments saying he was a hot dog, a wing nut, and a flake are true, he raises his eyebrows to vertigo heights, lets a big grin bloom on his face, spreads his hands in mock surprise, and answers, "Come on, shit, I was a goalie, for Christ's sake. What do you expect?"

He has me there, and I tick off the list of netminders I know. A strange breed indeed. Gary "Axe" Smith, who on any given night could be found ranging up the ice as far as the red line, a runaway armoured stork methodically stickhandling through traffic and ultimately dumping the puck into the other end, as if to show his defence how to do it. The powers that be eventually put in a rule to curtail his wanderings. Bruce Gamble, eyeballing pucks into the net like a batter watching a third strike, claiming he didn't get paid to stop pucks at practice, and besides, he'd say, "When the time comes, anything I can see I can stop." Gerry Cheevers and his goofy mask crisscrossed with stitch marks like a Dr. Frankenstein paint-by-number kit. Kelly Hrudey's karate headbands. Patrick Roy's nervous head gyrations and neck stretches before every face-off, recalling a scene from *The Exorcist,* or a cowboy fighting his first shirt and tie. Need I say more?

But our conversation today ranges over several topics, such as how unflaky Mike was in real life.

"The night before a game — no drinking, none. Got my sleep, and I'd think about the game, about the guys I was going to face and what to expect. I was dead serious, man." The last comment is said through the usual underlying grin, complete with big eyes that almost deflect the moment into a sly laugh. Passing on the urge to question the remark, I move on to his relationship with Punch after Imlach's return to Toronto.

"Punch was okay. We never had a problem until it came to 'Showdown' [a *Hockey Night in Canada* bit featuring three-man hockey and skills competitions]. Sittler, B.J. [Salming], and I were selected, and Punch let it be known he didn't want us to play. 'What the hell happens if one of you gets injured?'" Mike asks, mimicking Imlach's sharp, piercing tone almost to perfection. "'The goddamn team is the one who'll suffer, not you assholes.' He couldn't stop us, but he made it clear he was against it. I told him, 'Give me the same dough I could win if we go all the way [$10,000] and I'll make sure I miss it, stay at home,' but he wasn't about to match the money, so I played. Wouldn't you know it, the first damn minute I get caught out behind the net, Borje dives in and makes a phenomenal save, spearing a shot with his glove. Cracked a bone in his hand or something, and it was all downhill from there with Punch."

Next, he shifts gears and tells me how he didn't want to leave Toronto. "Some of the media said it was money. Bullshit, it was the length of the contract. I wanted three years with an option. They offered two and an option. To go elsewhere would involve compensation. We looked around — Detroit and L.A. were interested — but then there was the matter of compensation. The Leafs never made another offer. They just sat there and waited for me to come around, I suppose. Suddenly it came down to interest from the Capitals, and the compensation didn't worry them, so the deal was done. It was August of 1980, and here I was going to the arena I felt was the worst in the league. I hated the Capital Centre. Blue ice, bad lighting, the puck could get lost in the crowd background, but I learned to handle it and, in looking back, I loved living in Upper Marlboro, Maryland."

He relates how he and girlfriend [now Mrs. Palmateer] Lee Dantzic went to look at furniture for their new apartment in the D.C. area. The salesman, after writing up the bill, asked Mike what it was that had brought him to Maryland. Mike told the man he was a hockey player with the Capitals. "Hell, yeah . . . yeah, I thought I recognized you. Jeez, I saw you play last year. You were great, just great."

With the payment put through on Lee's credit card, the salesman happily put the other foot in his mouth. "All the best and have a great year, Mr. Dantzic," he sang out, a hockey fan to the very end.

But the two seasons Mike spent with the Caps weren't a lot of laughs. The first year he suffered through a pulled hamstring, ankle ligament damage, and bone chips in his wrist. The second year his knee began to show the strain, giving out periodically despite the opinions of the Washington medics that it only needed some rest. About six games into the second season it was obvious the knee wouldn't respond, and an arthoscopic probe was scheduled.

Wayne Stephenson was just returning from an injury of his own the day Palmateer was being wheeled into surgery at noon. Suddenly a nurse barged into the operating room and said, "Hold it. Don't start." She explained to the doctors that Stephenson had been injured in the game-day morning skate and Palmateer, the guy stretched out on the gurney in white socks and a surgical gown, was going back to play that night. They wheeled him out and shipped him back in an ambulance to the Landover arena dressing room, where he nodded and snoozed, thanks to the effects of the relaxants he had been given, right up until game time. The Caps and Palmateer lost 5–2 to the Quebec Nordiques.

The surgery was performed the next day. The results: nothing out of the ordinary was found. However, the knee continued to collect fluid, and after five days, when they wanted to simply drain it, Mike refused and got Alan Eagleson on the phone. Then he flew to Toronto where Dr. Jackson confirmed the goalie's worst fears. "Crushed bone, pieces of cartilage, gone for the season" was the verdict.

The repair operation was done over the ensuing summer, and Palmateer headed back to the Leafs for $1, conditional on his knee standing up to the rigours of the NHL. It was the option year of his contract, and the Toronto GM was now Gerry McNamara. Palmateer was willing to settle for less money on the strength of a two-year contract, but the Leafs balked and the deal went to arbitration. Palmateer got more money, plus his one year and an option. Opening the season slowly, he eventually went down to St. Catharines to become part of Trivial Pursuit lore, and followed that up with the best win-loss percentage of any goalie over the final half of the season.

But the writing was on the wall. He admitted to being unable to cover pucks on the right side of the net. His knee wouldn't allow him to do anything but flop or sit down to cover up. The hockey career, for all intents and purposes, was over.

But on this sunny May morning the grin is still plastered all over his face, the eyes still have the glint, and the walk is still that of a guy with fewer years on his shoulders, or knees.

As a parting question, I ask if he's belatedly learned of any fears he might have harboured, any part of goaltending that in retrospect makes him wonder about his choice of position. The eyes widen and a grin blossoms.

"Jeez, the only thing that ever scared me was when Jim McKenny cut through my crease on his way up the ice. Goddamn, that was scary!"

A lot of us were scared, too, Mike.

90-SECOND ALL-STARS

G — **Tony Esposito** *". . . my idol."*

D — **Borje Salming** *". . . never let you down, always sacrificed himself."*

D — **Ian Turnbull** *". . . in this situation [90 seconds] he'd be a bonus offensive threat."*

C — **Darryl Sittler** *". . . if we weren't in their end, his man wouldn't score."*

RW — **Lanny McDonald** *". . . great man in the clutch."*

LW — **Steve Shutt** *". . . he's so dangerous when the chips are down."*

John Ferguson

Dirty Harry on Ice

MY ONLY SIGHTINGS of John Ferguson as a player were images of him intimidating some poor soul, or shots of him in the penalty box, mopping his brush cut with a towel. His expression was permanently "pissed off," and he resembled a testy, tethered falcon anxious to get back to the blood sport before all the prey was gone. It was a familiar sight to all hockey fans.

He was in his final year when I was in Buffalo for the Sabres' first season, but even then I only vaguely recall encountering him as he left practice. Even though I was doing player profiles and articles back then, I found it easy to get the subjects I needed for the entire season without approaching the seemingly unapproachable, snarly, inhospitable Ferguson.

Over the ensuing seasons our paths rarely crossed, which, according to others who knew him, wasn't such a bad thing. His reputation always preceded him.

Surly, terse, scowling, and menacing, Fergie preached "no fraternization with the enemy." The enemy consisted of anyone who played against Montreal, and the credo covered both winter and summer. Again, through those who knew him best, the rule was inflexible, as far as John Ferguson was concerned.

John Bowie Ferguson: "surly, terse, scowling, and menacing."

He was a hard-ass, and few around the league would question his claim to the title of "top policeman." Each team had one, and John was inserted into the Canadiens' lineup to serve and protect back in the early sixties when the proud Habs grew tired of playing also-rans to the Toronto Maple Leafs and the Chicago Blackhawks over four Stanley Cup outings.

Ferguson arrived in Montreal in 1963, a fresh face from Cleveland of the AHL, where he had just capped off a third year of apprenticeship with a respectable 38 goals. But Big John didn't attend training camp based on his slick moves, double-toe loops, or never-miss, top-shelf backhand. It was the 179 penalty minutes that caught the eye of GM Frank Selke, Sr. Ferguson started his eight-year NHL tenure tentatively with a modest but respectable 18 goals and 45 points, which in the days of the six-team league were commendable numbers for a rookie. He also posted a meagre 125 minutes in penalties, but from that point on it was all free-wheeling for Fergie.

The job of a "policeman" in Ferguson's heyday differed slightly from that of present-day pretenders. Familiarity bred long-lasting feuds and classic matchups, but the role of the resident policeman was to make sure the other team realized that anytime they overstepped the mark with one of the less pugilistic players, they would have to pay the piper. It could be sooner rather than later, depending on the score, the time of the game, and the standings, but often several meetings came and went before the bomb detonated.

Nowadays fights are billed ahead of time, and punchers take on other punchers for no apparent reason other than that they're "there." Back when helmets were for test pilots, agents were strictly spies for another country, and no one man could carry a TV camera, anyone messing with Henri Richard, Jacques Lemaire, Bobby Rousseau, or the regal Jean Beliveau knew they'd be dealing with John Bowie Ferguson. Make no mistake: the moment would arrive, inexorably, like closing time in a last-chance bar. That's how Fergie earned his spurs. Inexorably. With five Stanley Cup rings in the bargain.

In the pre-expansion period, clubs would play one another a dozen or more times a season. And, as Dave Keon was heard to express one

night, "There aren't many trick moves you can pull up here after playing a team 14 times a year. You just have to do them better."

From a numbers standpoint Fergie's best season was 1968–69, the
fourth Stanley Cup year when he banged in 29 goals and set a playoff
record of 80 penalty minutes in 14 games. There was one more Stanley
Cup in 1971 to close out his career, then, at the age of 33, he joined the
civilian population and took stock of his options.

By the fall of 1972 he was, to some, the surprising choice to be an
assistant coach to Harry Sinden as Canada and Russia set out to do battle at the pinnacle of hockey. With over 35 top candidates for only 22
jobs, someone was going to have to show the colours, and that someone
was Fergie. As tough-minded a coach as he was two-fisted as a player,
he gained the respect of most of the members of Team Canada through
hard work, astute observation, and a single-minded, one-track team loyalty. The makings of a general manager and coach were there, and it
wasn't long after the Canadian storybook victory that opportunity came
knocking in the form of the New York Rangers of the seventies, which
eventually led to his long run with the Winnipeg Jets in the eighties.

But, like all jobs in sports, there are limits. New regimes come in
and coaches come and go. During those bumps in the road, John went
back to his love of standard-bred racing in Montreal and southern
Ontario. Fergie wasn't one to sit around and wait for the phone to ring.

The first time we met face-to-face was when the retired members of
Team Canada '72 got together once again to play their visiting Russian
counterparts. Four games were scheduled in Ottawa, Montreal,
Hamilton, and Saskatoon, with a series of warm-up practices at St.
Michael's Arena in Toronto.

The magic of that Canadian team was still evident during those
practices, and the fans were out in force along with the press. It was a
nostalgia trip pure and simple. Autograph seekers crowded the glass
and waited patiently. Radio personalities patrolled the exits to the
dressing room, mikes at the ready and tape decks clutched like purses.
TV minicams sprouted everywhere around the glass, and players and
media paired off like dancers to various areas of quiet in the northeast
corner of the arena.

The practice over, Fergie made his way toward a three-step drop leading to the dressing room door, but was buttonholed by a curly-haired young man toting an over-the-shoulder recorder, complete with call sign on the microphone. He couldn't have been more than age eight back when Paul Henderson popped the winner. Now he was a Ryerson College grad wearing a Cathedral football jacket, and it was assumed he was from Hamilton.

Ferguson didn't accede to the young man's question orally, but simply stopped in mid-stride, stone-faced, looming stolidly in acceptance of the price of fame. The cub reporter fiddled and fumbled with his personal checklist, making sure the mike was jacked in, the battery registered full, and a tape was indeed in the machine, before clumsily pressing record and play just like the manual said. While he took one last look at the call sign to assure himself that he had it right, Fergie remained motionless, apparently neither inclined to leave nor to stay.

Meanwhile, out on the ice, Pete Mahovlich, Dennis Hull, Gary Bergman, and Stan Mikita continued to cavort at the far end like otters on a frozen creek. The boys were intent on trying to shoot from behind the far goal line, bounce the puck off the boards or glass, and successfully bank the disc into the net at the other end. Later we all agreed the deed was done by someone other than Dennis Hull, for if he had fired one of his patented lasers with the same result, it's doubtful that Ferguson would have been able to complete the series, let alone go on to a future job with the Ottawa Senators.

Approaching "go" status, the young reporter turned Ferguson slightly to the side, supposedly to eliminate the noise of pucks cracking off the glass. Had he left things as they were the puck might have passed between them. Instead, just as he asked his first question about the reunion, the runaway puck cleared the glass and started its descent, hitting Ferguson on the hand that was firmly clutching a clipboard. Fortunately the blow was a glancing one, but nevertheless it was still severe.

Ferguson's reaction was to spin away in pain for an instant before whirling back, while the reporter tried desperately to keep the microphone close to his face. The junior newshound succeeded. He also got every one of Fergie's magic obscenities full force. Then John rotated again in pain and anger, and the clipboard was fired like a Nolan Ryan fastball into the stairwell, breaking in half against the wall. Our young reporter never missed a beat: the mike was still inches away from Ferguson's face.

Down at the other end of the ice three players had ducked behind the net, while a fourth was slinking through the players' bench door. By this time some of us, including the redoubtable Dick Beddoes, were reduced to tears of laughter as Fergie stormed into the dressing room, the kid following like a child's pull toy. I think he felt he had a scoop, a definite shot at the lead story on the evening news with this unexpected answer to his simple question, "What do you think of the upcoming series?" Apparently he was unaware Fergie had been hit by a puck.

At that point, for reasons known only to himself, Joe Veres, an auto sales manager and future partner with Dennis Hull in a new Chrysler dealership in Welland, Ontario, retrieved the two pieces of clipboard. He wondered aloud if John would autograph the souvenir.

Beddoes only laughed harder and suggested that anyone taking the clipboard into the dressing room now would probably emerge in a few seconds with the offending merchandise "wedged up their ass like a dorsal fin." Tricky Dick had to stop and wipe his eyes.

Later I went into the dressing room, observed Ferguson removing his hand from a pail of ice, and watched Joe Sgro, the longtime Leaf trainer and Team Canada member himself, apply a dressing to the aggrieved finger, which by now resembled something smashed by a hammer.

I never heard a complaint from Ferguson, nor any mention of being the victim of horseplay. To him it was merely a natural occurrence if you want to stand around a hockey rink.

The next day, famous clipboard in hand, I entered the dressing room and asked John if he would be good enough to sign it for a buddy of Dennis Hull. Without so much as a mild protest or comment he signed the item and added "Best wishes, Joe." Smiling, he then handed it back.

Somewhere in Joe Veres's office at Rose City Dodge in Welland the clipboard reposes as a tribute to John Ferguson. Although Fergie's reputation was still intact, I was beginning to see another side of him, one I'd see again.

The second time we met was at a sports celebrity dinner in Goderich. The head table consisted of myself, Rob Ramage (then captain of the Leafs), Toronto goaltender Allan Bester, a great little comedian named Royce Elliott from Peoria, and John. There was also a local MC who shall go nameless.

This annual event included a golf game, but Ramage, Elliott, and myself had to miss the tournament. As we checked into the hotel in the late afternoon, Ferguson came through the door, limping as if he'd been two-handed across the foot. The fact that he didn't acknowledge us was because of the intense pain he was suffering, or at least we wanted to think so. As he struggled up the staircase to his room, we figured he'd be a scratch from the head table lineup.

A little later I ventured up to his suite and found him with his foot propped on a chair, resisting instructions from a golf partner to call a doctor. Even to my untrained eye the foot was either broken or sprained. Perhaps it was my bug-eyed look at the bare ankle that convinced John, but in a few minutes we had the dinner chairman, Craig Davidson, working the phone to get a local MD to pay a house call.

That night at the dinner John sat through what seemed to be an interminable auction, awaiting his speaking turn without expressing any evidence of pain or discomfort, although it was obvious that, modern medicine aside, not much had changed except for some ice packs and a taping.

To me it was understandable that someone in his condition would be impatient, snarly, and ill-tempered. But not John. Even the faux pas delivered by the MC didn't rattle him.

On introducing Fergie the gentleman tangled up his words a tad and said, "So not only was this guy a goon, but a pretty good hockey player, too!"

I was sitting between Allan Bester and Ferguson. Almost in unison Bester and I looked at each other and silently mouthed, "Not only was this guy a goon . . ." Then we covered our eyes with our hands and waited.

But Ferguson gave no indication that he had even heard the remark, although we knew he must have. Instead of being offended, he proceeded to give a tastefully delivered talk with class and style.

More recently I saw him at a card show in Toronto with Dennis Hull. Unlike Hull, who meets and greets all comers with open warmth, the Ferguson I observed at the card show was taciturn, rarely offered any conversation, yet still replied to every question directed his way. Far from the menacing ogre he normally portrayed, he was what you'd call your "basic reserved." Where Hull would participate in photo opportunities, laying on a ready smile through misfires and blinding flashes, John was always reticent. As the day wore on and the lineups became shorter, he sensed an imminent completion of his duties and began to loosen up slightly.

Obviously his forte wasn't people, certainly not those who come for the 15 seconds of spotlight it takes to sign a name. And I thought how unfair it was to saddle someone with the responsibility of being all things to everyone simply because he happens to be a celebrity. John Ferguson became a celebrity for several reasons, none of which involved being a greeter with gobs of bonhomie.

First, he played on five Stanley Cup–winning teams. That should be reason enough, but there's more to being a star than appearing on TV in the late spring, lining up for a new championship calendar photo, or rehashing the goals one contributed. Fergie delivered much more than tangible contributions to build his claim to celebrity. He brought his indomitable spirit, the backbone he loaned to others, and the fire he lit under teammates with better skills but occasionally fainter hearts.

But sometimes people get their priorities scrambled, and in my opinion John Ferguson's greatest accomplishment occurred when he took on his very first coaching job with Team Canada '72. Quite simply it was the greatest single series in hockey history.

That day at the card show the fans rarely asked him about Team Canada '72, not within my hearing, anyway. Nor did they present team pictures to be signed. Across the room, meanwhile, Dennis Hull was often asked about the Summit Series, and many action photos and the old artwork lithographies of the team were put forward for his signature. I even saw several carefully preserved front pages of the *Toronto Sun* with the headline "Canada Wins." Ferguson, for the most part, was bypassed, although he signed his share of the usual mixed bag of cards, pucks, books, programs, and the current "picture of the day" on sale at the front desk.

Typically he didn't mention the omission later as we stood talking among ourselves. And as he walked away down the hotel corridor, I thought how unfair and fickle the public perception can be, remembering Dennis Hull's answer to my general question about Team Canada's reversal of fortune in the Soviet Union: "It was the best coaching job I ever saw . . . bar none."

So, with all respect to Harry Sinden, John Ferguson was there, too. We should remember that.

90-SECOND ALL-STARS

G — **Glenn Hall** "*. . . his style was unique. He made the Hawks a contender.*"

D — **Bobby Orr** "*. . . revolutionized rushing defencemen.*"

D — **Serge Savard** "*. . . more defensive-minded than Orr, but just as valuable.*"

C — **Jean Beliveau** "*. . . he had class, great puck skills, a winner.*"

RW — **Gordie Howe** "*. . . strongest, best right winger of all time.*"

LW — **Dickie Moore** "*. . . great scoring ability and a fearless competitor.*"

Glenn Goldup

Tinseltown Biker King

I'M SURE IF SOMEONE tossed a 1973 photo of Glenn Goldup onto a table, no one would have much trouble picking him out of a crowd even today. He's still a solid six feet, and maturity has added a few more pounds to the 187 he admitted to in the *NHL Official Guide* 20 years ago. The "sideburns forever" have changed to a full head of businesslike hair, and the moustache remains, although now it's neatly trimmed.

He looks the way an ex-hockey player is supposed to look and act. There's a slight deflection on the bridge of the nose, an almost imperceptible gimp when he first starts walking, his manner is still a tad abrasive, and his responses are a touch testy. However, like the rest of us, the years have added a braking system, which means he doesn't flare up as quickly as he used to. And that's good in Glenn's case because he was one tough guy, a player who made his own room, as well as room for others in the same sweaters, all through his career.

Goldup comes by his hockey prowess honestly. Father Hank played on the 1941–42 Maple Leaf Stanley Cup–winning team and rolled up six NHL seasons with the Rangers and Toronto. Aiming himself in the same direction, Glenn came through the Marlboro chain, from Shopsy Pee-wees to the Marlie juniors, winning the 1973 Memorial Cup with Mark Howe, Bob Dailey, Wayne Dillon, Paulin Bordeleau, and Mike Palmateer.

Glenn Goldup: "a free spirit who was unwilling to unbend, a man who constantly snarled and chafed at his tether."

Those were the days of Fred Shero's Broad Street Bullies in Philadelphia. The big bad Bruins were in vogue, too, with tough, aggressive wingers. In such a hockey world Goldup might have been picked in the first round of the 1973 entry draft. Denis Potvin, not surprisingly, went first overall, followed by Tom Lysiak, Dennis Ververgaert, and Lanny McDonald. It was too early yet for a tough, grinding, two-way winger. His gigantic defensive teammate, Bob Dailey, went eighth, while Rick Middleton and Ian Turnbull were 14th and 15th.

Then, bingo! The first pick in the second round belonged to Montreal, and the Canadiens took Goldup. That started the best and worst of times.

In early September of 1973 Glenn, along with his younger brother Paul, who had been drafted by the Junior Ottawa 67's the same summer, sat around the table with their dad, discussing hockey and futures. Hank's fatherly advice aside, Paul was later to attest that he had to follow his brother's "popularity" in arenas throughout the OHA.

From Peterborough to London, from Windsor to Niagara, "every damn place I went I heard, 'Goldup, you asshole,' and a lot of 'Goldup, you prick, they're gonna kill you.' Shit, I wanted to tell them, 'Hey, it's my brother you want. Lighten up.'" Instead he settled into a routine of watching his combative defence mate, Behn Wilson, step into Glenn's vacuum. It's all part of the experience of hockey.

You have to remember that players who make the big league are a product of a very small world that, given the talent, keeps expanding, widening, to expose their abilities to more competition, better opponents, and larger challenges. As such, these select teenage players become catered to and garner most of the good things like equipment and coaching. They're used to being the best at any given age, whether in house leagues, Peewee, Bantam, or Midget. Then, if they survive the cloned, NHL-like Junior draft and the training camps that follow, they move up to professional hockey, where they're revered at home and jeered when away, eventually becoming hardened, polarized, and pampered.

It's a contradiction that they grow up quickly but still not fast enough. They're the cream and they know it. Confidence, always a prerequisite in any athlete, may slide a notch higher than reality. It's a common malady.

I have always likened the experience to that of being the big kid in grade eight, then plummeting to a lowly freshman in high school. It's hard to go back to being the nerd, the new kid on the bigger block. The good ones go on to be the high school hero, only to become the frosh again in college.

For Glenn Goldup school was over. Montreal was the biggest stumbling block now. They had won the Stanley Cup in the spring of 1973, but Philadelphia was looming on the horizon, making Goldup's debut as a winger seem like perfect timing.

Six games with the Habs were the beginning of his NHL career, the balance of the season being spent with the Halifax Voyageurs affiliate in the American Hockey League, where he popped in a respectable 18 goals and 15 assists in 44 games. He was called up for the Canadiens' playoffs, but as many others had done before, he sat them out.

At the 1974 training camp he was trioed with Peter Mahovlich and Yvan Lambert, but by January, after nine games and one assist, he was back in Halifax for another 49-game stint and the playoffs.

The Voyageurs became a permanent home by the 1975–76 season. Glenn would endure occasional call-ups to watch from the press box, but he logged 65 games in the AHL, scoring 23 goals and making 22 assists. In the spring of 1976 he led all playoff goal scorers with eight and headed the penalty parade with 33 minutes in nine games. The Voyageurs won the championship Calder Cup that year, and Goldup, in his first full season in one spot, turned in a career-altering year, one that caught the attention of other teams.

By then he had "barked" his way into the Canadiens' doghouse. He was a free spirit who was unwilling to bend, a man who constantly snarled and chafed at his tether. He knew he could play and contribute. The confidence was there, almost to the point of cockiness, but he was an acknowledged member of the "black aces," continually yapping, "Play me or trade me." That was a liability in the Montreal offices.

Little wonder that he was overjoyed to return from a Guadeloupe holiday with sidekick Rick Chartraw, a Voyageur running mate for two seasons, to find he'd been traded to Los Angeles. The two buddies went to Montreal to celebrate, then bought another week and returned to the island. Partying aside, it was sobering to be given up on, to be dealt away in three short years for a third- and first-round pick somewhere down the road. Ironically Chartraw would go on to have his name engraved on the Stanley Cup four straight times.

Yet to this day Goldup still has high regard for the Canadien organization. "An unbelievable group, from Sam Pollock all the way down to the trainers. Pollock cared about the team and the players, and I have nothing but respect for him and them. Hell, they put great hockey minds together, like Ruel, Bowman, Currie, Blake . . . Al MacNeil. There's a coach I had a lot of respect for. I loved him. He got the best out of me because the respect ran both ways. I don't blame Montreal. They have a handle on everybody. Shit, there are more spies in that city than telephone poles. Every goddamn fan is a spy. If you did anything, I guarantee it wouldn't be more than four hours and the brass would know what little stunt you'd been up to." He shakes his head and grins at the pleasant recollections of past escapades by a wild young player.

From his side the trade to L.A. was a new lease on his career. It was no secret that the Kings needed toughness combined with a winning attitude, but it was the truculence they needed most. So in 1976 he found himself at the Kings' camp and, it seems, the victim of culture shock.

"It was like an old boys' network," he now says. "Some of the players were more interested in not making waves among the veterans, this little gang whose members weren't supposed to lose their jobs. After five days in camp, I was leading the scoring. Then I took a cheap hit from Neil Komadoski on the knee. I had fired a slap shot at the top of the face-off circle and was past the bottom of the circle when he caught me. It was so long after, so obvious a late hit, but," he adds philosophically, "I had a lot of time to think about it. You know, not one player came to visit. Shows you how it was."

After rehab he played seven games in Fort Worth, then 28 with the Kings to finish out his first year on the West Coast. Despite the doom and gloom of a recovery, the hours of therapy and playing himself back into shape, and the eventual return to the big team, it wasn't all down-in-the-mouth time. He had a few years of fun and games to go.

In the L.A. suburb of Manhattan Beach there's an area the Kings call the Bermuda Triangle, supposedly because of the number of players who have gone missing in action over the years. It consists of three corner bars at the intersection of Rosencrantz and Hyland: Orville & Wilbur's, Pancho's, and Brennan's. The trick was to make all three in one evening *without* going MIA.

On one occasion, just to start the evening off right, Goldup drove his motorcycle up a three-stair entranceway, circled the bar, kickstanded the bike at his favourite stool, and ordered a drink.

More shenanigans occurred at a team party at Brian Glennie's place on the beach. The players' wives and girlfriends were in attendance, and cameras were hauled out of purses and bags for those onetime shots of a good day. Later, as the evening waned, the pace became less hectic, the mood more creative, and Glennie and Goldup decided other photos should be taken of the auspicious occasion. With as many cameras as they could hold in their arms they retired to a little-used washroom in the big home and proceeded to take bent-over close-ups of each other's butt and genitalia.

"We musta taken 30 pictures," he says, guffawing. Three days later the rest of the players kept turning up at practice with the photos, laughing and openly praising the two models.

One convulsed player said, "My wife asked me, 'Which one of those assholes is this?' And she's holding up a picture of Glennie's private eye," he gasped, waving the offending picture over his head.

And if there's one thing constant in every player's life, it's when a little humour develops in the person of another player who is able to make you laugh as soon as he enters the room. For example, Vic Hadfield had Chuck Arnason. For Pit Martin it was Dennis Hull. For Dennis Hull it was Dale Tallon. For all-time comic great Jim McKenny it was Tim Ecclestone. For Glenn Goldup it was Butch Goring.

"Seed," as Goring was known, never fails to bring tears of laughter to Goldup's eyes. The nickname stems from Butch's rep as a seedy dresser, a guy who went on one-week road trips with little else but the clothes on his back and a toothbrush. When Goldup is goaded into relating one of the stockpile of Seed stories, he often returns to the one about a trip to Montreal.

Sitting in the Rose Saloon in Etobicoke, hunched over like a lawyer conferring with defendants, Glenn says, "We stop at O'Hare in Chicago for an hour, get off, and go for hot dogs. They've got the best goddamn airport hot dogs goin'. Seed is wearing a powder-blue — what do you call that shit? — corduroy, yeah, a powder-blue cord suit and a white turtleneck."

"Where's his shaving kit?" a bystander pipes up, having heard the story previously.

"In his fuckin' suit pocket," Goldup snaps from the side of his mouth, undaunted. Then he continues. "We pile on the crap, onions, relish, all that stuff, yeah, mustard, too. They got this special mustard, really good. Then Seed takes a big chomp and whoosh, a whole blob of mustard slides down the fuckin' front of his turtleneck. I mean, from here to here." He indicates a stain as big as a tie.

"He wears it all the way through the trip, on the plane, on the bus to the hotel, moppin' at it like it's gonna go away. I mean, mustard is forever, for Christ's sake." Goldup heaves a sigh and looks around for anyone who might tip off the ending.

"Next day, you know, we go to the Forum in different cabs. We're in the dressing room. I'm startin' to put on my equipment, and in comes Seed, turtleneck white from top to bottom. He takes off his fuckin' suit jacket, and there's the goddamn stain all down the back!" The group at the bar howls. "Wore the son of a bitch backward for the next four days — to Long Island and back to L.A.," he adds, topping it off for the shaking heads and jowls.

Juvenile? Maybe so, but that's the kind of thing athletes in every sport have been doing for decades, long before Glennie and Goldup took up photography. It's a way out of the mind-numbing schedule, a way to escape the knowledge that every game might be the last.

Over the next five seasons Glenn moved from side to side, line to line, through three different coaches and a myriad of incoming and outgoing personnel. He played a total of 291 NHL games, with 52 goals and 303 minutes in penalties. He played in 16 playoff games and collected seven points, four of them goals.

In retrospect it's a nondescript record. There are a few highs, some lows, an almost career-ending knee injury that undoubtedly played a large part in the ultimate results but, as they say in Tinseltown, he did have a part in the big picture.

Nothing would match the euphoria of going to Montreal as their second selection way back in 1973, and nothing in the numbers would justify the pick. Other than heart, nothing else kept him there but hard work and a harder attitude.

Yet listening to him talk 10 years removed from the scene about the places and the people he met along the way, you know this isn't an unhappy man. He goes down the list as if reading a TV schedule — Halifax, Montreal, Rick Chartraw, John Van Boxmeer, Los Angeles, Marcel Dionne, Bob Pulford, Ron Stewart, Mike Murphy, Charlie Simmer, and Brian Glennie.

The final whistle came in New Haven. "I came home, threw my equipment bag under the basement stairs — always kept my equipment under there, even as a kid — and said to myself, 'This is it.' I was in a fog, because the realization had hit me. I didn't have a job, didn't even know what I could do. I had a big-time withdrawal problem."

Today Glenn works in the marketing department of the Toronto Argonauts. But in spite of the downside of retiring, when I ask if he has any regrets, any things he would like to change if he could, he shakes his head slowly, contemplating the myth that people have tried on since time began.

"No, it was the best . . . the very best 10 years of my life," he says softly with conviction.

90-SECOND ALL-STARS

G — **Ken Dryden** *". . . aggressive, intimidating, difficult to find an opening."*

D — **Guy Lapointe** *". . . things happen with him on the ice."*

D — **Bobby Orr** *". . . need I say more."*

C — **Bryan Trottier** *". . . a rock, the leader."*

RW — **Guy Lafleur** *". . . played in both ends, never squawked."*

LW — **Rick Martin** *". . . he was dangerous, anytime, from anywhere."*

Pierre Pilote

Hawk on the
Blue Line

I ONLY GOT TO SEE Pierre Pilote live and in colour twice, both times with the Leafs. At the age of 37, at the end of his career, he wasn't up to the benchmark of his peak years. He was even wearing a helmet. It was like seeing the Blue Jays' Pat Borders with a bulging cheekful of tobacco. Disgusting. Regardless, I was impressed by what I saw.

Many years later I would invite him to play on the newly formed NHL OldStars travelling team, which led to our first face-to-face meeting at a practice. He took some convincing to be lured out of retirement, but once he got there, he rarely missed a trip. I considered that an accomplishment.

As a youngster, I had adopted the Chicago Blackhawks as my team, something to do with the change in uniforms and the fact that I had been brought up on a continuous, nauseating diet of the Leafs and the Canadiens. The day the Hawks emerged in their incredible Indian-head, crossed-tomahawk, red, white, and black livery, I was smitten. As the sixties began, my favourite player was Pierre. When Chicago won the Stanley Cup in 1961, Pilote was better than great as he led all playoff scorers in assists and total points. Had Conn Smythe taken his hands out of his pockets long enough to invest in a trophy back then, Pilote would have been a shoo-in.

Pierre Pilote in later years: "even in his fifties he was the consummate defenceman, the one who could carefully manage his slightly diminished physical properties to the utmost."

Where did he come from and how did he get to the top of the pile? He came from St. Catharines, that hockey anvil on Lake Ontario where the Teepees would become the Blackhawks. When the parent Hawks purchased the Junior team, they changed the name and assured themselves of an incubator for Bobby Hull, Elmer Vasko, Stan Mikita, Chico Maki, and Ab McDonald, who would all play on the Cup winner.

In those teenage days Pilote was known as a banger, a prodigious hitter, and a fighter to boot. As good as he was, he didn't make the big team when he turned pro, even though the Hawks languished, almost perennially, in the never-never land of the NHL basement. Instead he moved 20 minutes down the Queen Elizabeth Way to the Buffalo Bisons of the AHL, spending the better part of four seasons and coming under the tutelage of Frankie Eddolls during his second and third years. Eddolls, an astute observer of the game and an eight-year veteran of the NHL himself, made a significant change in the rambunctious Pilote.

"Eddolls taught me that the game was simple, uncomplicated, if you played it right. The short pass rather than the long, rink-wide kind was the key to movement, the key to the attack. But I'd still get into pissing contests down there. Like Billy Juzda and Bill Ezenicki. They were tough guys at the end of their careers, and we'd hammer on each other every time we met. I was full of piss and vinegar, they were experienced and smarter, but I figured I could outlast them. Finally Eddolls said to me, 'Those two old fuckers will wear you out and you ain't provin' anything to them or me, so cut the shit and get back to playin'. And that's when I learned to pick my spots, you know, just cork 'em when the chance came up instead of goin' looking for trouble."

To say he wasn't an influence on Chicago's emergence as a hockey power would be to ignore the defensive facts. From 1950 to 1956 the Hawks finished fourth only once; the rest of the decade saw them place sixth. Their goals against peaked at 280 in 1950–51, but generally hovered around 240. In Pierre's first full season, along with Junior partner Elmer "Moose" Vasko (1956–57), the Hawks again finished last but with 225 goals against. The next year saw the addition of goalie Glenn Hall from Detroit, and the Hawks began to lower the opposition scoring steadily and raise their standing until they copped a third-place finish, a goals against of 180, and a Stanley Cup in April 1961.

Pierre was 30 years old and at the top of his game; his career and preeminence as a defenceman were sandwiched between Doug Harvey and Bobby Orr. He had eight consecutive All-Star selections, five times on the first team. From 1962 to 1967 he won the James Norris Trophy as the best defenceman in the NHL three straight years and was runner-up in another three.

But, although the Hawks flirted with greatness, finishing first once and getting to the final two more times, by 1968 they were back to fourth and 222 goals against. The long ride for Pierre Pilote was over.

At home, on a late Chicago summer afternoon, Pierre got the call he thought would never be his to handle. It was the *Toronto Star*'s intrepid Red Burnett on the trail of a story. "Whadda ya' think?" Red rasped, using up one chunk of a reporter's W5.

"About what?" Pilote queried, using one of his own.

"About the trade," Burnett said with a touch of surprise. Before long Pilote was set straight and informed of his imminent move to the Toronto Maple Leafs.

Dejected, Pierre could only ask, "For who?"

"Jim Pappin," Burnett told him.

"Red told me Punch always liked me, said he had some youngsters on defence to bring along, like Pat Quinn, Jim McKenny, Brian Glennie, Mike Pelyk, Rick Ley, kids who were gonna need some help, so he put out a feeler to Tommy Ivan. To tell you the truth, the more I thought about it, the less I liked the idea. My style wasn't compatible with the game Toronto played. Besides, all my career I had played hard against the Leafs. Shit, they'd hated me for 13 years. I'd taken all of their best on at one time or another, runnin' them, fighting, scarin' the crap out of them every chance I got.

"I wanted to finish in Chicago, and I only wanted to play one more, maybe two. Ah, but what the hell? I figured I might as well go, you know? You think you have your life pegged, planned out, and then, well, that's fuckin' hockey, eh?"

Pilote was eventually, and officially, informed of the trade an hour later by Don "Fast-food" Murphy, Blackhawk PR director extraordinaire.

It wasn't until later, much later, that Punch told Pilote what Tommy Ivan had said to him. Apparently Ivan "wanted to get at least something for Pierre." So, loyalty aside, at 37, the best defenceman ever to play for Chicago was considered expendable. Although he would perform commendably in his last NHL season, with three goals and 21 points over an impressive 69 games, it was the last stop.

And Pilote was right — he had an uncomfortable season and never really fitted in with the Leafs. Most of them considered him distant, an all-for-one, one-for-one kind of a guy. The old guard of the Leafs — Tim Horton, George Armstrong, Bob Pulford, Dave Keon — found the ex-Blackhawk aloof, distant, and wary. Pilote felt the same way and chalked it up to past animosity, hard feelings, and old grudges. As a result, the majority of young Leafs found him unsociable, self-interested and, as one phrased it, "Tight. Pierre made Johnny Bower look like a spendthrift."

Almost 15 years later, in the early eighties, I called to see if he was willing to join the OldStars road team, and while he didn't throw money around in our league, either, he was anything but aloof. Over the years he took a lot of razzing, as we all did, but he took it good-naturedly and gave it back in kind. Even his permanent roomie, Pat Stapleton, called him "the old fella." We had other names for him like "Tollgate" (you always had to pay to get by him on the ice), and one of my own personal favourites, "Turnstile." That nickname came about after Pierre, bending over to pick up his errant stick in the goal mouth, was run into by a crossing player, who spun him in a complete circle. Still bent over, he again tried to retrieve his stick and was banged into by yet another player with the same result. It was "Turnstile" for the rest of that trip.

But even in his fifties he was the consummate defenceman, the one who could carefully manage his slightly diminished physical properties to the utmost. On some trips, when we'd play four dates in a row, he was no worse for wear than any of the other "kids" on the team. There were nights he would break up a rush with a deft, classic poke check, and in two quick, trademark running strides would lead a return rush, moving smartly to centre as the playmaker. Whenever the obvious opportunity arose you'd see the genius come to the fore. He'd move forward in the familiar straight, heads-up skating style, eyes and mind sifting through the situation in front of him, then with a look-off any NFL quarterback would be proud of, or a sneaky head fake and stutter step, he'd feather a soft pass through skates and sticks to a man suddenly open and in full flight. He was a master.

One Sunday afternoon we played in Halifax, following a Saturday night game in Bridgewater. It was a quick turnaround, and our opponents were the young and frisky Dalhousie University varsity team, sporting a Bobby Hull in their lineup. Bobby junior. Following the game, their coach approached me to say they had a video camera in the stands and a VCR replay setup in their dressing room. He explained they had focused on our defence pairings and now had considerable footage of Pilote, Stapleton, and Bill White gaining control in our end and breaking out. "It's gonna be required watching for all our players," he enthused. "Picture perfect, classic stuff. They caught our forecheckers in deep time after time." Then, after a chuckle and a shake of the head, he added, "That Pilote, he's a goddamn marvel. Bet he didn't take 100 steps all night. Just glides around the ice and lets the puck come to him. I had to kick our defencemen in the ass every once in a while to get their attention. They couldn't take their eyes off him."

But he could still be irritable and crotchety. In a game against the Windsor Spitfires there was a certain winger who either didn't hear our usual pregame agreement and instructions about no bodychecking and keeping the sticks down or just didn't give a damn. He ran around the ice as if the game were his express ticket to the NHL. He'd hack, chop, hook, grab, run our guys into the corners, and generally lay on the body. Sensing an undercurrent of discontent on our bench, I went down to their dressing room between periods, had a chat with their coach, and reiterated the premise that people came to see hockey, so maybe we could get "Mad Dog" or whoever to chill out and stay on his side of the white line. I assured him we were following the script and in turn was given a guarantee they would do likewise.

However, midway through the second period the unrepentant one charged through centre again like a Rototiller on casters, cutting a swath through the zone. As he arrived at the blue line, he looked up long enough to see number 3 just before Pierre cartwheeled him with a perfect, low shoulder check.

Most of the guys on our bench turned away or ducked behind the boards, laughing, with the exception of Eddie Shack, who giggled, then roared through his moustache, "Stick that one in yer crease, big boy!" All I could do was stand there, hands turned outward, as if to say it was a surprise to me, too. Meanwhile Pierre had stopped, stooped, and inquired if the winger was okay, even helped him to his wobbly feet, brushed snow off his jersey, and offered apologies. For a while I thought there might be the makings of a slugfest, but apparently the message was delivered and received. In the dressing room Pilote weakly claimed innocence, offering several different versions of excuses, smiling all the while. None of us believed him, especially me.

Pilote liked to keep the lines between management and players open and would often ask me in a nasal, plaintive tone how I thought the team was playing. More specifically he was looking for some positive stroking, a few favourable comments about his own play. Invariably I would reply, "You're doin' great, Pete."

He would cock his head to one side, squint, take on a pained look, and whine, "Wellllll, as long as you're happy."

Then a dozen or so winks and hidden smiles would light up the dressing room. Everyone used to wait for Pierre's question. On one trip Dale Tallon wanted to start a time pool on it.

But Pilote was also protective of the team's quality. For a scheduled game in Charlottetown I had conscripted Errol Thompson, a Summerside native, to play with us against the Junior A Islanders, and intended to use him in a second game against Don MacAdam's team at the University of New Brunswick. It was Errol's first time around with us, and to be kind, he had a career-worst game in P.E.I. I don't think it was nerves, or new faces, but a simple case of rust. As he remarked later, playing pickup hockey with the locals is a lot different than getting back in with pros. Pierre approached me after the game and asked,

"What the hell did you get him for?" I think his irritation had something to do with a pass from Pilote that "the Pearl" failed to convert into a goal.

"He'll be okay," I reassured him, but I could see that didn't cut any ice with Pierre.

In Fredericton Errol was on his game and stole the show. Pierre, obviously assuaged, simply said, "I see why now." Then he added, "Nice hands," in reference to Thompson's stickhandling. The two of them were so typical of the makeup of that Original Six team. Although they came from different eras, Pete retiring a year before Thompson joined the Leafs, they became buddies on the road.

Over the six years the Original Six team was out there, we put on a lot of miles back and forth from Victoria to St. John's and every Canadian valley in between — the Annapolis, Ottawa, Peace River, Okanagan, and Fraser. Not surprisingly, the opportunities to talk on planes or buses were endless. There was always something, or somebody, new to talk about. As different players joined the team over the years, stories about this guy or that coach, teammates and opponents, would surface constantly, much to the amusement of regulars and occasional players alike. It was never boring.

Yet if there's one memorable line I've always remembered from Pierre, it was about a player he never got to suit up against.

Sitting across the aisle from him on an "iron lung" headed for Regina, I asked him what qualities made a player better than another at a given position. Just what was it that earned a player the Norris Trophy and allowed him bragging rights as the best at his position. I expected a tale of hard work, practice, dedication, or a corny story about his father building a backyard rink and using the Lawn Boy as a Zamboni. Or at least a tale of cagey coaches like Frankie Eddolls, Rudy Pilous, or Billy Reay.

Pierre looked out the bus window at another 85 miles of Saskatchewan horizon, then said, "Tommy Ivan once told me I could see things other players couldn't." He swivelled in his seat and faced me, leaning over and speaking softly, as if we were plotting a new prank. "You know, I recognized situations and reacted before they happened. I could see a play forming, recognize a dangerous rush, or — how should I say? — a good scoring pass to the wrong guy, a little sooner than other players. I don't know. Maybe Ivan was right." He shrugged, as if the whole thing were still an enigma to this day. I paused to let the thought sink in, to dissect the mystery of seeing scenes in your mind that hadn't happened yet.

"So, having said that, what do you think of Gretzky?" I asked, sliding into the next obvious question. Pete looked out the window again and, after a moment, frozen in a squinting, painful evaluation, wistfully said to the Prairie farmscape, "That fuckin' guy sees things none of us can see."

In his 14 NHL years he played bigger than his physical stature, hit heavier than his weight, won the elusive Stanley Cup so many others never achieved. The All-Star selections, the Norris hat trick and, inevitably, the Hall of Fame were but a few of the awards he garnered over his career. Yet, according to Dale Tallon, one recognition outdistanced all the rest.

Dale, always intuitive and observant, deadpanned the opinion: "He was the only player in NHL history to have his picture on the front of his jersey."

90-SECOND ALL-STARS

G — **Glenn Hall**

D — **Doug Harvey**

D — **Tim Horton**

C — **Henri Richard**

RW — **Gordie Howe**

LW — **Bobby Hull**

"Do I have to explain six guys in the Hall of Fame?"

Mike Walton

Whirling Dervish
for Hire

IF ANYTHING FITS Mike "Shakey" Walton to a T, it's his final
record in the *NHL Official Guide.* A salmagundi of numbers
and city names, asterisks and designations, bold and regular
type, the whole mess reminds one of a Dunn & Bradstreet credit report.

Mike is as frenetic as the record shows. He doesn't discuss subjects;
he attacks them orally in a torrent of talk that's salty, brazen, earthy, and
liberally sprinkled with words like *unbelievable, incredible,* and the all-
encompassing *classic,* which is his adjective of choice when describing
anything or anybody dumb, great, ridiculous, or awe-inspiring.

He sees most daily occurrences as humorous or depressing, with no
middle ground. Things are either with him or against him. To know
him is to understand that the obscenities are merely intensifiers. He
uses the word *fuck* as it was intended, as a noun, verb, adjective, or a
singular synonym for praise. He punctuates accolades or criticism
with eye rolls and a laugh closely related to the signature chuckle of
Eddie Murphy, except Murphy's air is drawn in, while Mike's is
expelled — "Ahaw . . . haw . . . haw!"

If you can catch him in his restaurant/bar, he's usually on the phone
or riffling through a briefcase that looks as if it's been packed for a
one-week stay that turned out to be a simple overnighter. He screens

Wild man Mike Walton: "Salty, brazen, earthy" — an original.

calls with an "I'm here" or "I'm not here" to the staff and, depending on their judgement as to the importance of the call, he can be swayed and detoured from whatever task is at hand.

Shakey's sits on the south side of Bloor Street West, midway between Jane Street and High Park in Toronto. There always seems to be a Walton on the premises — brother Rob, the day-to-day manager, or daughters Connie, Michelle, and Jackie, either behind the bar or working the tables.

It's a home for a collection of photographs mounted on every available inch of wall space not already sporting a neon beer sign. Mike is probably in 90 percent of the pictures, an All-Star dressing room here, a Stanley Cup dressing room there, in a tuxedo here, a sport jacket or sweater there. Alan Eagleson's in one photo, Phil Esposito, Wayne Gretzky, Bobby Orr, and Bobby Hull in others. And there's a drawing of Don Cherry and Blue. Team Canada photos abound, as do shots of the Marlboros, Leafs, Bruins, and Saints. On the way down the staircase to the washrooms is a wood-mounted collection of old *Weekend* magazine colour pictures, the ones of NHL stars standing unnaturally on a variety of backdrops to off-set their uniforms. Their hands are always on their sticks, as if they're impersonating shepherds, while their jerseys and socks are crisp and spanking new, down to the gloves, pants, tape, and skate laces. Harry Howell, Andy Bathgate, Pierre Pilote, Alex Delvecchio, and Norm Ullman stare happily at you as you approach the whizzer.

The thought occurs that perhaps Mike has a personal photographer lurking in the background, or that he's been a victim of the dreaded paparazzi, like Madonna or good ol' Sarah Ferguson.

On one occasion I recall walking into the establishment to find Mike busing tables, piling dishes, and feverishly readying places for the next round of patrons about to arrive when the movie ended at the theatre just steps away.

"Must be tough," I said, standing directly behind him. "I hear the tips here are horseshit."

Whisking a damp cloth over the tabletop, he grunted, "You oughta know all about that, buddy." He didn't even look up, and the comment was worth two sets of "Ahaw . . . haw . . . haw" when he did turn around.

To those who don't know him, Mike seems to fly by the seat of his pants. He even walks in a permanent quick-step like many of the people you encounter in airports, zipping along as if they might miss the plane, but too cool to run. He eases into familiarity. In fact, I can't remember ever being formally introduced. I was simply one of the Suit & Ties around the dressing room, one of the "civs" the other players seemed to know. Eventually I became acceptable enough to exchange hellos with him, even share a laugh from time to time. I can still picture him leaving the dressing room in his Maple Leaf days, coat open, collar up, hotfooting down the hallway, sometimes braking abruptly when requested by reporters, sometimes not stopping at all, tossing off comments over his shoulder, begging off requests because of a vague chore awaiting somewhere up ahead.

Nothing has changed. Today we meet after several misfires. A balky back problem has slowed him down to a relative crawl, the result of a cold and windy golf tournament with play-by-play man Bob Cole in Newfoundland. Although his pace is measured, the activity around him at the bar is normal, and hectic. Questions go back and forth over the bar like tennis serves, and the phone rings incessantly. More questions come from daughter Connie about pay envelopes for the staff, then the phone rings again. When it turns out to be nothing, we continue our disjointed talk. At that moment a regular walks up, needing a minute concerning an upcoming Blue Jay junket, and a bill is submitted from the kitchen for supplies, while an earlier-than-necessary waitress skulks in the background, awaiting the promised payday, checking her watch, obviously on the bank's schedule, not her own. Then there's another phone call, and this one generates a groaning response. "Excuse me. I have to talk to this fuckin' jerk." Picking up the receiver, he lowers his voice conspiratorially and turns his back to the bar crowd.

We herky-jerk through a seemingly never-ending series of interruptions until a tipsy visitor wants to talk hockey. "Them good Leafs, you wuz one of them, weren't yah?" Finally we leave the bar and go downstairs, where I notice two missing *Weekend* photos, ragged screw holes the only reminders of the former occupants. The "office" consists of a desk, two chairs, a customer's cased guitar for safekeeping, and more pictures stacked on top of and around other pictures. The eyeballs and heads in a row of players peek over the edge of a smaller frame in front. The title reads "Minnesota Fighting Saints 1973–1974," prompting another replay of his record in the *NHL Official Guide.*

Walton's hockey roots go back to the Toronto Marlboros, where he played on Jim Gregory's 1964 Marlie Memorial Cup winners, leading all scorers in the series. The team included up-and-coming Maple Leafs Pete Stemkowski, Ron Ellis, goaltender Gary "the Axe" Smith, and a teenage version of Jim "Howie" McKenny.

I ask Mike if he really did have a beef with Punch Imlach at his first training camp, the one where he was told to shave his sideburns and cut his hair. The story, dutifully carried in the papers, was that he had refused, just as Turk Broda had when ordered to lose weight years before, or Bruce Gamble when told to shave off his muttonchops at a later date. By the last few days of the Peterborough training camp everything was resolved among Imlach, mediator King Clancy, and Walton, but the whole issue only fired up veterans Tim Horton and George Armstrong. Getting into Walton's room one night, they first cautioned Mike's roommate to keep quiet, then mugged the sleeping Walton. Pinned in the vise of Horton's arms, Mike had his sideburns and a fair bit of hair above the ears neatly removed by Armstrong.

"I was furious. It was fuckin' unbelievable. I called those two bastards every name under the sun. They claimed they were paid $100 to do it by the other players. I didn't speak to them for a couple of years. Later they asked me to help shave other guys, but I told them to go fuck themselves. I was just, oh, man, I get pissed thinking about it even now."

We run through some capers Walton has been cited for, such as the time he and three other unnamed members of the Bruins were alleged to have removed an eight-foot wooden Indian from the foyer of a downtown Boston bar, loaded it into a convertible belonging to one of the boys and, with the top down, drove through a snow squall to the front door of Bobby Orr's plush downtown condo. Orr, still at the restaurant, was greeted by "Tecumseh" when he arrived home. The statue supposedly remained there for a month.

I tell Mike the story reads like an episode of *Cheers*.

"Yeah, it was unbelievable. The snow was falling. We're wavin' at people. A fuckin' classic. Cops pulled us over, laughed about it when they saw who we were — incredible. Honest to God, it's the truth. Fuckin' thing musta weighed a ton."

He fidgets with an elastic band, stretching and twisting, worrying it to death, until I start to cringe, fully expecting a snap and sudden blindness in one eye. I slip on my glasses in defence.

"Don't mind me. Go ahead and talk," he says. Then unexpectedly he reaches behind him for a chequebook and a set of labelled envelopes. Apparently the staff is going to get paid despite my visit.

I ask if it's true that he dived into a pool in full uniform.

"Yeah, it's true. We were in L.A. and had to dress at the hotel, you know, like a Bantam team, ride the goddamn bus to some rink in the suburbs. Really big league stuff, eh? So when we came back, we had to walk past this enclosed pool, and one of the guys, [Ken] Hodge or somebody, said, 'I bet you wouldn't dive in.' They dared me, so I did, right off the goddamn board. I fuckin' near drowned. I mean, get this, I was in full gear, jock, shin pads, even had my gloves on. Almost deep-sixed, trying to butterfly to the shallow end — an absolute classic."

"How about your time in the WHA?" I ask him. "Did you cause a riot in San Diego?"

"Wasn't a riot. The fans just threw about 100 gallons of beer on the ice, is all. Most of it on me. We went in there for the last game before the playoffs. I'm leading the scoring. Andre LeCroix — he's with San Diego — is one point behind me. So in the first period I come from behind my own net, go right down the ice into their end, pass out in front, and Teddy Hampson or somebody taps it in. I say to the ref skatin' by, 'I got one, okay?' He nods, but when the announcement comes, they say it was unassisted. I ask the ref and he says he told the scorer.

"I go over to the timekeeper's bench and get on the phone. They had to pass the thing to me through the hole in the glass. Now I'm arguing with this asshole. He's saying it was unassisted. I'm sayin' he has to be nuts. He says I don't know my ass from page four. I'm sayin' he must be blind *and* dumb, that I took it from one end to the other and the only two fuckin' guys who touched the puck were me and Hampson. Now he's telling me I'm full of shit. I go nuts, a real tantrum, yank the goddamn receiver out of the dialer, and fire it across the ice. It was incredible."

A knock sounds on the door, catching Walton between an "incredible" and an "unbelievable." It's Connie with a reminder about the cheques. Apparently staff members are beginning to pile up around the bar upstairs.

"Fuck 'em!" Mike growls. But he's not serious. Laughing, he starts to sign, then says, "Bring him another beer and get me the usual, and tell her not to go overboard. I got a meeting later." He turns to me and says, "Don't mind all this. Go ahead, ask away, but I gotta sign some shit. Son of a bitch, do you believe this? Unbelievable! How many people we got on this payroll?" He throws up his hands in a gesture of challenge, but the question is rhetorical. The pen scrapes busily across the paper.

"What about the riot?" I persist.

"I told you it wasn't a riot. More like a beer bash. Well, the next period I'm out there killing a penalty and I get the puck behind the net. But this time I carry it end to end through their whole team, and I score — no pass, nothin'. I go directly over to the timekeeper before the ref even arrives and scream, yeah, scream, at the guy, 'You gonna give me that one, motherfucker?' Whoa, the crowd went nuts, absolutely crazy, ahaw . . . haw . . . haw, and I'm puttin' on a show, you know, skating around the ice, hands over my head, egging them on. They were running out of their seats to get down by the glass and throw beer on me. I didn't give a shit, just kept skating around, but I had to go in and change my goddamn sweater. I was soaked to the ass. Harry Neale comes up to me and says, 'Calm down, Shakey, fer Christ's sake. Calm down. Leave it alone.' And that was the night I won the scoring championship."

"And you don't consider it a riot?" I ask, trying to keep the amazement out of my voice.

"Naw, it got worse when we went back in for the playoffs. This loon comes up to the glass, maybe in the second period. He keeps waving his arms, reaching over, trying to grab at me, so I'm complainin' to the ref, and he just keeps waving me off. Anyway, I get pissed about it, and this shithead is screeching in my ear now. So I reach up and butt-end him on the head. He goes down like a stone, and they call the medics. Now the crowd goes apeshit. Classic, incredible, unbelievable. And how about this one? The asshole lays formal charges and I gotta make a summer court appearance.

"I get my Toronto lawyer, and he finds me a guy in San Diego. Meanwhile the WHA office is making big noises, telling me I won't spend any time in jail. A lot of those geniuses fuckin' knew. Even Bobby Orr came down with me just for the trip. We figured, what the hell? Show up, back home the following day. Next thing I know I'm in court, arraigned on attempted murder, and I'm being held in custody. They fingerprint me, pictures, the whole bag. They do a strip search, look up my ass, everything. They put me in a holding cell with about 30 other guys — armed robbers, rapists, even a guy who OD's. Then a big black guy comes over, and I'm literally shittin' myself. He asks me what I'm in for, so I say attempted murder, and the fuckin' guy backs right off. Doesn't even wanna talk to me. A classic, Roscoe. A real classic."

Connie returns with the drinks and begins to collect the completed cheques, stuffing them into the envelopes. "Can you get these finished, Dad?" she asks, more an order than a question.

"Yeah, hey, I thought this asshole quit." He points to a name on the list.

"No, Dad, he just came in late a couple of times."

"Can you believe these fuckers?" He signs the cheque and tears it along the perforation before dropping it carefully near an envelope. "Make sure he's in here on time from now on." Then he looks over at me, his eyes askance. "Unbelievable, eh? These guys want their money on time, but they don't wanna show up."

Overall it was a helter-skelter career for Shakey Walton, much like what's happening now. He could score goals, was incredibly competitive, and contributed everywhere he played, but he was saddled with a tag: troublemaker. He was timely in that he survived in Toronto long enough to be on the team's last Stanley Cup winner in 1967. In his 31 games after elevation from Rochester he scored only seven goals. Yet in the playoffs he put in four goals in 12 games. He was shunted off to

Boston in time for their Cup win in 1972, and before moving to the WHA he would undergo the most traumatic period of his career.

On a western road trip the Bruins arrived a day early in St. Louis with everything except Walton's luggage. Stuck with only the clothes on his back, he cut a deal with pal Bobby Orr to use some of the defenceman's clothing for the evening dinner in the hotel. "My roomie was either Gerry Cheevers or Eddie Johnston, but they were out when Orr — Jeez, did I say he was in the adjoining room? Okay, I go in the shower and Orr gathers up all my clothes, even my shoes, goes into his own room and locks the connecting door. Now I'm asking, naw, begging, swearing at him, to open the door. Jeez, all I got in the world is a fuckin' towel, and he's laughing at me. So I go out on the balcony to look around the dividing wall and see if I can get in from there. But Orr spots me and I see him pick up the wastebasket. I know goddamn well he's going to fill it with water and drown me.

"Anyway, by this time I've figured out it's goddamn cold. Hell, it was winter, and I'm too high up to be climbing around like Spider-Man. So I get really pissed off just about the time Orr comes back with the bucket of water. I bolt for the door, but I don't notice it's rolled almost shut. I hit the door in my panic to get out of the road, and it breaks. I must have hit it perfect. Plate glass falls all over and cuts me here." He peels back his shirt collar to show a puckered throat scar. "My feet and both knees were sliced open to the bone. My arm, too." He displays another red, angry-looking line. "And fuck, I'm bleeding bad, just pumping it out.

"Bobby heard the glass smashing, and I guess I said a couple of things — I don't quite remember what — but by the time he and a few of the guys got to me, I had crawled to a chair and was sitting there, gushing like a fucking pig from everywhere. The boys are running around getting towels, trying to stop the blood. Hodgie [Ken Hodge] is on the phone trying to get the desk clerk to call an ambulance. Finally, after a wait, he gets on the phone again and threatens the guy's life if he doesn't come up with an ambulance. I think the clerk thought they were bullshittin' him. Then, at last, the medics arrive. Shit, we found out later the hotel made them come through the back door and up the service elevator rather than through the lobby.

"Once I'm in the hospital and the guys find out I'm not gonna die, they loosen up, and Pie [Johnny McKenzie] comes into the emergency room where the doctors are gonna sew me up and says, 'Holy shit, Shake, look at all the needles and scalpels. Jesus, man, this is really gonna hurt.' Nice guys, eh? Took four pints of blood to fill me up again. Thought I was gone, but for some strange reason I was probably the calmest guy there."

Despite the hundreds of stitches and rehab, he made it back to participate in the playoffs. But the rumours persisted that he had been carved up by a jealous husband, or that he had charged headfirst through the front lobby door in a drunken stupor, anything but the truth.

Which brings me back to why Mike Walton resembles his stats. In his 15th and final season he went out in true Walton style — mile-a-minute, here-there-and-everywhere to the end. In 1978–79 he played for no less than five teams. Two AHL clubs — Rochester, where it all began, and New Brunswick — then NHL stops in St. Louis, Boston again, and Chicago. For those five teams his totals were 70 games, 19 goals, 23 assists, and 42 points, and he added four more Stanley Cup playoff games with Chicago, scoring one goal.

As we finish our drinks, I wonder aloud if he has second thoughts about his whirling dervish approach. He becomes thoughtful for just a moment, then says quietly, "I had my ups and downs, but hockey was good. Imlach got the best out of me, even though we locked horns. I used to love to aggravate him, but I know I did my share everywhere I played. I was a player's player."

Suddenly, impulsively, he changes directions and points at the missing *Weekend* pictures — Bob Nevin and Stan Mikita — which are reclining against a file cabinet. "Can you believe these assholes? A guy on his way to the john tried to steal the fuckin' pictures. I mean, look at who they tried to take. Bobby Nevin, for Christ's sake. Can you fuckin' believe this shit? Ahaw . . . haw . . . haw! Nevvy! An absolute classic."

90-SECOND ALL-STARS

G — **Gerry Cheevers** *". . . played everything like it was the Cup."*

D — **Bobby Orr** *". . . a genius, a classic."*

D — **Doug Harvey** *". . . he'd stay at home with Orr up the ice."*

C — **Wayne Gretzky** *". . . nobody better."*

RW — **Gordie Howe** *". . . no mystery here, folks."*

LW — **Bobby Hull** *". . . what can you say — greatest?"*

Dave Keon

Maple Leaf Galahad

IWAS ASKED TO DESCRIBE Dave Keon recently and I went through my usual routine. "He's compact, bigger than Theoren Fleury, smaller than Eric Lindros, bilingual, and lives in Florida." The questioner pointedly suggested I expand the description, and we finally got around to what I felt were the real goods.

"Yeah, he can be aloof, a little distant, but only to those he doesn't know. He has an aura of privacy around him, the same as Bobby Hull doesn't. When you see Hull, you think it's okay to go up and start chatting. Dave isn't like that. He's got his place, you've got yours," I offered, realizing I might have hit the nail on the head. Then I added, "Dave Keon is *not* a funny guy."

Oh, he has a good sense of humour, I went on to explain, and he appreciates humour, considers it a part of his everyday existence, but it's more the self-deprecating kind, as in Jim McKenny's, more like counterpunching than delivering haymakers. You say something, he comes back with a zinger and adds to the story line. In a nutshell it's a hockey player's viewpoint of humour which, as explained elsewhere in this book, is along the lines of seeing fun in life's little tragedies. We used to call them "true-life adventures," the kind of stuff that can break up a full dressing room when a

Dave Keon: one of the Maple Leafs' all-time great captains and a gentleman to boot.

player tells someone about another's misfortune. Hockey players love to make fun of pain, inadequacies and, especially, their own shortcomings.

For example, I recall a charter I took with the Leafs to Boston. The Bruins then were big, and bad, too. They were also the reigning Stanley Cup champions. On the flight down it was rumoured that Bobby Orr was having another bout with his recurring knee problems, that his level of play would be down to just a notch above ordinary — good news for the fourth-place Leafs. During the game, with Toronto shorthanded, coach Johnny McLellan sent out Keon to kill the penalty. At one point Keon, a master at cutting off the ice, herded Orr back to his own end like a border collie herding sheep, finally pinning number 4 to the end boards for a face-off. The penalty almost over, he returned to the bench and told McLellan, "He can't turn to his right very well."

A few minutes later, out for his regular shift, Keon found himself again corralling Orr in the Boston end. He shaded his coverage of Orr's strong side, and as they approached another Mexican standoff along the boards, Keon moved in for the pin, only to find himself staring through the glass at Boston fans, while Orr made a quick twirl and led the Bruins away on a rush up the ice that resulted in a Boston goal. A red-faced Keon sat down hard on the bench and said to McLellan out of the side of his mouth, "He seems to be okay now, John."

McLellan was the one who related the story to me, and he always got a good chuckle out of it, adding cryptically, "It happens all the time up here [the NHL]. The best ones fool the other best ones. That's why they're the best."

Keon was a member of the elite from the day he left St. Michael's College. Like most rookies, he didn't know if he fitted in as a member of the Leafs until Toronto's third game of the 1960–61 season. They had opened on the road with a 5–0 loss to Montreal, then had a Saturday home opener against the Rangers. He played only briefly in each game, then it was Sunday in Detroit and Keon was beginning to consider asking for a trip to Rochester, reasoning he'd rather play and learn than ride the bench. But a funny thing happened on the way to the Hall of Fame.

"Both teams were two men short, and I'm sitting in my reserved spot at the end of the bench. I'm wondering to myself, What the hell is Punch gonna do now? Then he taps me on the back and says, 'Get out there.' I remember pointing at myself and saying, 'Me?' as if I hadn't heard him right. I was still sitting down. 'Yeah, you,' Imlach says, and walks away. I go over the boards with Stan [Allan Stanley] and Timmy [Horton], look up at the clock — it's about the ten-minute mark — win the face-off, and we score. Never missed a shift after that. Never thought about Rochester again, either."

He had a first year that seldom happened to kids straight out of Junior in those days. Bob Nevin and Keon joined the Leafs at the same time, although Nevin had spent a couple of years fine-tuning his game in the minors. They were the last pieces to Punch Imlach's puzzle. Keon would get 20 goals, Nevin 21, an even rarer occurrence for first-year players when the league consisted of only six teams. Keon would win the Calder Cup as rookie of the year; Nevin would be the runner-up.

Dave's second season was even better than the first. He heeded Allan Stanley's advice in training camp: "Get Bert [Olmstead] the puck. He'll get it back to you."

He scored 26 goals and added 35 assists. His two penalty minutes nailed down the Lady Byng Trophy as the league's most gentlemanly player, and he was selected to the second All-Star team. Pretty heady stuff for a 22-year-old, not to mention the Stanley Cup, Toronto's first in ten years.

"It was a home final against Chicago. We won our two, they won theirs, then we beat them in Toronto again. Went into Chicago and won the first away game by either team — 2–1. Man, we were wild at the end — jumping, skating around in circles, and I remember running down those stairs. You know the stairs to the lower-level dressing rooms, looking for the champagne, I guess, and there's only the trainers, stickboys, and Olmstead. Crusty ol' son of a bitch, sitting there, wiping off his skates, and I come in whooping and hollering. No fun here, so I make a U-turn to head back up to the ice where the action is. I mean, I'm so damn excited, but Bert reaches out and grabs me. 'Sit down,' he says. 'There'll be lots of these for you. Don't be making a goddamn fool of yourself. Now sit down and watch what takes place.' And I did. Hell, he'd already been on four winners himself. I didn't know it then, but it was his last game. When we got back to Toronto, he packed up and drove home to Saskatchewan the next day. Didn't even stay for the big parade. Bert had some different standards."

Keon began to think Stanley Cups were a normal spring bonus as the Leafs went on a tear and won two more. As other pundits have said before, it could well have been six or seven in a row had Punch Imlach not mortgaged the future for the present, which brings us to the subject of Imlach and his mystique.

"No mystery about Punch. He simply treated us all equal — like dogs. Worked everybody hard — old guys, young guys, didn't matter. But back with the Leafs in the sixties Punch couldn't foresee problems. For instance, he thought a power play specialist was what the team needed in '63, so instead of grooming somebody from our organization — and we had a lot of guys who could do the job — he went out and got Andy Bathgate. But we had to give up Nevin and Dick Duff. Sure, we won the Stanley Cup, but we didn't do it again until three years later.

"We had *the* team, *the* people to win year after year. I still say he didn't have to tinker with the team, and as far as him being a motivator, I don't think so. See, he never had to motivate me. I could do it myself. A lot of the other guys could, too. You didn't have to beat us with a stick to get our attention. We knew what we had to do, how much it took to get the job done. As soon as Punch got a player a little more complex, in terms of moods, he'd have big problems. Couldn't fathom or handle guys like Frank Mahovlich, Carl Brewer, and Dick Duff. Instead of dealing with the situation he'd rather eliminate it.

"Here's a good example of how he didn't take charge, although he wanted everybody to think he was the iron-fisted admiral of the ship. One of the Stanley Cup years toward the end of the regular schedule,

I'm getting a little tired, playing my regular shift, killing penalties, all that stuff, so Punch says, 'You don't have to come to practice, just the games.' He's supposedly giving me a break for the playoffs. So I say Okay, and I don't show up. About the third time I miss practice, he calls me and tells me I'm gonna have to come back because some of the players are bitching, saying they should have time off, too, and how can he keep them on the ice when I'm not there?

"Years later, when I'm with Minnesota, Glen Sonmor tells me he doesn't want to see me the last two weeks of the schedule except at the games, that they need me for the playoffs and I should get some rest. Having gone through this before, I ask Glen, 'Hey, what if some of the other players don't like the idea?' And he says, 'Too bad. I'm running the team and they don't have a say in this.' Could Punch have done the same thing? Well, he didn't, but he sure as hell liked to throw his weight around . . . until somebody blew the whistle."

Keon agrees faintly with an Imlach quote that said he and Keon had a good relationship. "We did, and why not? I played well for him." He also remembers Imlach in another light. It was 1963 when Keon's baby son, Richard, passed away. Keon came down to the Gardens to talk to Imlach in the morning, the day the team picture was scheduled. It was also the day he was to meet with cemetery officials to select a plot, a sad chore that couldn't wait until the day of the funeral. On his way to Imlach's office he ran into Harold Ballard, who wondered if Keon could wait until after the photo session, which to Ballard seemed a reasonable request, but Imlach told Keon to look after his family, get whatever had to be done attended to, and not to worry about the Leafs. "That's why the '63–'64 calendar has my head on Bill Collins's body," he now says. "They dressed Billy in my number 14, then took a photo of me the following week and doctored up the picture."

If there's one thing that exemplifies the Imlach era for Keon, it's the training camps, which resembled boot camps more than hockey teams. "He worked everybody hard — vets, rookies, didn't matter to him, and the off-ice mentality was military, as well. I'll always remember my first taste of pro hockey, wondering if I was gonna be able to outlast the routine. We'd be at it twice a day, PT in between. I'll never forget the first year because Johnny Bower arrived a couple of days late. Imlach had him on the ice *three* times a day, and he's out there busting his hump, new skates, new goal pads, new everything. I'm watching and I say to myself, 'This guy's gotta be 20 years older than me. If he can do it, I can, too,' And I know that just seeing him there, working his ass off to make the team, got me fired up."

But as he runs down the list of great Leafs, one stands out in his conversation like a lighthouse — Tim Horton. "Timmy was the glue of those Toronto teams. He was the one who could be relied on in any given situation to do the right things. He was a leader, the toughest, the strongest, bar none, in the NHL. On top of everything else he was fearless, but not crazy fearless, if you know what I mean. He was never intimidated or shaken to the point of distraction. He was a rock. Ask anybody. One night in Chicago, my first season, Elmer Vasko, all six-three, 230 pounds of him, drilled Pully [Bob Pulford] into the boards, and a scuffle started. Timmy, all five-ten, 185 pounds, waded in, and I could hardly believe it. The next thing I know Vasko is on his back with Horton on top asking, 'So how about this, Elmer?' To me Tim Horton was the Toronto Maple Leafs.

"I remember hearing about the time he was injured. Shit, injured, he was almost killed by Bill Gadsby. Timmy was coming through centre — he wore contacts back then, you know — and one of the contacts shifted or something. Gadsby caught him with his head down, broke his jaw, his leg, separated his shoulder, really did a number on him, and he missed the last half of the season. A lot of people thought he was finished in his fifth season. Hell, he went on to play another 19 years, was still playing when the end came."

The night Horton was killed in his car on the Queen Elizabeth Way in 1973 Keon remembers seeing him in the parking lot near the Gardens. Horton, now with Imlach's Sabres, was the worse for wear that night. "I was with my sister Pat, and we ran into Punch and Tim. He looked beat up, said he thought his jaw was broken. His face *was* swollen. I told him to get to a doctor, and he said he'd wait until the next morning in Buffalo. In fact, that's what he and Punch were talking about. He was hurting. You could tell. He didn't even play a shift in the third period, but he was still picked as the third star. Shows you what he was made of."

Horton, like others before him, was dealt unceremoniously to New York in March 1970, and Keon remembers the Leafs' slide from grace, a succession of drops in quality of players that characterized the seventies. "Between Imlach, Ballard, and Smythe the team was painted into a corner. One rebuilding scheme after another. Jim Gregory and McLellan had the mess dumped in their lap, then the WHA came along, and Ballard's attitude was 'Screw 'em, and screw the players.' We lost some good young guys — Rick Ley, Mike Pelyk, Bernie Parent, Brad Selwood, Jim Harrison. Then came my turn. It was '75 and I was into contract negotiations, looking for some continuity. I wanted three years. They only wanted to offer two at best. Finally Gregory and I met, and he told me they had no problem with the money but were uncomfortable with the second year. Well, we had exhausted all our cards. The fact I wanted to stay a Leaf didn't mean spit to them. Loyalty was a one-way street, and I had already been approached by the WHA. I told Jim, 'Well, you can be uncomfortable with it by yourself in Toronto, because I'll be in Minnesota.' And I was gone. I had no problem with Jim Gregory. He's a good hockey man, a person I knew and trusted. But the problem wasn't with Gregory. It was a little further down the hall."

And if the WHA wasn't great, it was fun. He went through two collapses of the Fighting Saints, making a brief stop in Indianapolis for 12 games the first time, landing on his feet with Hartford the second, and would get back to the NHL when the leagues merged in 1979.

Stanley Cups and Hall of Fame aside, Keon knows that stardom is fleeting at the best of times, and loves to tell a story about his first trip into Toronto with Minnesota to play the WHA Toros at Maple Leaf Gardens.

"I explained to the guys before we left St. Paul not to be upset if there's a mob of reporters at the airport wanting me to talk about why I left the Leafs, did I hate Ballard, did I regret the move, all that kind of stuff. Some of the kids on our team hadn't played in

Toronto, and I was only trying to get them ready for the media barrage. After all, I told them, I had played there for 15 years. We had won four Stanley Cups. Hell, I was the captain of the Leafs. I said it was natural the press would be after me more than them. Anyway, we arrive at Pearson — nobody, nothing. We go down to the Royal York — nobody, not one bloody press guy. The players are starting to laugh it up, saying stuff like, 'They got caught in traffic' or 'Maybe it's their day off.' Shit like that. Suddenly I spot a fellow I went to St. Mike's with, and he comes over. Joe Sorbarra, I think his name was. He sticks out his hand and says, 'I know the face, but sorry, I can't recall the name.' Well, the boys are rolling around the lobby floor by now."

Dave laughs at his own predicament. "That wasn't the worst. They kept it up even after I did some interviews at the rink. But the next day we flew to Edmonton, and when we got to the hotel, our trainer, Glenn Gostich, handed out envelopes with the room keys at the check-in, and said, 'Yep, sure are a big name here in Canada.' My envelope had the name 'D. Kenyon' on the front. The envelope made the rounds, too."

When the NHL–WHA merger occurred in 1979, all was forgotten and David Keon was reborn, at least in the eyes of the establishment, although he hadn't spoken to Harold Ballard in the five years since he'd left Toronto. In the first week of the schedule Hartford played a game against the Rangers in Madison Square Garden, and when the Whalers walked the rubber mats to the ice surface for the pregame skate, Ballard, in town for NHL meetings, was standing there. As Keon strode by, Pal Hal growled, "John died," referring to John McLellan, who had passed away only days before.

"He was just looking for a chance to strike up a conversation, get over the old sores without having to take any shit or aggravation. I'd seen it and been through it before, so I ignored him. I was walking ahead of Mike Rogers, and Ballard yelled out again, 'Hey, Keon, John died, yuh know?' I kept on going, and then Harold said loud enough for us to hear, 'Fuck you, then.' As we made the gate, Rogers said, 'You must hate that guy, eh?' I just stepped out on the ice."

But it wasn't all acrimony. Before the first game in Toronto as a member of the Hartford Whalers there was an odd request. Keon, almost dressed except for his jersey, was told by the trainer that there was a gentleman to see him. Keon distinctly recalls begging off. "'I don't wanna see anyone right now,' I said. 'I'm trying to get ready.' But the trainer persisted. 'I think you'll want to see this man,' he told me, and walked away.

"Next thing I know in comes Connie Smythe — homburg, spats, jacket, pants, and overcoat all the same colour, the works. He comes over slowly — he was getting on then — shakes hands, and says, 'You were a great player and a great captain. I'm sorry about what happened.' We chat for only a moment, and then he says he has to leave, that his driver is waiting to take him back to the farm. He came in just to talk to me."

Over all the speaking dates we did together, the miles in cars, the hours in restaurants, I got the feeling that this private man was as regretful as any Toronto supporter when it came to the fallen Leafs. Once, in Detroit, we watched Toronto score the first goal, then bow to the Wings 4–1. Standing in the corridor after the game, waiting for the crush to thin out, a man wearing a Maple Leaf hat and sipping a last beer absently said, "I used to be a Leaf fan. I used to bleed blue." Davey grunted, looked directly at him, and said, "So did I."

Recently Dave and I spoke at a Rotary club luncheon in Brampton, where the usual Q and A followed. Keon tried to convey the feeling of being a Leaf back when the Leafs were *the Leafs,* comparing it with his last years in the blue and white. He also tried to get across his regret, especially for the fans who had to see the demise of a great franchise. He even got in some humour when he rhymed off the names of those sixties heroes — Bower, Horton, Baun, Shack, Pulford, Armstrong, Nevin, Mahovlich, Kelly, Sawchuk, Stewart, Hillman. The names rang crystal clear, and I could see smiles of appreciation from a group of people who had lived through the Toronto triumphs. Keon said the lineup was very strong, even to this day, and he suggested, "We might even do okay in the NHL now, if we could get clearance for our 70-year-old netminder." That was another dig at the venerable Johnny Bower, the guy who had inspired him 30 years earlier.

I had heard all the queries many times before, and God only knows how often Keon has listened to them come up, but a couple of them still have merit.

One man asked, "To what do you attribute your clean play and subsequent Lady Byng nominations in a career that only shows 135 minutes in over 1,600 total games?"

"Take a look at me," Dave replied. "I'm not a very big guy, and I was taught at St. Mike's to make the most of my style of play, to apply my talents as much as I could. If I did, I'd help the team and succeed. Same thing happened to Stan Mikita when he came up. First few years he was hacking and spearing, fighting and yacking, but he had to change. He won two Lady Byngs in a row. Jeez, when he came up, he wasn't very good looking at the best of times. After a couple of those rowdy years, he didn't look a hell of a lot better. I got the message as a kid. Stan got the message a little later."

The second question led to more insight into Keon and how he looks back on his great career. "How come you picked number 14? Most kids back then picked number 9. Nobody had 14."

"When I first got to the Leafs, I was wearing a training camp number — 24. When I made the team, I knew I couldn't have 15. That was my cousin's number. Remember Todd Sloan? Anyway, 15 belonged to Billy Harris. The trainer wanted to assign me 24, and it was okay with me. But they said it didn't come in the new set of sweaters, so they gave me 14, which I didn't want at all. It was the number they usually assigned to a guy up from or going back to Rochester — a transit number. But one thing always made me happy later. I still saw kids playing hockey in the road or at hockey schools in the summer, and some of them wore number 14. That made me feel good about what I'd done in hockey."

At that very moment I suspected the entire room felt good about what David Keon had done for hockey.

As the luncheon ended, there was one last autograph to sign. A gentleman approached with a white jersey in hand — number 14, Hartford

Whalers. In an age where 77s, 66s, 44s, even 92s abound, it was nice to see a traditional 14 again, even though I suspected we all would have preferred to see a blue-and-white Maple Leaf 14.

For the nostalgia, if nothing else.

90-SECOND ALL-STARS

G — **Johnny Bower** *". . . he could take care of himself, and no soft goals."*

D — **Bobby Orr** *". . . the guy could lug the puck."*

D — **Tim Horton** *". . . in a tight game you could trust Timmy to do the right thing."*

C — **Jean Beliveau** *". . . he could handle the heavy going in the slot."*

RW — **Guy Lafleur** *". . . this guy could score on you from the blue line."*

LW — **John Bucyk** *". . . his corner work and scoring touch."*

Bob Kolari

Arbiter of Anarchy

BOB WHO? That's exactly what I asked the first time the name came up.

Actually I asked, "What's a Kolari?" Little did I know at the time that he would become an integral part of the Labatt's Original Six road team, an indispensable cog in the "big wheel," as Dallas Smith referred to the team. Dallas was one of those farm boys who had an analogy for everything.

After a win, he would say, "The big wheel just keeps rolling, eh, fellas?" as if it were important that we won. When we lost, questions were asked about the big wheel, and ol' Dallas would say, "A minor nail in the snow tire of life, boys." So, if the team was a radial tire, then Bobby Kolari was its air pump.

We had always intended to use our own referee in the Original Six games. Too many things hinged on our being able to control the pace and open up holes for our gimmicks and tricks. After all, this was show business, and there were the penalty calls. Kolari would call Pierre Pilote for "going too slow in the fast lane" and get Tommy Williams for the exact opposite. Following a once-a-game Dennis Hull slap shot from the red line onto the glass behind the net, a chilling sight to any amateur goaltender, an incensed Kolari would give Dennis two minutes

Bob Kolari: "an arbiter of reason in a volatile environment, he never leaves the ice, never misses a shift, never even gets a drink of water during a period, and he has to be cool in the face of real danger."

for "attempted murder." He always banished one of the opposition hot dogs "for impersonating a hockey player," and at some point in the game would give our guy a penalty for "hugging" his man and their player another for "liking it." We had rigged penalty shots, goaltending changes, and stoppages in play that were necessary and had to be called at the precise time. There were setups for their team, for our team, and for the fans. It was imperative for us to have our own whistler.

Our first referee was a good one — Ron Ego, a former NHL linesman and later a WHA ref. I always told him he improved the officiating in both leagues by making one move.

In the very first game the Original Six ever played we went up against the Thunder Bay Twins, Allan Cup champions or finalists, I can't recall which, and Ego set a new record. From the opening face-off we played nine minutes and 37 seconds without a whistle. Our players changed on the go every time they came near the bench. It was great for the fans, but it almost killed us. I thought I had had a handle on the officiating, but it was obvious we had to talk about it again. At the end of the period I walked down the hall to the officials' dressing room, put my hands out, and cried, "Ronnie?"

"You said you didn't want me to be the whole show," he said in his own defence. "You said they came here to see the players."

"Yeah, but I didn't expect you to pull a vanishing act," I countered. Somewhere in between lay the right amount of striped shirt, and from that point on, through six years, the refs were a force in our team presentation.

There came a time after two seasons when Ron couldn't make it because of business commitments. We had never had to consider the option, but he suggested another fellow he had worked with and could recommend. That's where Bob Kolari comes in.

He was big and robust, and many of our players knew him from the WHA days. But to others, including me, he was a mystery man. However, he was an immediate hit with the players and the fans and became one of the boys overnight. He took officiating to another level, or lowered the standard to new depths. From our side, though, he was an innovator and a major part of our game, largely thanks to his knack for entertaining staging.

Bob fell into refereeing at a late age, 27, and like most guys who take up officiating, he began as a walk-on. It's an old scenario: a ref doesn't show because of a snowstorm or something, so you yank somebody out of the stands. Kolari wasn't a stranger to the game, by any means. As a Junior defenceman, he was good enough to get a try-out with the Guelph Royals, and at one stage he was paired with Bob Plager. But as he admits now, "I missed the cut by a lot."

Realizing he had an aptitude and a definite liking for the referee's role, he started with local games, graduated to Junior B, then moved up to the major Senior and Junior leagues. When a business transfer came up, moving him to British Columbia, he became one of the top officials in the Western Canada Junior League. At the age of 35 he was told by the NHL that he had appeared on their scouting reports so often that the league was wondering why he wasn't in the pros. There was a very good reason, money.

Attending his first NHL training camp, he discovered he had a job as a linesman if he was willing to spend eight months on the road, give up his present job, and take a one-third pay cut. Not being totally star-struck, or dumb, he returned to Vancouver and took up where he had left off — content and relatively wealthy.

In 1972 the WHA loomed on the horizon. The new league didn't have the same mind-set, and they offered Kolari an appreciable pay hike over his combined job and officiating assignments. Bob completed a refereeing quartet that included Ego, Bill Friday, and Brent Casselman. Bob Sloan and Ron Harris, all NHL conscripts, would join later.

As a player, you never appreciate what it takes to be a good official. We know they're around, some seem to be better than others, and a few even seem downright regular guys, but we still don't appreciate their ability. I know I never did until I had two I could call my own. Any player who has ever been pressed into service as a referee can tell you he suddenly finds he's out of position, out of condition, out of recollection of the rules, and out to lunch because he usually doesn't know a penalty unless it happens to him personally. A player turned ref will tend to "watch" the game rather than call it.

The world of the referee is one of control and posture. An arbiter of reason in a volatile environment, he never leaves the ice, never misses a shift, never even gets a drink of water during a period, and he has to be cool in the face of real danger. His only physical protection is whatever light equipment he can wear under an oversize sweater and pants. His only avenue of escape is to scale the glass, because he operates in a narrow, imaginary, unseen corridor no more than four feet from the boards. The official is a participant in all the fights whether he wants to be or not, and the only friends he has in a game are the other officials, and sometimes even that's debatable.

Soon after he started with us, Kolari was nicknamed "Bobo," or just plain "Bo," by Pat Stapleton, who had spent some time in the WHA with the Indianapolis Racers and the Chicago Cougars. We logged a lot of miles listening to stories about the glory days of the breakaway league and its long list of characters. Despite the images of Bobby Hull, Gordie Howe, Wayne Gretzky, Frank Mahovlich, Paul Henderson, Dave Keon, and other established names, the WHA was still a bit primitive, a little strange to the outside observer. But Bo loved the rebel league, and since he was my roomie on the road over four seasons, I got to hear all his "A" material.

"The best thing about that league," he once told me, "was that the bottom team could beat the top team on any given night. I'd go on the road for a month at a time, start out with a set of standings, and by the time I got back the whole list would be reversed. It was wild! One night in Indianapolis Dave Dryden was in goal for Edmonton. Somebody takes a screened slap shot and hits Dryden square in the nuts. You could hear the thunk as it hit the cup. Every guy on the ice cringed, believe me. Dryden goes down like he's been shot, and the Oilers corral the rebound and take off.

"They know it's not a goal, and I sure as hell know it's not a goal, but the goddamn goal judge turns on the light. I guess he thought it sounded like the puck hit the bar in the back of the net. I don't know. Anyway, the light is like a fucking Christmas tree, which the rest of us are ignoring, but the fans start screaming, the play comes back down to the Edmonton end, and Dryden's still down, trying to locate his jewels.

The goddamn light is going around and around like a cop car's, and now the goofy bastards are starting to throw stuff. It's comin' from all sides, and most of it at me, because I keep waving the goal off and glaring at the dumb-ass goal judge, who refuses to turn the light out.

"Finally they freeze the puck, get a whistle, and it starts to pour all kinds of shit. As I skate to the timekeeper, the shower gets worse because I'm closer to the boards. So I just yell at the PA announcer. You know, no goal, for Christ's sake, and still the asshole leaves the light on. And it's really getting ugly. They're throwing hats, beer, programs, hell, I almost got conked with a Zippo lighter. Finally the guy makes the announcement and the goal judge turns off the light, but the ice cleaners can't keep up with the garbage.

"Jacques Demers is the Indy coach, and he can see it's getting out of control, so he sends out Rene Leclerc to argue, or so I think. He skates right up to me, and I'm really pissed off by this time. He says, 'Don't throw me out, Bobby. Demers sent me out here to pretend to yap with you. He said if we stand together and we have a nice little talk, they won't throw anything. They don't wanna hurt me, eh? Then they'll settle down once I give you some shit — wave my arms around, point a few times, okay?' And that's how we got out of that screwup. Smart man that Demers."

Gordie Howe was a bigger-than-life presence, according to Kolari. "He really watched over his sons. I did a game between Minnesota and Houston when Billy Butters came over to me and said, 'C'mon, Bob, you gotta call something on those Howe kids. Shit, we can't touch the bastards, or the old man'll kick our asses.' Dad was one tough mother, I'll tell you. I don't care how old he was.

"So about the middle of the second I get Marty for cross-checking, and out comes the big boy off the bench, skating directly toward me. I held up my hand and told him not to come near me or I was gonna have to toss him, too. I said I didn't want to hear anything about the penalty, that it was over, and final. He skated by me and said out of the side of his mouth, 'Your fly's open, Bob.' I just laughed, ignored him, and thought, Nice try, slick. A few minutes later the two linesmen crowded around me and one asked, 'What are you doing, trolling?

Your fly's open.' Goddamn. I had to do it up right on the ice with them screening for me. Gordie was sitting on the bench, just grinning at me, the son of a bitch."

But his most memorable anecdote was from Quebec City. Minnesota was in town, and as usual there were problems on the ice and penalties were being called one after the other. Suddenly a melee broke out behind the Minnesota bench. "I could see [coach] Harry Neale almost into the crowd, beating on somebody with a hockey stick, hitting the glass, right into it. By the time I got over there, the players had Harry back on the bench, a little roughed up but okay, and things were being handled in the crowd by the cops. I asked what the fuss was about, and Harry said, straightening his tie, 'Nothing. I was sticking up for you, Bobby. The guy called you a cocksucker!' The whole bench broke up. Me, too. I just skated away and got the game going as quickly as I could."

We never had anything like that happen with the Original Six, but Bobo did stumble onto an incident in St. John's one night that made its way into the team's permanent repertoire of stunts.

Newfoundlanders take their hockey as seriously as anybody, and in the case of one particular leather-lunged woman, the game was a way to vent frustration. It was obvious from the outset that she was going to have her say. A foghorn voice capable of warning ships in Torbay reverberated around the arena. She was a gifted and dedicated referee baiter from way back, and she took a distinct dislike to Kolari. "Who the hell's the ref?" she boomed. "King Kong? Ain't he a big 'un?" Bobby's size was the first victim, and he hadn't even dropped the puck.

"C'mon, lard-ass. Call da damn penalty. Fill up dem fat cheeks and blow, boy." Bobby's weight was the second target.

The night continued that way to the delight of the crowd, which seemed to catch on to the custom of "no penalties." Even if Bobby called one, the drill was to go into the box, then, as soon as the play started, return immediately to the ice. It was done that way because we reasoned no one had come to see players sit out for two minutes, theirs or ours, and for the most part the players were playing hard and fast but noncontact, no dirt. It was usually to their advantage, not ours, so it was fair. Unfortunately the first three penalties Kolari called were on us. Ms. Foghorn came close to expiring each time our player stepped back onto the ice. She'd bellow, almost frothing, "Them goddamn cheatin' buggers is at it agin." And every time Kolari passed by, he'd look at her momentarily, which didn't go unnoticed.

"Why yuh lookin' up here, fer Jay-zuz sake, yah goofy lookin t'ing yah?" she raged, standing up, waving a menacing fist. We thought she might wind down eventually, but obviously her larynx resembled a paving stone, and she kept it up without losing a decibel. Suddenly, without any prearrangements, Kolari whispered some instructions to both teams at a face-off in the corner, and as the puck was dropped, Tommy Williams slashed the stick out of the hands of the St. John's Blue Caps winger.

Ms. Foghorn let go with a roar, probably scaring people still in the rest rooms. She screamed and screeched at the terrible injustices on the ice. Kolari skated up to her and patiently tried to explain that he was doing his best, that he certainly didn't have an easy job. Meanwhile Williams had thrown the loose stick over the glass. She wailed at this further foul while Kolari continued to appease her, his back to the play.

Then Bill White almost mugged one of the home side players, clutching and grabbing as only White could, almost stripping the poor guy's pants off. She went apoplectic, the cords in her neck stuck out, eyes bulged, spittle flew, and by the time Bobby turned back to the play, naturally everything was fine again. The crowd was in on the act and laughed appreciably, but Ms. Foghorn didn't notice. She could only weakly croak, "Yer a disgrace, buddy, a goddamn disgrace." After that we used the routine whenever someone took the game a tad too seriously.

It was always a pleasure to watch Bobo go through his "referee" routine, the one where he acted the part of a serious dispenser of justice, an impartial overseer of the game. Today I frequently ask myself who was having more fun. And I often wonder how Ms. Foghorn is doing.

90-SECOND ALL-STARS

G — Jacques Plante

D — J. C. Tremblay

D — Pat Stapleton

C — Dave Keon

RW — Gordie Howe

LW — Bobby Hull

"They were great players wherever they played."

Alex Delvecchio

Motor City Fats

SITTING ACROSS FROM ALEX DELVECCHIO at a table in the Airport Marriott Hotel lobby café in Toronto, I have a perfect view of "Fats." He looks exactly the same as he always has, even though his hair is now completely white: the face is still tanned and the build is more or less the same. And, as usual, he looks laid-back. Then I bring myself up short. It can't be. Maybe it's my glasses, or perhaps now that I've gotten older I've begun to make allowances for other people's advancing years.

Alex has greeted me with "Hey, left-hander," and the salutation takes me back to when I first crossed paths with him as a kid in Thunder Bay. I lived on Cummings Street, while he lived three blocks up on Dease. I was 10 or 11 and just beginning to master the craft of road hockey; he was playing Junior for the Hurricanes. They played their games on the only indoor ice in the twin cities — Port Arthur Arena — and to say he was light-years ahead of our gawky group is an understatement. I only saw him play Junior twice; tickets plus transportation to a Junior contest were costly, not to mention the amount of time consumed. Anyway, I realize I'm not being fair to either of us by trying to delude myself that we look the same in days gone by.

Alex Delvecchio: "he may have been underrated, but I have a feeling that's exactly the way he always wanted it."

We commiserate about Thunder Bay, rehash some old hockey stories, trade tales of old friends, and wonder whatever happened to so-and-so. There was no shortage of local hockey heroes back when the universe was in tune and Thunder Bay was Fort William and Port Arthur. The Leafs had the "Fort" line of Gus Bodnar, Gaye Stewart, and Bud Poile. They were followed by a succession of hometowners: Lee Fogolin, Sr., Danny Lewicki, Rudy Migay, Dave Creighton, Benny Woit, and Steve Black. In 1949 New York's Pentti Lund won the Calder Trophy as the NHL's best rookie, while another stylish Ranger, Edgar LaPrade, won the Lady Byng the next year.

It was 1950, my dad was a foreman on the construction site of the new Fort William Gardens, and I was posing as a so-called carpenter's helper, which consisted of me parading around the site with a hammer in one hand and a piece of scrap plywood in the other. Guess how I got the job? It was the year I perfected my dodge of looking resolute while not going anywhere, a trait that has always served me well. It was my last summer before entering high school. Leo Boivin, a future Hall of Fame member, was playing for the Port Arthur Bruins, and Larry Cahan, who would go on to 13 NHL seasons, was another teenager up on a ladder installing signage at the front of the unfinished Gardens.

Delvecchio had just completed his final Oshawa Generals Junior season, in which he and linemate Lou Jankowski finished one-two in the OHA scoring race. Jankowski's first-place total of 124 included a league-leading 65 goals, while Fats put up a league-high 72 assists and came in with 121. Not hard to figure out! That September I went on to school dances with real bands, had dates with assorted baby-sitters, and tried to become a hockey hero on my own.

Delvecchio? No surprise there. He turned pro and attended the Detroit Red Wings' training camp. Rarely did a rookie make the big club in those days, regardless of the numbers, so it was no downer when he was assigned to Indianapolis. In nine games he banged in three goals and made six assists. That was enough for another Fort Williamite, Jack Adams, the longtime general manager of the Wings. He moved Alex to the Red Wings . . . for 27 years, 24 of them as a player.

By 1952 Fats returned home with a Stanley Cup, after a crushing eight straight wins in two playoff rounds over Toronto and the mighty Montreal Canadiens. The final series saw the Wings score 11 goals, but the Habs managed only two. A definite pressure cooker, especially for a first-year centre.

Did we at home care? Oh, we preened and strutted a bit when the announcers mentioned Fort William, or scowled and snorted when they said Alex was from Oshawa. As a community, I suppose we were happy, since we'd been returned to the map. But as for treating Delvecchio differently, naw, he was just a guy who left his home on Dease Street to play hockey, and we had a ton of those. Back in Fort William he was just Fats.

You have to remember that most of us hadn't seen much of him since he was 16. Every summer he'd return, get a job, and play some baseball, just like the rest of us.

It was through baseball that I got to know him best. He was a some-time first baseman and shortstop. Come to think of it, he could play any position, and somewhere in the attic of my memory I seem to recall him catching a few times, too. When I first saw him on a ball field, I was a 14-year-old pitcher playing Junior, and thank God he was on our side. He could hit and had a loosey-goosey way of walking, a relaxed batting stance, quick hands, and a great eye for balls and strikes. He made hitting look effortless and could get you extra bases or spray the ball to all fields. Fats never seemed in a hurry, and while baserunning wasn't his forte, he picked his spots and wasn't caught very often.

In 1953 he came home with a fifth place in NHL scoring and selection as the second-team All-Star centre, but no Stanley Cup. He moved up to Senior ball, where he belonged, but he was still just good ol' Fats to us.

The next year he came home with another Stanley Cup under his belt, I remained in Junior ball, where I belonged, and we won the championship. To prove the Wings weren't a fluke, he came back with his third Stanley Cup in 1955. That was good enough for me, so I moved up to Senior ball, too. But, more important, somewhere along the line he had nailed down a job as a Carling brewery rep. Stanley Cups and All-Star awards were okay, but if you had your priorities straight, Black

Label beer addressed itself to any immediate problem. So when he arrived in Thunder Bay in May 1955 and discovered that our team, ANAF (Army, Navy, and Air Force), was going to fold, he bought the team, and in a brilliant marketing stroke became the owner, manager, permanent shortstop, and any other position he wanted to play.

By the end of August we were locked in a seven-game playoff against the Port Arthur Red Sox. I was having shoulder problems and was only good for a few innings, if that, when Fats called me into a game in about the fourth inning. We were losing large when I arrived. He handed me the ball without a word, then trotted back to his position. The warm-up went well, but adrenaline got the better of me and I fired the first two pitches into the dirt about six feet in front of the plate. The batter must have thought he was in a cricket match. My catcher, Maurice Gelmych, called time and trotted out to me, saying, "Just keep it in the strike zone." Already frustrated, as well as embarrassed, I nodded sulkily. Fats arrived about the same time, took the ball from Gelmych, and proceeded to rub it up. "Just throw strikes, for Christ sake," he said impatiently, staring down at the waiting batter.

That's when I lost my temper. I was so damn angry about the unnecessary, facetious, not to mention redundant remark. "What the hell do you think I've got here?" I demanded heatedly, pointing at my shoulder. "A fuckin' on-off switch or somethin'?"

When Fats got pissed off, he had this habit of nodding, all the while looking blankly at the source of his irritation. After my outburst, he looked at me, his head working overtime. Then he slammed the ball into my glove and walked back to his infield position. He never said another word to me, and somehow I got through two innings, but as soon as my name came up in the batting order, he replaced me. And rightfully so. We were now down 3–2 in the series.

In the next game we came back big and blew them away, forcing a seventh game. For this tilt we had our ace pitcher all rested and ready. He was so rested that he never woke up, coming out of the first inning down 4–0. As we went down one, two, three in our half, Alex suddenly said to another pitcher and me, "Go get ready." As far as I was concerned, it was an exercise in futility, considering my last outing and my clash with the big guy. Also, he didn't need 10 or 20 pitches from a sore-armed sorehead. Maybe later, but not now. But when our ace couldn't get anyone out and loaded the bases, Alex called a halt, whistled, and said, "The left-hander."

Until I heard the familiar nickname he always used when he wasn't calling me something worse, I had been throwing lazily, nonchalantly, strike after perfect strike, with batting-practice ease, no pressure and no inkling that I would be in at this early stage, if ever. When I arrived on the mound, slightly flustered, he was rubbing up the ball again, and all he said was: "Keep us in this thing."

Five innings later, the seventh, I turned over the ball to my relief and left the game down 5–0. I recall receiving a poke in the ribs and a slap on the butt from Fats, as I walked away. We lost the game 13–0.

I've never forgotten those two incidents over all the years. He could have yanked me for being an oversensitive idiot the first time, yet he buried his anger and carried on, giving me a chance to do the job. He didn't have to give me the opportunity in the second instance, but he again put aside all the rancour and did what was best for the team.

I suppose the lesson I took from his actions, the reason it has stuck in my mind, even grown in stature over the years, is because he was so far above us in maturity and experience. Here was a man who had surpassed the pinnacle of any athlete I ever knew, asking me to dig down and find something in myself to bring to the game. I don't think we ever understood his capacity for leadership, his hidden drive under the laid-back surface.

More than once in those baseball years I heard different players grouse about his no-nonsense approach. "This ain't fuckin' Motor City, yuh know" was a common mumbled retort to his exhortations. He brought the same quiet fire, the same internal heat to the local yokels and their pretenses at being "the best," as he did to the NHL, although the comparison would have seemed farfetched even to him. After all, this guy was a 24-year-old member of the best hockey team in the world. I'm sure he expected more of us than we were capable of, certainly more than we were grudgingly about to give. All he was really saying was: "I'm doing it. Why aren't you?"

No one realized back then that he would set a longevity record with one NHL team and that he would win three Stanley Cups and three Lady

Byng Awards. I doubt any of us even knew there was going to be a Hockey Hall of Fame, or that he would be in it and give me the chance to regale my pals with the story about the day I told him to shove off.

He came through and survived in the golden era of hockey. He was in the top ten scorers 11 times, nine of those in the six-team league days, and was selected as an All-Star at both centre and left wing. But he wasn't without his adversity, his slumps and hard times.

Moving from line to line, where and whenever management decided to either shore up a struggling pair of wingers or offensively load up others, he spent the first half of the 1964–65 season mired in a goal drought. The Wings were rolling along at a first-place clip, but Delvecchio was stuck in neutral, with no goals. His plight made the radio, TV, and papers. It also raised a few eyebrows in the Wings' front office. He had only missed two games in 12 seasons coming into 1964, with the exception of 1957 when he suffered an injury and missed 22 games. Maybe he had succumbed to the "old-age flu." After all, he had been burning it up pretty consistently over 13 seasons.

People sent four-leaf clovers, rabbits' feet, lucky pennies, and silver dollars that had brought good fortune in Vegas. There were rosaries, prayers, and Ouija board predictions. But the best was an offer too hard to refuse.

Over the holidays Pam Aldred, the reigning Miss America, personally offered an emerald brooch she had worn for luck the night she was crowned at the pageant only a short time before. Carefully fastening the jewellery to the flap of his jockstrap, Delvecchio went out on New Year's Eve in Madison Square Garden and popped his first goal of the year behind Eddie Giacomin.

"I got 24 in the remaining half of the season to finish fifth overall," he says now with a chuckle. When I ask if he kept the lucky memento, he answers, "Shit, no, I returned it. Took it over to her place myself a few days into January. Those were real goddamn emeralds."

The talk turns to coaches, and his favourite was Sid Abel. "He was a players' coach. Always willing to experiment, always willing to take a look at things from a different angle. He was the guy who assigned a specific player to watch Bobby Hull — Bugsy Watson — and it worked. And there was the year we had the good road record. He told me to come back and literally stand beside [Terry] Sawchuk. Shit, you know I couldn't just go back and lounge around, but the defence needed the help and we only did it on the road. It was too boring at home."

When I ask him about his 1,549 regular-season games, a 24-year average of 65 a season, he only shrugs. "I attribute it to conditioning." He waves a hand in resignation. "I don't know. I would show up at camp no more than eight to 10 pounds over, and we'd get at it."

As our time grows short, I ask a question that's been bothering me since "road hockey" in Thunder Bay. "Where does the name Fats come from?" Over all that time, and even sitting here today 15 years or more removed from his last game, he still looks decidedly unfat.

"My Uncle Pat called me 'Fatty' as a little kid. Might have had something to do with these cheeks." He strokes his face and laughs.

But my favourite memory of Alex Delvecchio occurred at my own wedding reception. Half the beer at the hall in the East End of Fort William belonged to Fats, the rest to our baseball teammate and old friend Eddie Cox, who sold the stuff for the local Doran's Brewery. My grandmother attended, and she was a big hockey fan. I knew she hadn't met many real players in her time, certainly none as illustrious as my buddy Fats. But she was one of those Toronto adherents weaned on *Hockey Night in Canada* radio broadcasts and was a staunch believer in the high-pitched vocal offerings of Foster Hewitt. As a fan of the Leafs, she was what you'd call "rabid." And her loyalty to the blue and white knew no bounds. The Leafs were saints, choirboys on ice, occasionally misunderstood by referees, but good, clean kids one and all. The rest of the teams were staffed with misfits, miscreants, degenerates, dirty, snivelling, and loathsome riffraff. Even players who were traded to Toronto took some time to be cleansed of their previous ways. Yet she never swore, not even a "hell," and with the exception of those who weren't Maple Leafs, I can't remember her having cast aspersions on anything, man or beast.

When Alex and wife Teresa arrived at the reception, I took it upon myself to introduce the matriarch of my group. After making Mrs. Delvecchio known, I dutifully said, "Gram, this is Alex Delvecchio."

She took the extended hand and replied softly, "Yes . . . yes, you're one of those dirty Detroit sneaks, aren't you?"

Fats only blinked in response. In my grandmother's world the term *sneak* was about as low as you could get. She had a great laugh over the encounter afterward, and I firmly believe it mended his ways and sent him on his way to an injury-free career.

Our Sunday afternoon meeting is all too brief, too scattered to make much sense out of later, but one thing I do come away with is the belief that Alex Delvecchio was an underrated player. We get up to leave the coffee shop but linger in the lobby to exchange phone and fax numbers, then chat some more about today's good new players and the changes in basic philosophy behind their attitudes. Then, after a final handshake, we go our separate ways to parked cars.

I can't help but compare Delvecchio to "stars" I've met at hotels, golf tournaments, airports, dinners, and chance meetings, especially the recent ones. I run down a list of names, people who have been interrupted in mid-sentence for autographs, yet here's a player who's on the NHL's all-time scoring list, ranks ahead of the likes of Norm Ullman, Jean Beliveau, Mike Bossy, Daryll Sittler, Frank Mahovlich, Henri Richard, Rod Gilbert, Lanny McDonald, and Dave Keon. But not one person has confronted him with paper and pen during the time we spent in the café. He is the most unsung player over two decades, a fact agreed to by his peers, who sometimes have to have their own memories jogged.

Now, I think as I get into my car, he's an underrated civilian, too. After I turn on the ignition, I catch a glimpse of the familiar, ambling stride as he heads to his own car.

He may have been underrated, but I have the feeling that's exactly the way he always wanted it.

90-SECOND ALL-STARS

G — **Terry Sawchuk** *". . . had a permanent playoff style, very reliable."*

D — **Doug Harvey** *". . . could play offence and defence."*

D — **Bobby Orr** *". . . the best defenceman, period."*

C — **Milt Schmidt** *". . . could do it all, and very tough."*

RW — **Gordie Howe** *". . . wasn't anybody like him in the game."*

LW — **Ted Lindsay** *". . . in a clutch situation, you needed Ted."*

Epilogue

S O THERE THEY ARE, only a few of the hockey people who for one reason or another are unique. There are many others to be sure, but for now these personal observations and insights are the ones that come to mind.

An acquaintance once asked how I kept all the anecdotes and tales on tap, and I simply pointed to a notebook on my desk, dog-eared and scruffy, a constant companion through the telling of these stories. From the late sixties on I've always kept notes to remind me, to shed a ray of recollective light on original scribblings appearing on the backs of envelopes, paper scraps of all shapes and sizes, and a disturbing variety of bar coasters.

From those jottings I uncovered my notes on the last time the Leafs trained in Peterborough when I first observed the camaraderie among members of the fifth estate. Being on the other side of the fence for so long, I suspect I had the corny, prejudged conviction that they were all out for scoops and that the rivalry was more intense and underhanded than anything on the ice. Not so. Beat writers and broadcasters are a supportive, self-contained group. Yes, there are some fifth wheels, as with any other social caste, but for the most part they operate as a quasi-fraternal club.

Dennis Hull (centre) parks himself in front of the net: he "tends to look at things in *a more pacific way, it's the humour in being shunted aside, being slighted, despite a distinguished 14-year NHL career."*

Two supposed "rivals" who caught my eye immediately were George Gross of Toronto's *Telegram* and Red Burnett of the *Toronto Star*. Cynical Red, whose trademark fedora only lacked the hatband Press card to make him a reporter out of a Bowery Boys movie, had seen them come and go for a lifetime. Gross, an escapee from behind the Iron Curtain, was a dapper, moustachioed, no-nonsense writer. He was known as "the Baron" for his regal, not to mention Prussian-like bearing, but personally he favoured "the Coach," since it was his, and Burnett's belief, that *they* had won four Stanley Cups for the Leafs. This was their considered opinion, and with tongue in cheek for everyone else's amusement, they implied that Imlach had only followed their manipulations, strategies, and game plans.

"If I didn't want a guy to play or dress, all I had to do was file a story saying he was a cinch to be in uniform, or at least on the power play. Punch would either scratch the player or sit the poor bastard on the bench for as long as he could, just to prove me wrong."

While in Peterborough we stayed at the Holiday Inn, and with Red flu-bound in bed, George made special room service runs and relayed information from the day's workouts so Burnett could write a creditable story. "Can't let the old bugger expire," he'd say, heading off with aspirin and hot soup. "Wouldn't be the same without Red to lead the bitching for the rest of us."

That was a revelation for me at the time, and it was great to hang out with the likes of broadcasters Fred Sgambati, Brian McFarlane, and Ron Hewat, an outstanding play-by-play man and one of the best after-dinner MCs I've ever heard. There were the "ink-stained wretches," too: the zany, often eccentric Dick Beddoes; Frank Orr, who always managed to get the word *splendid* into his game story; Bob Pennington, the guy I once saw without a pipe clenched between his teeth and didn't recognize; the Proudfoots, Jim and Dan; and Paul Dulmage, who wrote the best lead paragraphs about the NHL.

If the media types were a surprise to me, the players weren't. They remained the same regardless of the level of competition. Players, as always, came and went, performed and retired, the new ones much like the old ones after a period of adjustment. If anything, my contention was reinforced that hockey players are the toughest people in the sports world.

They make light of injuries that put most other athletes away for the count. To the boys of hockey injuries are the cost of doing business, and peppered throughout my notebook are the examples — an interminable litany of surgical procedures and rehab drudgery. Bobby Hull, playing with his broken jaw wired together, a couple of teeth sacrificially removed to enable drinking a concoction of pureed meat and other nutrients. Brian Glennie, taking a first-period slap shot off the stick of Philadelphia Flyer Bill Barber, again resulting in a broken jaw and necessitating numerous stitches and repairs to a severed facial artery. Pat Stapleton absorbing over 300 stitches to close a cut extending from eye to jawline after a face-first collision with a skate blade. The bloodletting, the continual clash of muscle and bone, happened on a daily basis. Yet they all came back to play again, the scars and the lingering limps put aside, ignored, each player still able to engage in the seemingly small, painless, trivial diversions of life.

A notation I came across recently concerns Bobby Orr. Without argument Orr is considered the standard to which other defencemen, hell, other forwards, aspire. His achievements on the ice are legendary, beyond comparison, made all the more incredible given that his knees have seen more than their share of needles and knives. We all wonder how one athlete can be so gifted, but to him there are other, more important accomplishments than commonplace hockey feats.

He played only one ballgame with the ProStars at Exhibition Stadium in Toronto, along with add-ons Phil Esposito, Henri Richard, and a kid with good moves at shortstop named Wayne Gretzky. Twelve years later Orr and I met again while on our way into Don Cherry's Mississauga restaurant for a two-show taping of the *Grapevine* TV program. I commented on his diamond debut. "You had three hits that night," I enthused, recalling his success at the plate, pleased with my remarkable powers of recollection.

"Four," he shot back without hesitation. "Yep, I got four," he repeated, obviously a memory of some importance to him.

And that's how it should be — memories. For Bobby Orr, with all his awards and accomplishments, it may be an obscure softball game.

For quarrelsome Tony Esposito, it might be the humorous disparity of a doping test in Germany. For Dennis Hull, who tends to look at things in a more pacific way, it's the humour in being shunted aside, being slighted, despite a distinguished 14-year NHL career, which naturally pales beside the Golden Jet's, as well as that of his nephew Brett. In fact, Dennis has made a successful secondary speaking career out of being ignored and snubbed. Many times I've listened and laughed while Dennis, hockey's 200-pound version of Rodney Dangerfield, relived another in a long life of ultimate slurs.

Once, when he and I were going our separate ways after a red-eye flight from the West Coast, I reminded him of a put-down he had received on the opposite side of the country in Kentville, Nova Scotia. We had completed our speaking chores and were asked to participate in the Hall of Fame awards given out at the end of the evening. I drew a local boxer of note, Rick Anderson, and Dennis was assigned the task of presenting an 83-year-old with a citation for his contributions to the game of hockey.

"He looks like a nasty old bugger, but I think you can take him in a KO," I said by way of caution as Dennis readied himself for the ceremonies.

The man reminded me of the little bald-headed sidekick on Benny Hill's old show. Dennis walked over, chatted for a moment, then roared with laughter. The gentleman only blinked rapidly, obviously agitated.

Later I asked Dennis what had happened. "I introduce myself, and the man says, 'Yeah, okay,' like I have to pass a test or something. I ask him about playing in the old days. Did he only play locally? Jeez, he gets real snarky and says, 'Yeah, all my damn life, so?' Now I'm standing, waiting, but he doesn't say another word. I ask him what position he played, and do you know what the crusty old bastard says? He says, 'I played all positions except goalie, and all of them better'n you.' Besmirched," Dennis lamented, using a word we designated as the severest reputation killer.

Then there was Russia and game six of the 1972 Summit Series. The combative Bobby Clarke and reliable Ron Ellis are on the ice to kill a penalty, something they have done together with merit and much success. So far. Coach Harry Sinden plays a hunch and sends Dennis over the boards to replace Ellis and to check Alexander Yakushev. Clarke is already into his patented three-point stance: a gloved bottom hand at the heel of the stick, his butt higher than his head, eyes burning a hole in the puck held by the linesman. Straightening, his intensity put on hold with the change, he notices a sheepish Hull skating up to the face-off circle. Dennis isn't convinced the change is such a good idea, either.

Centres have certain places for their wingers on critical face-offs, so Hull looks at the sweaty-haired, determined Clarke and asks, "Where do you want me, Bobby?"

Clarke curls his lips, revealing the gap between eyeteeth fangs, and rasps with finality, "On the bench."

"No respect again," Dennis groans, laughing.

If there's a reason for inadvertently saving these items through the years, through the plane rides and bus trips, the waiting at boarding gates, the eight-man sessions around bar tables, it's because of Dennis, Jim McKenny, Larry Cahan, and Eddie Shack. They and others like them were people whose comments on the sport and the scene at hand were pertinent, relevant, and interesting. I felt I had to write them down because I was the lucky guy who was on the inside, the one who was able to listen and learn.

In the course of finalizing this manuscript I discovered that not one of the interviews had ended in anything but an appreciation for the time spent in hockey despite injury to either body or ego. Every player expressed his feelings of gratitude for the opportunity to play, to be with "the boys." None regretted the money situation of their era; not one resents the good times — make that better financial times — of today's crop of players. Their attitude is: that was then, this is now.

To me they are collectively epitomized in the pride Don Cherry takes in his AHL colleagues, the lunchpailers of the game, the ones who slug it out in lesser towns driven by the dreams of one more crack at the top. He loves them and lauds their abilities and character. You can feel the pride when he talks of his days in Rochester.

Jim McKenny feels the same way. Despite his considerable skills, he spent time in the minors, flying in DC-3 "gooney birds," the planes the players referred to as "knucklers" because they'd dip, dive, sink, and sidewind like a baseball change-up. He fondly remembers goaltender Bobby Perreault, Bill Sweeney, Barry Watson, Rock Godfrey, Barry Watson, and Red Armstrong who, McKenny claims, could have easily played themselves in the movie *Slap Shot.* As Shakey Walton would say, they were "classics." McKenny feels those who never spent time in the minors missed a great experience. At the time I recall saying to myself, "Yeah, right, bullshit."

But, as usual, McKenny and Cherry are right, if a bit ahead of the point. I woke up to the realization that "life" didn't begin and end in the NHL. The elusive, continuous thread I originally missed back when I was looking for a theme had been there all the time.

As I said at the outset, they came from the same hockey background, the starting point common to all who have ever laced on skates. Two-room playground shacks where nails served as coat hangers and tubs of snow were melted to serve up humidity. Where potbellied stoves glowed red and often the smell of wool too close to the heat permeated the air. Where new sticks were a rare commodity, a status symbol, stick tape was something you hoarded, and an errant puck could be lost in the snowbank until spring. There were skeletonlike pipe nets, wearing only remnants of netting. Steam came off hot faces in subzero weather, and runny noses were standard equipment. They played in ill-fitting uniforms, grab-bag equipment, games where ice time was regulated by a buzzer, dutifully ruled by referees who worked four morning games in a row. They came from arenas where it was cooler inside than outside, the lines were buried hazily under layers of ice, and the snowy residue along the bottom of the boards was rarely swept away.

Every year, the day after Christmas, new unbloodied sweaters would appear like spring tulips.

And nobody knew which one of the kids skating on his ankles would go to the NHL.

Eventually the best graduated to carpeted dressing rooms, physiotherapists, media guides, the smell of A-535 and new leather, Gatorade, an abundance of tape, nothing but new sticks, and sweaters that actually sparkled.

To a man, each and every one of them played that last minute.